Castle

on the
Island

TD Cochran

Library of Congress: TX 8-212-028

ISBN: 978-0692814550

For …
My Mom, My Dad & My Sister
My Best Friend, Tara
My Spy Story Friends

With Gratitude to the Authors & Producers who came before …
Ian Fleming, John LaCarré, Len Deighton,
Harry Saltzman, The Broccoli Family, Bruce Geller

With Respect to…
The real world spies who work day after day, but don't get to have as
much fun as Léa & Tara.

T.D. Cochran
The Pit - 2016

CONTENTS

PROLOGUE: Best Friends   1

PART ONE: THE HAUNTED CASTLE

1	Friday	6
2	The Smartest Kids In Town	10
3	The Road North Of Town	16
4	The First Night	21
5	Saturday	29
6	Breakfast	35
7	Lunch	38
8	Trapped In A Dungeon	44
9	Waking Up	55
10	The Next Morning	62
11	The Old Man	72

PART 2: HOW IT ALL BEGAN

12	The Daily Sentinel	78
13	Handbook Number 10	81
14	Lights, Camera, Action!	85
15	Dinner And Some Secrets	90
16	The Train To Liverpool	96
17	The Boat To Dublin	101
18	An Underwater Surprise	105
19	Silent Running	109

PART 3: SPY SCHOOL

20	The First Day	114

21 Welcome To Spy School   120

22 Tour of The Castle   125

23 Guns and The 'Net   127

24 Movie Night   134

25 Janet Austin   139

26 Are We Still Friends?   145

27 Spy School, Day Two   150

28 Good, Evil, And Richard Burton   154

29 Spy Sex Interrupted   159

PART 4: THE UPPSALA MISSION

30 The Train To Paris   162

31 Mission Briefing   165

32 Léa's Morning   173

33 Tara's Morning   178

34 Breakfast   183

35 The Hunt Begins   188

36 Hostage   193

37 Natural Cover   196

38 What Are Best Friends For?   201

39 Juice And Bikes   205

40 Bike Chase   210

41 We're Not So Hot   218

42 Tara's Secret Code   221

43 Pulling The Plug   228

44 What's Really Important   234

EXTRAS

Tara's Code Book   237

Léa's Links   239

TD's Playlist   240

EPILOGUE: An Unusual Meeting   241

PROLOGUE: BEST FRIENDS

Trafalgar Square, London
(Ten Years After Our Story Begins)

Tick ... Tick ... Tick ...

"Something's not right," said Léa Taylor to herself.

Tick ... Tick ... Tick ...

"Something's not right," Léa whispered to her best friend, Tara Wells.

"Yeah, I just don't know what it is. But look where we are and what we're doing," Tara whispered back.

A cold, light London rain started to fall as the two women crouched near the base of Lord Nelson's Column in Trafalgar Square. Four bronze lions crouched on stone pedestals surrounding the famous column.

A dedication plaque lay on the ground, revealing a small, hole under one of the lions. A medium-sized black travel case was centered in the hole. The case was open. Its contents were the things nightmares are made of.

Tick ... Tick ... Tick ...

Léa said, "The last time I heard a nuke tick—"

"Wait a minute. When did you ever hear a nuke tick before?" Tara sarcastically interrupted.

"As I was about to say, the last time I heard a nuke tick was in an old James Bond movie."

"Wait, don't tell me. Goldfinger, right?"

"You've been paying attention on movie nights," said Léa.

"At least James had a timer ticking down to double-oh-seven. I've got no idea how much time we have before this thing blows up in our faces," said Tara.

A shiny metal sphere was centered in the middle of the suitcase. Two car batteries filled the lower half of the case. At the top, two computer boards were taped to a hunk of plywood. It was just two circuit boards with no display counting down to the explosion.

Two wires snaked up from the batteries to the electronics. Five wires went from the board into the shiny metal sphere.

Tick ... Tick ... Tick ...

The light rain picked up, and water began dripping into Léa's eyes. She shook her head sharply in an attempt to shake the rain away. She looked over to her best friend.

The two women had been friends since childhood. Now, they were in their mid-thirties and were just as close as they had been as children.

"When did you ever hear an electronic trigger ticking like mechanical clock?" said Léa.

"I'm guessing someone's playing mind games with us. So where's the real detonator?"

Léa pointed her screwdriver at the small plywood board holding the electronics to the side of the suitcase.

"I think, there," she said.

"Funny how it's sitting a few inches off the back of the case," said Tara.

"I'm guessing our annoying little clock is ticking just below that board."

"Annoying?" asked Tara.

"Kinda sounds like that tree outside my bedroom window back home."

Léa smiled as she thought back to the night before her life changed forever, a memory etched deep.

Tap ... Tap ... Tap ...

The bare tree branch lightly tapped the bedroom window as wind and rain gusted on-shore. Off the coast, a big Atlantic storm was raging. The dark skies were brilliantly lit by occasional bolts of lightning.

Tap ... Tap ... Tap ...

The branch continued to tap annoyingly against Léa's bedroom window.

This has to be the kind of "dark and stormy night" that desperate authors dream about when they start a new novel, Léa thought to herself.

Tap ... Tap ... Tap ...

It was two o'clock in the morning, ten years before Léa would find herself at the base of Lord Nelson's Column. She was home on vacation from grad school, visiting family. Léa was also in town to catch up with friends, to make a little money, and to do something she'd been planning to do since she was a little girl.

Léa's childhood home was on the Orkney Islands north of Scotland. The family, including her mum, dad, and a black cat named Gracie, lived just outside the small port town of Stromness.

Just as Léa looked away from her window, the room lit up with a flash of lightning. Léa closed her eyes to readjust them to the darkness. When she opened her eyes, she saw Gracie's large, green eyes staring down at her from the tall chest of drawers.

"Here kitty!"

Gracie blinked her eyes but didn't move.

Typical cat, Léa thought.

Tap ... Tap ... Tap ...

The bare tree branch continued tapping against her window. The branch reminded her of something she'd seen before. It hadn't been at school. It had been at night. It hadn't been her room. It was a movie. But which movie?

Léa reached for her iPhone and tapped out a quick message.

You awake?

A few minutes later, her friend Tara responded.

I am now!!

Sorry ... Can't sleep ...

You okay?

Yeah ... The storm ...

What's Up?

That movie with the branch hitting the window?

Dr. Zhivago.

That's it! Thanks ...

Why?

There's this branch hitting my window ...

Cut it down and go back to SLEEP!!

Even with Tara's desire to go back to sleep, the texting continued for the next hour, until both phones' batteries finally started to give out. After a few more messages about the next day's plans, Léa's phone beeped, then shut down.

The phone charger was in Léa's backpack on the desk across the room. She pulled on the socks she kept beside her pillow for nighttime trips across the cold hardwood floor. Once the socks were on, she jumped out of bed and ran over to the desk. Léa quickly retrieved the phone charger and turned back toward the warm bed as another bolt of lightning lit up the room and the countryside through her window.

With the flash of light, Léa could clearly see outside her window where she and her friends would be spending the weekend.

The old castle was on the north end of the island. It had some goofy name that Léa could never remember. More importantly, it had a sinister history. Nearly everyone in town had a "castle story" to tell.

Tap ... Tap ... Tap ...

Spending a weekend at the castle was a Stromness rite of passage. Almost everyone did it. Actually, almost everyone tried.

Léa's eyes were still fixed on the castle's location when another bolt of lightning lit up the sky, and she saw every detail.

Tap ... Tap ... Tap ...

No one ever spent the weekend at the castle alone because the place was haunted. Or so the stories went.

This weekend, Léa and her friends would find out if the stories were true.

Tap ... Tap ... Tap ...

As Léa turned away from the window, lightning lit up her room, and she caught sight of herself in the dresser mirror, wearing only her socks.

Not bad, she thought.

A shiver ran down her spine from the typically cold, Stromness night. Léa dove back into her warm bed.

Back at Trafalgar Square, Léa's smile faded as the sound of the ticking timer broke through her happy memories.

Tick ... Tick ... Tick ...

"You still haven't cut that branch away from your window, have you?" asked Tara.

"Well, we have been a little busy these past ten years."

"It's just one, tiny little tree branch." Tara shook her head.

"You might cut me some slack about the branch and concentrate on our little problem here." Léa nodded to the bomb.

"Oh, this old thing? Okay, if you insist." Tara smiled.

Léa smiled back. "You've figured something out."

"Sure have." Tara was still smiling.

"So tell me."

Just as Léa looked back to the bomb, the lights on the computer boards began to flash, and a hidden speaker beeped loudly.

Léa and Tara looked at each other.

"We may be about out of time," they both said.

PART 1: THE HAUNTED CASTLE

CHAPTER 1 - FRIDAY

Stromness, Orkney
(Ten Years Earlier)

"Will you just look at that," said Pattie McNally through the food window.

"Wha's that you're sayin' woman?" Her husband shouted from the kitchen, raising his voice over the noisy dishwasher.

"Young people these days," said Pattie, shaking her head.

The object of Pattie McNally's disgust sat in the corner booth by the window. Tara Wells knew she was being looked at. People always looked at Tara. It was what she wanted.

She reached for her cup of coffee, the heavy metal bracelet on her wrist hitting the table with a loud *clank*. As she drained the coffee, her other hand shot straight up over her head. Without looking toward Pattie, Tara snapped her fingers and pointed down to the empty coffee cup halfway to the table.

Her bracelets—one on each wrist—*clank*ed again as she rested her hands on the keyboard of her new MacBook Pro. Tara thought for a moment. Then her fingers began to fly over the keys, and for the next five minutes, her hands were blurs.

Then, as quickly as she had begun typing, she stopped. Without looking over her work, Tara exported the project to a PDF file, attached it to an email, and pointed to the *send* button.

"Ka-ching," she said loudly as she clicked *send*.

Tara reached for the coffee cup and saw it was still empty. She huffed, raised her hand, and snapped her fingers again. Then she returned her attention to the computer.

5

Pattie grabbed the coffee pot and shuffled over to the table. Tara slid her cup around the laptop without breaking eye contact with her computer screen.

As Pattie topped off the coffee cup, she looked down at Tara and asked, "Can I bring you something to eat, love?"

Tara responded by reaching for her iPhone and turning up the volume on her earbuds. Her eyes remained fixed on the computer screen.

As Pattie waited for the answer she knew would never come, she looked over the small, thin girl, wearing heavy black boots, tight black cargo pants, and a shiny black leather jacket. The girl's black hair matched her dark sunglasses and her black-painted fingernails. Other than her pale skin, the only things on her that weren't black were the heavy, brushed metal bracelets.

As Pattie turned to leave, she noticed another glint of brushed metal around the girl's neck. The heavy metal collar appeared to be locked with a padlock. Pattie's eyes continued down the mostly open black leather jacket and could tell the girl wore nothing underneath.

Without moving her head, Tara glanced at the back of the older woman shuffling away. She realized she had earned the woman's disapproval, and a small smile appeared just below her black sunglasses.

"Mission accomplished," Tara said quietly.

"And what mission was that?" Léa asked.

Tara looked up as her best friend slid into the booth, across from her. Léa Taylor reached into her backpack, pulled out her laptop, and opened the lid. As the system powered up, she plugged her earbuds into her phone. Then she waved at Pattie, pointed at Tara's coffee cup, and smiled.

Tara watched her friend reach into her backpack for a plastic folder full of paper, a pen and, a legal pad and arrange them on the table. As Pattie approached with a fresh cup of coffee, Léa looked up and smiled again.

"How are you today, Mrs. McNally?" Léa asked.

"Right as rain, love. Will you be wanting some biscuits to go with your coffee, dear?"

"Yes, thanks," said Léa.

"And how about your friend? She really is frightfully thin. Some of Mr. McNally's biscuits and gravy might be just the ticket."

"Don't know. Anything to eat, love?" Léa asked Tara.

Tara stared coldly back.

"I guess that'll be a 'no, thanks,'" Léa said.

"Right then. I'll leave you to it," said Pattie as she turned away.

Léa continued the stare-down with Tara for a few more seconds before breaking eye contact and unzipping one of the many pockets on her backpack. She pulled out a mini bottle of Bailey's and stirred it into her coffee.

Tara tried to keep from smiling. She knew what was coming next. As if on cue, Léa shut her eyes and ever so slightly snapped her head from side to side.

Totally predictable, thought Tara.

Tara called it 'clearing the cobwebs,' and Léa did it whenever she was confused, frustrated, or angry. If she looked up, she was frustrated. If she looked down, she was mad. Some things never change, and Léa's cobweb clearing was as regular as the rain on the island.

This time, Léa didn't look up or down. She stared straight ahead for a few more moments.

Léa held the coffee with both hands, enjoying the aroma before taking her first sip. Freshly brewed coffee was one of her favorite scents. It was even better with Bailey's.

Tara's gaze remained blank as Léa cradled the coffee under her nose. After glancing quickly at Tara over her coffee cup, Léa turned to watch the rain hitting the window.

Drops slowly ran down the glass. Léa's eyes followed one of the rivers of water. Without looking away, she reached for her backpack, unzipped another pocket, and pulled out her camera—not just any camera. It was her professional-grade DSLR.

Photography had been one of Léa's passions since she'd received her first camera from her parents. Again, without looking, Léa's hand disappeared into another pocket of her backpack. When it reappeared, her fingers carefully clutched one of her lenses.

From lots of practice, Léa was able to remove both lens covers, attach the lens, and flip on the power without looking. Her father had taught her to never take her eyes off her subject so she wouldn't miss the shot. Now she always got the picture she wanted.

Click ... Click ... Click ...

Léa snapped three quick shots and looked down at her camera. The LCD screen displayed the last shot, and it was just what Léa wanted. Smiling, she spun the camera to show Tara.

Tara continued to stare at her friend and didn't look down at the camera.

"Well done. You've managed to capture rain falling," she sneered.

No question this time. Léa looked down as she cleared the cobwebs.

Definitely pissed, thought Tara to herself as she looked toward the kitchen.

Mrs. McNally appeared to be busy brewing a fresh pot of coffee, but Tara knew she was keeping a close eye on the two young women sitting by the coffee shop's big window, watching Tara's every move.

This better fucking be good enough, you old bitch, thought Tara.

Léa had clearly given up on the stare-down and was looking out the window again. Tara's bad attitude had definitely hurt Léa, and Tara felt

7

awful.

This is not what I signed up for.

Tara looked down at her computer and tried to look as though she was working. Behind the sunglasses, she kept watching her friend.

Léa inhaled the aroma of her coffee before taking another sip. As she stared out the window, Léa wondered what happened to her friend.

Tara's perpetual bad mood had begun about this time last year. Without a word, she had disappeared for a few months. After reappearing, Tara had said she'd gone to London to check out the big city and find herself. But the friend who had left was not the woman who returned.

Setting her coffee cup aside, Léa cleared her throat.

"Forgive me for saying, but the angry bitch act is really getting quite tiresome. Is there any chance I'll ever get my best friend back?"

Tara didn't say a word.

Léa picked up her iPhone and tapped out a quick text. A few seconds later, Tara's phone buzzed.

You'll text at night but won't talk to me now?

Tara looked down, and one corner of her mouth bent into a smile. She typed a response.

People change ...

Léa looked up from her phone.

"Not like this. If I didn't know any better, I'd think I done something to make you angry with me. But I'm smart enough to know it's not that. You're treating everyone with equal contempt, and we're all getting quite tired of it."

Léa picked up her coffee and turned her attention back to the rain hitting the window. A few minutes later, her phone buzzed.

Just give me a little time. It'll be okay ... promise!

Léa looked up. Tara had nudged her sunglasses down her nose. The two friends looked at each other, then Tara smiled and winked at Léa before pushing the sunglasses back into place. Before Léa realized what had happened, Tara went back to work on her computer.

For an instant, Léa felt the warmth of her old friend. But almost as quickly, the cold stranger returned. Léa turned her attention back to the rain falling outside.

At the kitchen window, Pattie looked at her husband and whispered, "Did you see that?"

Her husband nodded as he turned his attention back to the stove.

"I think we can give her a break this time," he whispered.

"No we can't. That'll never do," said Pattie quietly.

"Now, now. This is different." Her husband began wiping down the grill.

"That's awfully generous considering how long you were in the hospital because of her," said Pattie.

"You can't carry a grudge forever."

"I guess," Pattie said.

Tara glanced at the kitchen and saw Pattie staring at her. She glared over her sunglasses, her eyes like daggers. Then she turned back to her computer.

Léa had been watching the rain through the front window of the coffee shop. In the distance, she saw breaks in the clouds and even a few rays of sunshine. Léa started to reach for her camera when she spotted three of her friends. She put down her coffee.

"Here comes Pat and the Twins," said Léa.

"About time." Tara didn't look up from her computer.

Léa sighed and stared back out at the rain.

CHAPTER 2 - THE SMARTEST KIDS IN TOWN

That Same Morning

"Looks like Grumpy Cat and Nice Girl beat us here, guys," said Pat Morris over his shoulder.

The two young women sitting by the coffee shop's front window looked like they were from different worlds. One looked pretty much like everyone else in the small island town. The other looked like trouble from the big city.

Charlie and Cindy Martin glanced through the window at Léa and Tara.

"More like Bondage Cat. See the hardware on her wrists and around her neck? Those cuffs aren't cheap," said Charlie.

"It's not like she doesn't have the money," said Pat.

"Thanks to her, we all have money for pretty much whatever. So she can dress however she wants," said Cindy.

"I guess." Pat reached for the coffee shop's door.

Cindy eyed Tara through the window.

"It's her perpetual bad mood that I'm getting sick of," she said.

"Yeah, but behind that bad mood her scheming brain's making us some good money. We just gotta make sure we don't do anything to set her off," said Charlie as he followed Pat through the door.

"We'll be okay," said Cindy, following behind them. "It's Léa I feel bad for."

"Why do you feel bad for me?" asked Léa as the group gathered around the table.

"Because your best friend has gone all Lisbeth Salander on you," said Pat.

Charlie huffed. "That's putting it mildly."

"Lisbeth Salander?" asked Cindy.

Pat started to answer, but Léa cut him off.

"The Girl With the Dragon Tattoo. I know you're the movie expert, but the comparison isn't even close. Lisbeth Salander had been badly abused her whole life. Tara's just had her mood superglued in nasty mode."

"And more importantly, we're not here for movie chat," said Tara.

The bell over the door jingled as an old, skinny man shuffled into the shop. He wore an old Inverness coat and a knit driving cap and carried several newspapers. He snapped his umbrella closed, dropped it in the small basket by the door, and started walking toward a table in the corner.

"Hullo, Mrs. McNally. Be a nice girl, and bring over a pot of hot tea, with some toast and jam," he said loudly.

"Good morning, Mr. Dennis. You'll be wanting something more than just toast," said Pattie.

"Just the toast and jam, thank you."

Everyone in the shop watched as he shuffled across the room, threw his coat and hat on an empty chair, and sat with a heavy thud.

"You can't just live off of tea and toast. You need some meat on your bones for the winter," said Pattie.

Mr. Dennis adjusted his glasses and shuffled through the stack of newspapers on the table until he found the one he wanted. Then he smiled up at Pattie.

"Never mind about me. I have all I need here with my newspapers, my tea, and your excellent strawberry jam," he said.

"You're going to dry up and blow away." Pattie shook her head and shuffled back to the kitchen.

All the kids watched Mr. Dennis as he took a sip of tea and opened his first newspaper. He looked up briefly and smiled at them.

"Don't mind me, kids. I won't be interfering in your plans for world domination today," he said.

Pat and Charlie looked at each other with traces of concern in their eyes. Léa looked at Tara, who actually seemed to smile at old Mr. Dennis' comment about "world domination."

"Did you see that? Grumpy Cat here almost cracked a smile," exclaimed Pat.

Tara glared at him, her barely-there smile fading entirely.

Léa broke the silence. "Perhaps now would be a good time to begin discussing our plot to dominate the world."

"What about our plot for tonight?" asked Charlie.

"Let's make some money first," said Tara. "I just finished Jared Carlson's history paper. Who's going to be coaching him for the final exam?"

"That's me," said Pat.

Tara started tapping on her computer.

"Not that it'll help that idiot's test scores, but I'm sending the paper your way so you can at least remind him what he wrote about," said Tara.

"As long as his parents' credit card doesn't bounce, who cares if he passes or not?" Charlie quipped.

"Maybe we should care. If he's turning in well-written papers, then flunks tests, someone might catch on to our plot to dominate the world," said Cindy.

Léa shrugged. "In which case, nothing happens to us. We're not doing anything illegal. But we'll have to figure out another way to fill our bank accounts."

"Thank you. Can we get back to making money?" said Tara.

After a few moments, Charlie said, "I've got something."

"Let's hear it," said Tara.

"I got stopped on the way out of the pub last week by David Minor's mum."

"The David Minor who's on the track team?" asked Léa.

"The very same." Charlie nodded. "He may be a star in sports, but he doesn't seem to have the brain power to make it through algebra."

"Just our kind of sports star. This sounds like a job for our Queen of Numbers. Want to take him on?" Tara looked to Cindy.

"Sure. Why not?"

"*Ka-ching!*" said Tara.

"Careful, Grumpy Cat. You're going to ruin your cranky reputation," said Charlie.

Tara shot Charlie her best hatchet eyes. She softened them after a few seconds and addressed the group. "Anyone else have any new money?"

Across the room, Pattie watched and listened as her customers continued discussing their amazing money making scheme. She leaned closer to the kitchen window.

"Just listen to them. How did they get so smart?" she whispered to her husband.

"We were just as smart when we were younger. We just didn't have them fancy computers or the Internet," he said.

"Not that smart. We never would have thought to help other people's kids with their homework like that."

"We also didn't have mums and dads willing to part with cold, hard cash to buy their kids good grades," he said.

Pattie had been listening to them for several years now. The whole idea had sprung up when they were still in school on the island. Then they all graduated and went their separate ways. But they still managed to meet every few months and continue their money-making scheme.

Every now and then, the conversation was punctuated by a loud "*Ka-ching!*" from the foul-tempered girl dressed in black.

"I hear they're heading up to the castle tonight," Pattie said.

"All their fancy gadgets won't do them much good up there, will they?" said her husband.

"About as much good as that old hunting rifle Gerald Wells took with him all those years ago."

"That fuckin' idiot." Her husband laughed.

"Language."

Her husband grinned. "Here it comes. Another chorus of 'profanity is merely the attempt of a weak mind to express itself forcefully.'"

"He was pretty pathetic shooting that old gun at a solid stone wall." Pattie smiled.

Her husband laughed, remembering that priceless ghost story. Attempting to spend a night at the castle was a rite of passage for people in this town. Most left long before morning.

Everyone in town grew up hearing stories about pathetic cries of anguish from long-dead, suffering prisoners coming from the castle's empty dungeon. They heard stories of people finding fresh blood on the centuries-old torture equipment. And they heard stories of people trapped for weeks in a maze of solid stone passages.

But David McNally and his wife never had the chance to check out the ghost stories for themselves. They grew up far from Stromness and their childhood was far from happy. David often wished he had grown up on the island.

"Where did you go?" asked Pattie.

"Just thinking back to my first visit to the castle."

Pattie smiled at her husband through the kitchen window.

"Any of them nasty ghosts give you nightmares?" she asked.

"No. I wish it were ghosts that gave me my gray hair and nightmares." He sighed.

"Me too," said Pattie.

He turned his attention back to the big pot of stew boiling on the stove.

"I wish it had been ghosts," he said sadly.

"*Ka-ching*! Is that it? Anyone else? No? Good!" Tara started packing up her laptop as everyone else's gazes lingered.

"So what about tonight?" Charlie asked.

"What about it?" Tara zipped her backpack and started to slide out of the booth.

"Tonight's the night. You know, the castle?"

"What about it?" Tara said again.

Cindy spoke slowly. "It's the *thing* everyone in town does. The *thing* most people only do once. They never go back again."

"Maybe we want to, you know, figure out what we're gonna do in case we see a ghost," said Charlie.

Tara turned and lowered her head, nearly touching her chin to her left shoulder. Even through her dark sunglasses, they could tell she had closed her eyes.

"Now you've done it. She's going to be mildly irritated with us again," said Cindy.

Tara stood in silence while everyone waited for the explosion of crankiness.

"I, for one, could care less whether she's irritated with us or not," said Léa.

Everyone turned to Léa.

"For years, people here in Stromness have been talking about that dirty old castle," she said. "They've been scaring their kids with ghost stories, and tonight's the night we all planned to find out what's really going on up there."

Now, even Tara was looking at Léa, and with less than her usual amount of attitude.

"Everyone used to call us the 'Smartest Kids in Town,' and we're heading up to that dirty old castle in less than twelve hours. I don't believe in ghosts, and I don't think any of you do either. But most everyone else on this cold little island does, and they're going to be watching us to see what we do."

Léa took a breath, closed her eyes for a few moments, and then looked at Charlie.

"So you make sure that we all have plenty of flashlight batteries and that your video camera and recorders are fully charged."

She turned to Cindy.

"You get all the camping stuff from your dad's attic, and don't forget the cold-weather rain gear."

She took a breath and turned to Pat.

"You bring your camp stove, lights, and portable heaters, and please don't forget extra stove gas."

Léa looked down and began stuffing her laptop and papers in her backpack. She took another breath. "Each of us needs to bring dry, warm clothes and something to sleep in. I'll bring plenty of water, trail food, and a hot dinner for what I suspect will be a cold night in that damp, dirty castle." Léa snapped the backpack zipper closed, then looked directly at Tara. "As for you, leave that ridiculous costume and hardware at home. And if you don't mind, I think we'd all appreciate it if you'd shove your nasty little attitude up your skinny little ass, at least for this weekend."

Léa looked back down at her backpack. She took a deep breath and nodded once.

"I think that about covers it. See you all this afternoon," she said.

Without looking at Tara, Léa stood up and strode out of the coffee shop.

Everyone sat in stunned silence. Even Mr. Dennis had stopped reading his paper and was watching as the door closed behind Léa. The kids all looked at Tara, whose face remained a frozen mask of indifference.

Charlie stuffed his laptop into his backpack and stood up. As he slowly zipped his jacket, he spoke to Tara. "I'd better get busy making sure all my batteries are charged up."

Pat followed Charlie toward the door, neither of them looking back at Tara.

Cindy packed up her own laptop and slipped out of the booth. She threw some money on the table and zipped her jacket.

"Guess we're done here," said Cindy.

Mr. Dennis smiled at Tara, alone beside the empty booth, then returned to his newspaper. Mrs. McNally looked at her with a *you deserved that* kind of smile before turning away to start a fresh pot of coffee. Her husband only briefly glanced at Tara over the boiling pot of stew.

Old Mr. Dennis looked up from his paper just as the small girl paused at the door.

Before reaching for the doorknob, she wiped away a tear behind her sunglasses and walked out into the rain.

CHAPTER 3 - THE ROAD NORTH OF TOWN

The Castle - That Afternoon

Pat pointed down the road. "Here come Cindy and Charlie."

Two kids on bikes appeared at the top of a distant hill before disappearing behind the next rise, following the road that circled the island.

"Right on time," Léa said. "Seen Tara?"

"Not yet. But I'm sure we'll feel her cranky disturbance in the force any minute now," said Pat.

Léa shook her head tiredly. She walked a few steps down what had once been a road leading to the castle. Now, it was more like a goat path.

The wind had been picking up all afternoon as another North Atlantic storm began churning up the sea and slowly moving ashore. A strong gust of wind and sea spray whipped the kids as they waited by the side of the two-lane road.

Léa and Pat turned their backs to the sea as the wave of wind and spray hit. Cindy and Charlie weren't so lucky. The strong gust struck them just as they stopped their bikes on the road's gravel shoulder.

"Whoa!" Cindy yelled as the wind knocked her into Charlie's bike.

Charlie planted his foot in the gravel just in time to prevent both riders and bikes from being blown over by the wind.

"Thanks for that," said Cindy.

"I was just trying to save the food," he said.

"I should have known." Cindy pushed her bike over to Léa.

"Hey." Léa greeted them briefly before returning her attention to the castle in the distance.

"What do you think we'll find up there?" Cindy asked her.

"No idea. Like I said this morning, I don't believe in ghosts. But everyone in town does, so something must be going on,."

Charlie and Pat pushed their bikes up the path. When they reached the others, Pat reached for Cindy's hand.

"So, here we are," he said.

"Here we are." Cindy smiled. "I hope you realize you have an important job tonight."

"Don't worry, I brought the stove and gas," said Pat.

Cindy rolled her eyes. "Good boy. But your main job tonight is keeping me warm."

"No need to worry. That's a responsibility I plan on taking very seriously."

Léa grumbled. "Just see that you don't take it too seriously. Don't keep the rest of us awake while you two are staying warm."

"Yeah," said Charlie.

"And don't you be so quick to chime in," Léa snapped. "Maybe you and Tara should try to rekindle your romance. Keep each other warm, and thaw her icy mood."

"Not much chance of that. Tara's general bad mood includes me, too." He sighed and kicked the dirt.

In the distance, another wave of wind and sea spray hit the shore. The gray skies slowly darkened. An angry ocean was visible between the rolling hills as the storm whipped up the sea.

Charlie looked at his watch and back down the road. After staring at the empty road for a while, he checked his watch and turned his focus to the castle. "It'll be getting dark soon. How much longer should we wait for Little Miss Sunshine?"

Léa pulled out her phone to check the time. No messages.

"We're already running late," she said. "I'd rather have a little natural light while we get our bearings in the castle."

She tapped out a quick text to Tara.

Where are u?

She pressed *send* and stared at her iPhone screen. Pat and Charlie looked over her shoulder at the screen. No reply. A minute later, the screen dimmed, then went black.

"I'm not all that excited about waiting around much longer," said Pat.

"Me either. Let's go." Léa stuffed the phone back into her jacket pocket.

As the four friends picked up their bicycles and pedaled down the path to the castle, another blast of wind and sea spray headed inland. Cindy braked when she spotted the approaching gust of wind. "I am not riding into that."

Everyone hopped off their bikes and started walking.

"You know," Charlie said, "there are actually places where the sun shines, and you can ride a bike for more than ten minutes without getting soaked."

"On the other hand, how many cases of skin cancer do we get here?" asked Cindy.

"And we have that." Léa pointed to the castle.

As the friends pushed their bicycles closer to the old castle, another wave of sea spray made its way across the open field. Léa looked to the castle, remembering the strange stories she'd heard growing up—walls disappearing, people being trapped for days in rooms without doors, and cries of pain and anguish coming from the long-abandoned dungeon.

There were stories of people who had gone to the castle and never came back. No one actually knew anyone who had disappeared. But there were, you know, stories.

The most bizarre tales revolved around sightings of the bodies of prisoners who had long ago died horrible deaths at the hands of dungeon guards. The stories said their wounds were as fresh as if they'd been inflicted mere hours before.

The thing was, Léa had never heard a castle horror story from anyone who'd actually seen something firsthand.

"What's on your mind?" asked Charlie.

Léa's blank expression broke. "Huh?"

"You suddenly got quiet," Cindy said.

"Just thinking about that old place." Léa nodded to the castle as another cold blast of rain and wind whipped across the field. "It's like I was saying this morning. Ever since we were kids, we've heard awful stories about that dusty old castle."

"You suppose there's any truth to those stories?" asked Pat.

"That's what I was just thinking about," Léa said.

"In general, ghost stories seem to have one or two verifiable elements," Cindy chimed in. "That's how they get people to believe the un-verifiable elements."

"I just hope the ghosts are smart enough to leave us alone," said Pat with a glance to Cindy.

"I'm sure the ghosts will give us plenty of time." Cindy smiled at Charlie. "Too bad Tara couldn't make it."

"It wouldn't make any difference," grumbled Charlie. "She hasn't been interested in doing anything with me for nearly a year now."

"Now might be the perfect time for you to move on," Pat said. "I just happen know someone who's available."

"Seems like a good fit. After all, you two are the smartest, best-looking people on the island," said Cindy.

Léa scoffed. "Please."

"That has possibilities," said Charlie hesitantly.

"Not a bad idea." Pat nodded.

"You two would make a great-looking couple," said Cindy.

Charlie saw that Léa was clearly uncomfortable. "Maybe we should concentrate on being ghost detectives for now," he said. "We can talk about romance later."

Léa smiled at Charlie. "Sounds like a good plan to me."

"We're here," said Cindy.

Charlie looked up at the castle. "Wow, this thing is big."

"We're only at the first gate," said Pat.

"Wow, this thing is big," repeated Charlie.

Léa gave Charlie another smile. "Thanks for that," she said quietly.

Charlie smiled back as Léa turned to the castle entrance. Her smile faded into an expression of determination. She squared her shoulders and walked through the first gate of the ancient castle.

"Come on, you bloody ghosts. Let's see what you've got," she whispered.

Back on the main road, a lone motorcycle paused at the top of the highest hill before the castle turnoff. The rider, dressed in black, watched the four cyclists stop in front of the ancient castle. The motorcycle's engine idled as the four walked through the first castle gate.

Tara removed her helmet and shook her long, black hair away from her eyes. The gel that had held her bizarre hairstyle in place was gone. So were the heavy metal cuffs and collar. There was no trace of the neck tattoo or nose piercing.

A slightly sad, ironic smile appeared at one corner of Tara's mouth as she watched her friends walk through the outer courtyard and through the second gate, arriving at the main entrance to the castle.

Tara thought back to her first night at the castle, over a year ago. Her friends disappeared inside, and she put on her helmet, gunned the engine, and motored past the turnoff to the castle.

Tara continued almost a mile down the road before bringing the motorcycle to a screeching stop. She checked her mirrors to see if anyone was behind her.

Once Tara decided she was alone on the road, she took off across the damp field, zipping down a path leading back to the castle. The trail was bumpy, and Tara's motorcycle flew off the the small hills like ramps. Soon she arrived at the main outer wall of the castle and turned to follow it.

Still riding at breakneck speed, Tara bounced off a few more hills as she accelerated down the path running parallel with the wall. Rain and wind bit at Tara's helmet as she raced toward the cliff overlooking the angry sea.

Just as the path was about to disappear, Tara skidded the bike to a stop. She looked around to make sure no one had seen her. Holding the front brake tightly, she spun the back tire until the motorcycle pointed at a small hole in the castle wall.

Tara gunned the motor one more time and disappeared into the ancient castle.

CHAPTER 4 - THE FIRST NIGHT

The Castle - 8 p.m.

"This looks like a nice spot to camp out for the night," said Pat.

"Not bad." Cindy looked around the big room.

The large, round room was near the top of the castle. A fireplace was nestled beside several big windows looking out over the stormy sea. There was no furniture, just gray, dusty stone walls.

"There's another room just like this next door," said Charlie as he and Léa joined the others.

"Must have been his and hers bedrooms back in the day," said Léa.

"We'll take this one," Pat said. "You guys take that one."

"That way we can avoid an awkward double make-out session," said Cindy, snuggling up to Pat. "But we can still keep an eye on each other in case any ghosts show up."

"The light is almost gone," Léa said. "We better start a few fires and get the camp lights set up."

Cindy held Pat closer. "I'm all about starting a few fires."

"Fires of passion later. Hot food first," said Charlie.

Léa nodded. "Well said. We can light the fires of passion later. Right now, I'm starved."

"Yeah, you're always starving aren't you, skinny girl?" A hint of bitterness crept into Cindy's voice.

Pat laughed and touched her arm. "It's the blessing of having a super fast metabolism."

"Not such a blessing when you're always hungry," Léa said. "But don't worry, Cindy. My metabolism will come screeching to a halt one day."

A sudden gust of wind blew a ton of sea spray into the room. Once the air cleared, most of the room was soaking wet. Only the area around the fireplace remained dusty dry.

"Well, at least we know not to set up our sleeping bags by the window," said Pat.

"Let's go check our room and get that campfire going." Léa made her way toward the door.

"We're like five stories up." Charlie gazed out the window. "How could this much water make it all the way up here?"

"Looks like a pretty big storm out there," said Cindy.

"There's always a pretty big storm out there. But getting that much sea spray all the way up here still seems odd," said Charlie.

"Plus, if there's always a big storm out there," Léa said, "you'd think it would be blowing a ton of water in here all the time."

"So?" Cindy crossed her arms.

"So why is it so dusty up here? And why isn't there more water damage on those old wooden beams and floors?"

The group fell silent, pondering Léa's questions. The sound of wind whistling through the old castle seemed to grow louder.

"Well then. Now we have a few more questions to add to our list." Léa started toward the door and called over her shoulder, "Come on, Charlie. Let's go see how wet our room is."

"Catch you guys later." Charlie followed Léa.

Charlie was barely through the doorway when Léa called out from the other room. "Uh, guys. You need to come see this."

Cindy and Pat started toward the door. In the other room, they looked around, looked at each other, and looked at Léa.

"So, what do we need to see?" asked Cindy.

Léa gawked at her. "You don't see it?"

Cindy peered around the room. She glanced at Pat and Charlie and shook her head. "Looks like all the other dusty old rooms we've seen today."

"Except this one is bone dry, and the one right next door is soaking wet," Léa said.

Pat walked over to the window, leaned out, and examined the outer walls of the castle.

"They're damp, but not nearly as wet as the room next door." He walked toward the door and spoke over his shoulder. "Be right back."

Léa looked at Cindy. "Go with him."

"Why?"

"Because if he sees a ghost, I want you to see it, too." Léa didn't try to cover her impatience. "Hurry up."

Cindy scurried out of the room.

"I'd call that a curious development," said Léa.

"Maybe it's time for me to dig out my video camera and recorders." Charlie walked over to his bicycle.

"Good idea," said Léa.

She looked out the window at the raging sea. The waves crashed into the rocks at the base of the cliff. The gray skies on the horizon were turning dark with the setting sun.

"Better break out the lights, too," Léa called over her shoulder to Charlie.

As if to answer, a bright camp light came to life behind her. She turned and smiled at Charlie.

"Brilliant. Now set up the camp stove in the fireplace, and I'll get some warm food going," she said.

"What do you suppose happened to Tara?" asked Charlie.

Léa shook her head and began unpacking pots, pans, and food. "Don't know, don't care."

"Like I believe that. You two have been best friends since you were five years old," he said.

Léa's hands paused. "You're right about that. But until her icy new exterior thaws, I'm really not interested in thinking about her, worrying about her, or talking about her."

Charlie got the message. "Okay."

Léa went back to unpacking. Charlie worked at setting up two more portable lights, and soon the room was bathed in their warm glow. As the last light popped on, Pat and Cindy reappeared in the doorway.

"Don't tell us," said Léa. "Let me guess. The room is soaked, but the outside wall isn't."

Pat nodded. "You got it."

"This is going to sound a little silly, but we might stay drier if we sleep in the tents," Léa said.

"Not a bad idea," said Charlie.

Léa added, "And we might want to all stay in the same room so we can welcome any ghostly visitors together."

"*Mmm*, not so good of an idea," said Cindy.

"Yeah, we have plans tonight." Pat put his arm around Cindy.

"Suit yourselves." Léa started working on dinner.

Cindy snuggled into Pat. "It might be good for you two to start making a few plans yourselves," she said.

Charlie started to say something, but Léa cut him off. "We'll make our own plans, thank you."

Charlie looked over at Pat and Cindy. "There you go."

"What do you suppose happened to Tara?" asked Pat.

This time Charlie spoke up before Léa. "We've already been over that, too."

"Okay," said Pat slowly.

The room fell into an uncomfortable silence. Charlie played with one of his cameras. Léa stirred the pot of stew. Pat stood with Cindy near the door.

"Let's go set up our tent," he whispered .

After a brief hesitation, Cindy and Pat quietly slipped out. Charlie watched them leave, glancing at Léa before turning his attention to the video camera.

When she was confident the stew wouldn't stick, Léa tossed the spoon aside and reduced the heat on the stove. She walked over to the big window and looked out at the stormy sea. The temperature was dropping fast, and she pulled her jacket tightly around her.

Léa wasn't in a good place. Charlie had annoyed her by bringing up Tara. But the snotty attitude Tara had developed over the past year annoyed Léa, too. It left her hurt and confused. The two girls had grown up together, gone to school together, gotten in trouble together. They had always been there for each other.

When they were little girls, their parents had told them frightening stories about the old castle. For Léa, the stories sank in deep. After all, her childhood bedroom had a clear view of the old castle. The ghost stories had frightened her until Tara told her not to worry because they'd face those ghosts together.

Now, it was almost twenty years later, and it was time for Léa and Tara to explore the castle. But Tara wasn't here, and Léa desperately missed her friend.

Bloody hell, thought Léa.

She looked down at her shoes. Léa realized she couldn't do anything about Tara being gone. Even though she missed her friend, Léa needed to move on to something she could control.

She gazed out at the stormy sea and down at the surf crashing against the base of the cliffs. The castle, the ghosts, and the ghost stories were topics worth Léa's time.

Close your eyes. Take a deep breath. Let your mind go blank. Start with a clean sheet of paper.

That was how Léa solved problems. She began by turning her problem into the simplest question she could.

Léa opened her eyes, and the question popped into her head.

"What's really going on at this castle?" she whispered under her breath.

The next step in Léa's problem-solving process was to eliminate impossible explanations. She closed her eyes again and immediately crossed ghosts off her mental list. Léa didn't believe in ghosts, and, even if she did, there was no way that ghosts could do all the things people had reported over the years.

So who's responsible for rattling chains, shrieks of pain, soaking wet rooms, and magically appearing walls?

After eliminating ghosts, the culprit had to be a genuine, flesh-and-blood human—probably not just one human, either.

So how many people?

Not many. The castle ghost stories had been circulating around

23

Stromness for decades. What was really going on at the castle was clearly a secret, and most people weren't good at keeping secrets. So there likely weren't many people involved.

And the last question … Why?

Léa smiled.

That's easy, she thought. *They have something to hide, and they're using the ghost stories to keep everyone away.*

Léa breathed in sea air, slowly exhaled, and opened her eyes. She heard Charlie walk up beside her.

"Figure it all out?" he asked.

"Not all of it. But some of it."

"Well then. Let's hear it."

"Later," said Léa. She turned and walked over to the fireplace. Léa stirred the pot a few times, tasted the stew, and smiled. "Come and get it!"

An hour later, Pat tossed his metal camp bowl onto the stack of dirty dishes and leaned back against the fireplace.

"That was the best!" he said.

"Sure was." Charlie rubbed his belly.

"Amazing," said Cindy.

"Thanks," Léa said. "Now. Who's going to volunteer to do the dishes?"

No one said a word.

"Don't make the cook volunteer someone."

Charlie stood up. "I'll take care of it, but you still have something to do."

"I don't think so," said Léa.

"Sure you do." He smiled. As he started working on the pots, plates, and cups, the room grew quiet again.

"Okay, I'll ask. What else does Léa have to do?" said Cindy.

"While you two were setting up your tent," Charlie said, scrubbing a plate, "the smartest girl in town put her brain into high gear and figured out the secrets of this old castle."

"Oh please," said Léa.

"Really?" said Pat.

"Well tell us." Cindy's head bobbed.

"Yeah, tell us the secret of life," Pat said.

Léa rolled her eyes. "I still have a lot to figure out."

Charlie laughed. "Tell me another good one. I was standing right next to you, remember? I've seen you when you work something out, and you worked this out."

"Here. I'll make it worth your time." Pat pulled a small flask from his jacket pocket and tossed it to Léa. She unscrewed it and sniffed.

"Peppermint schnapps?"

"I figured this would make a cold, damp night just a little warmer," said Pat.

Léa grabbed the coffee pot from the stove and poured a cup, adding a shot of schnapps. She took a sip and gave him a thumbs up. "Good call."

Léa tossed the flask to Cindy, who took a swig and handed it back to Pat, who took a bigger swig.

"Save some of that for us working folks," said Charlie.

"Anything you say, mate." Pat winked at Cindy, took another big swig from the flask, and tossed it to Charlie.

"Take it easy," Léa said. "We don't want to be too bombed when the ghosts arrive."

"Speaking of ghosts, how about telling us what you figured out," said Charlie.

"Well, to start, I'm really not expecting to see a ghost." Léa peered into her coffee cup and began talking. Five minutes later, she looked up.

"So what do you think?"

"Sounds about right to me," Charlie said, just finishing the dishes. "But we're going to need to know a lot more to figure out what they're hiding."

"What if, uh, they're, like, dangerous?" Cindy pressed the words out slowly.

"Looks like my little sister is feeling her schnapps." Charlie smiled.

"You're twins," Léa said. "How can she be your *little* sister?"

"I arrived first."

"By about ... a ... a ... minute," slurred Cindy.

Léa reached into the bag of food and pulled out two bottles of water.

"I don't want you two hung over tomorrow while we're prowling around this old place. So knock off the schnapps and start rehydrating right now." Léa tossed the bottles to Cindy and Pat. Cindy made an attempt to catch hers, but Pat just watched as his bottle sailed through the air and landed in his lap.

Léa reached into her backpack for a bottle of Tylenol. She tossed it to Cindy.

"Take a few of those too."

"Thanks." Cindy opened the bottle and swallowed a few capsules with a huge gulp of water. She poked Pat in the ribs, opened his water bottle, and handed him the pills.

"Let's go, boyfriend."

"Cindy had a fair point," Charlie said. "What if you're right and there are people behind the ghost stories who are trying to hide something? Think they could be dangerous?"

"I'm not sure," Léa said, "but I don't think so."

"Why?" Pat downed his pills and tossed the bottle back to Léa.

Léa looked back down into her coffee cup, thinking. The room became silent. Cindy and Pat sipped their water.

"Hear that?" Charlie looked over his shoulder.

Cindy's and Pat's eyes followed his. "What?" they both said.

25

"Listen carefully, and you can hear the wheels spinning in Léa's head." Charlie smiled.

"Don't do that," said Cindy.

"Jackass," said Pat.

The room fell silent again. A few minutes later, Léa looked up from her coffee and grinned.

"It's really quite simple. People have been visiting this old castle for years. Most come back with fantastic stories of blood-curdling shrieks, rattling chains, skeletons in dungeons, and appearing and disappearing walls. Right?"

"Right," said Charlie.

Cindy and Pat nodded.

"But no one from town has ever disappeared, have they? Sure, there are stories about people disappearing. But do you know anyone who's actually disappeared?"

No one responded.

"I'll take that as a no. Add to that, no one has ever really been hurt here, have they?" said Léa.

"She's right," said Pat slowly.

"Yeah," said Cindy.

"So whoever it is, they're willing to scare people, but not hurt people," said Charlie.

"I'm not saying it's guaranteed. But I don't think we're in much real danger," said Léa.

"Maybe no one's been hurt yet because no one's been smart enough to discover this place's secret," said Cindy carefully.

Léa shrugged. "That's a fair point."

"So we still need to be cautious," said Charlie.

"That's tomorrow. For now, I'm ready for some special time with my girlfriend." Pat seemed come back to life.

"Think you can stay awake long enough?" Cindy laughed.

Pat stood up and extended a hand to Cindy. "Wanna find out?"

"You're on." Cindy let Pat pull her to her feet.

Holding hands, Cindy and Pat started toward the door. The schnapps made them both unsteady. Cindy's shoulder bumped the wall, and Pat stumbled into her, but they remained on their feet.

"Sweet dreams you two," said Cindy.

"Night," said Pat.

"You guys remember where your room is?" Charlie laughed.

"Don't fall down the stairs," said Léa.

Pat held onto Cindy's arm. "They're funny aren't they?"

"Funny," said Cindy.

They stood in the doorway for a few moments with semi-blank looks on their faces. Then Pat shook his head. "Okay, love. Let's go."

With that, they managed to successfully make it through the doorway and into their room.

"Maybe we should just peek around the corner to make sure they can crawl into their tent," said Charlie.

"I think we'll be able to tell if they have any problems." Léa began to turn off the camp lights scattered around the room.

"Yeah, I guess," said Charlie.

Léa yawned, picked up her backpack, and crawled into the tent.

"Be sure to get that last light," she told Charlie.

"Right," he said.

Charlie snapped off the camp stove and reached for his camera bag.

"Don't forget to bring your cameras and stuff into the tent," Léa said from inside the tent. "You know, just in case any ghosts show up."

"I'll do better than that."

"How?"

"Look and see," said Charlie.

Léa popped her head outside the tent as Charlie set a camera on a small tripod in the far corner of the room.

"This one has a motion sensor. So if a ghost comes to get us in the tent, it'll automatically take pictures of what's happening."

"Brilliant. But won't it be too dark?"

"No problem. It's got night-vision," said Charlie.

"Even better." Léa disappeared into the tent.

Charlie checked the camera controls and snapped off the last camp light.

"Be right back," he said, heading the door.

"Where are you going?" called Léa.

But Charlie had already left the room. Léa poked her head out of the tent as he returned.

"Just checking to make sure my little sister got home okay."

"Everything all right?" asked Léa.

"They're both passed out."

"Of course. Come on, then. Let's get some rest. I have a feeling we're going to need it tomorrow."

"Me too," he said as he crawled into the tent.

CHAPTER 5 - SATURDAY

The Castle, 3 a.m.

Léa rolled over in her sleeping bag and stared at the top of the tent. Her bladder was sending urgent signals to her brain.

"Of all the nights," she said to herself.

Charlie seemed to be sleeping deeply. Slowly and quietly, she felt for the jacket and socks she had left along the side of her sleeping bag.

Léa had never liked wearing much while she slept. Despite her better judgment, she had decided she would sleep better if she was comfortable. If a ghost suddenly appeared, it would just have to wait for her to get dressed.

Léa found her jacket and socks and wriggled out of the sleeping bag. Once she was halfway out, she pulled her jacket over her shoulders. After inching out a bit more, Léa pulled on her socks and reached for her sneakers. She took one more look at Charlie before quietly crawling out of the tent.

The room looked just as it had before bed. The camp chairs were where everyone had left them. The pots and dishes were neatly stacked, and Pat's flask of schnapps was right where he left it.

Léa looked out the window. The storm was still raging. The temperature had dropped, and the cold wind and sea spray stung her face and legs.

Léa turned and left quietly, pausing to peer into Cindy and Pat's room. She could hear them both breathing steadily as they slept.

Nice to know Cindy and Pat are okay.

Her bladder prodded her brain again, and she scurried into the last empty room on the floor. Pat had set up a portable toilet. The room's window looked like the ones in the other two rooms. In one corner, the stone wall seemed discolored.

After finishing with the toilet, Léa examined the wall. They weren't different colored stones after all. A spiral staircase was built along the wall. Léa looked up, her gaze winding along the stairs leading to the next level. Pulling her jacket tighter around her, Léa started climbing.

As she neared the top, a gust of cold wind loaded with rain blew through the opening and hit her squarely in the face. Her rainproof jacket kept her chest and arms dry. But her hair, face, and legs were soaked. Léa rubbed the water from her eyes and kept climbing.

She travelled the last few steps and found herself in a small stone room. To her right, a low door appeared to lead to the roof of the castle turret. Léa could hear the wind and rain outside.

She snapped her gaze behind her. She thought she heard something. She waited a few moments before deciding there was nothing.

When she decided she was alone, a small, wicked smile appeared on the corner of her mouth. Someday, someone might ask her about her visit to the castle. Personally, Léa didn't think anything would happen. But she wanted a story to tell.

"Why not?" she asked herself.

Léa unzipped her jacket and tossed it into a dry corner. In a single movement, she slipped the sock and shoe from her right foot, then the left. A blast of cold wind and rain blew through the opening. Léa shivered once, smiled again, and walked up to the roof of the castle.

Léa felt a surge of excitement and adrenaline rush through her body. She knew she couldn't stay in this cold rain more than a minute or so, but she was determined to enjoy every moment.

From the edge of the roof, Léa looked out over the dark castle. Another surge of adrenaline rushed through her body. Léa raised her arms over her head.

"Hey! You in the castle! I'm here, and I'm ready for you!"

Toward the stormy sea, all she saw were clouds and rain. Léa slowly turned, surveying everything, until she faced the castle again. Then she placed her hands on her hips and gave the castle an annoyed look.

"Didn't think so," she said.

"Didn't think what?"

Léa spun around to find Cindy standing the doorway.

"I thought I heard someone outside our tent. But I wasn't expecting to see a show," said Cindy.

"Neither was I." Charlie appeared behind his twin sister.

Léa raised her arms above her head and struck a pose.

"Was it good for you?" She smiled.

Léa headed toward the door and noticed her jacket and shoes in Charlie's hands.

"I'll take those," she said.

"What do you think? Should I give them to her?" Charlie asked his sister.

"I think we should demand an encore."

"Funny," said Léa.

She snatched the jacket away and slipped it over her shoulders before reaching for her shoes.

"Don't you want these?" Charlie offered her the socks.

"No, I want to keep as many dry socks as possible."

Léa slipped on her shoes and stuffed the dry socks in her pocket. She was halfway down the stairs when Cindy caught up to her.

"So what was that all about?" asked Cindy.

"Why not?" Léa walked faster.

"Hey, slow down. Your shoes are wet. You might slip," said Charlie.

"I'm freezing," said Léa, walking even faster.

Cindy laughed. "And they call you and Tara the smartest girls in town."

"I'm not expecting to get a ghost story out of this visit," Léa said. "So at least I'll have a semi spicy story to tell."

Charlie stopped on the stairs. "Brilliant."

Léa and Cindy turned to watch Charlie race up the stairs and disappear onto the roof. A minute later, they both heard him yelling at the castle.

Cindy shook her head, and Léa smiled.

"You're both mental," said Cindy, looking sadly up at the roof.

"You know, Cindy, we're only young once, and we really can't do things like this when we're older."

Charlie appeared at the top of the stairs, his clothes bunched in his hands. He was soaking wet, shivering, and smiling.

"Wow!" He passed Léa and Cindy on the stairs. "That was really cold."

Cindy glanced toward the top of the stairs. She looked back at Léa and grabbed her arm. "Come on, Smart Girl. Let's get you dried off before you catch cold."

As they reached the bottom of the stairs and left the toilet room, they heard the sharp *clank* of metal striking metal. The sound that followed would remain forever lodged in their minds—a sharp, long, animal howl filled with more pain than they had thought possible.

Léa and Cindy froze. Charlie was passing through the door toward his tent. He slowly turned to Cindy and Léa as the cry of agony faded.

Almost immediately, they heard another *clank* of metal on metal and another cry of pain.

"What the bloody hell is that?" Pat emerged from his tent and joined the others.

The second *clank* was followed by a third, a fourth, and a fifth. Each sound brought another anguished cry.

Léa spoke quietly to Charlie. "Go get your recorder and video camera."

Charlie stood in the doorway.

"Charlie!" Léa hissed. "Your recorder and camera. Now!"

Charlie dropped his clothes and ran into the room. As he returned, starting his digital audio recorder, another *clank* brought fresh howls of pain. Léa pointed at Charlie's recorder. He nodded and gave her a thumbs up. Just like before, five *clank*s spurred five animal howls of pain, and the castle went silent.

Pat started to speak, but Léa shushed him. In less than a minute, five more distant *clank*s and five more howls emerged from deep in the castle. A few minutes after that, they heard a loud *thud* and another long cry of pain.

Then dead silence.

No one moved for five minutes.

Not a sound.

Ten minutes passed.

Charlie caught Léa's eye and nodded in the direction of their room. Léa nodded.

"Come on, guys," she said. "I think the show may be over."

She started inside, and the others followed. "How about some light? And turn on that space heater, too," she told Charlie.

Charlie flipped on the camp lights and fished a few towels from the pack on his bike. He tossed one to Léa, who shed her jacket and began to dry off.

Pat snapped on the space heater and looked at Léa and Charlie. "What have you two been up to?" he asked.

"Later," said Léa.

She pulled dry clothes from the pack on her bicycle and started getting dressed. Léa glanced at Charlie, who was pulling on dry clothes of his own.

"Did you get that?" she asked.

"Hang on." He tugged on a sweater and reached for the digital recorder. When he hit play, the sound of *clank*ing metal and shrieks of pain filled the room.

Cindy put her hands over her ears and shivered. "Okay, we've heard it," she said.

Léa nodded, and Charlie quickly shut it off.

Pat put his arm around Cindy. "It's okay," he said.

Léa started the camp stove. She filled the coffee pot with water and tossed in a few tea bags. Then Léa pulled up a camp chair.

Everyone else sat down, too. Pat reached for his flask, opened it, sniffed, but closed it without taking a drink.

"I think we just had our first close encounter of a ghostly kind," said Pat.

"That wasn't any ghost," said Cindy. "That was some poor soul being tortured."

She was shaking. Pat moved his chair close to her and took her hand.

"It's okay," he said.

"I don't think so," Cindy whispered.

After a few moments of silence, Pat gestured toward Léa, who was staring at the ground. "See, it really is okay," he said. "The gears are spinning in Léa's head. She'll have this all figured out in no time."

The water began to boil, but Léa didn't notice.

"It's like she goes into a different dimension," said Charlie.

He inched over to the pot and turned down the heat. He was reaching for cups when Léa looked up.

"Let the tea steep for a few minutes before you start pouring," she said.

Léa looked down, and the room fell silent again. After a few more minutes, she reached for a cup and handed it to Charlie.

"Okay. The way I see it, nothing has changed since we talked about it earlier."

"How can you say that after what we just heard?" Cindy's voice was sharp.

"We don't know what we heard. It could be someone playing sound effects on an iPad," said Léa.

"It sounded real," said Cindy.

Charlie chimed in. "Lots of effects sound real."

"And more importantly, we didn't see anything," Léa said. "We just heard some spooky sounds."

"Okay then. Why?" Cindy asked.

"Well, it kind of fits with the theory of the ghost stories being meant to scare people away from this place," said Léa.

"Why?" Cindy asked again.

Léa took the cup of hot tea from Charlie.

"There's no way we can know that right now," she said.

Cindy's shoulders slumped. "So what do we do now?"

Léa leaned back and took a sip of her tea. "We really can't go exploring this old place till the sun comes up. So I think we should have some tea, warm up, and then try to get a little more sleep."

"Good plan," Pat said. "We don't know our way around. I'd much rather go exploring when it's daylight."

He handed a cup of tea to Cindy. She took a sip and nodded. "From now on, no one goes anywhere alone. Even to the loo."

"Good call," said Léa.

Charlie's head bobbed. "Yeah."

"Right then. Back to more important things." Pat took a sip of tea and leaned back in his chair. "What the bloody hell were you two doing running around this old castle without your clothes on?"

Cindy shook her head and took another sip of tea.

Charlie stared into his cup.

Léa's gaze flicked around the room, and her wicked little smile returned

CHAPTER 6 - BREAKFAST

The Castle, 8 a.m.

Léa was fast asleep when a sound outside the tent woke her. The tent flap flipped open, and Léa opened one eye to see Charlie smiling down at her.

"Room service," he said.

Léa rolled onto her elbows and rubbed the sleep out of her eyes. When she looked up, she saw Charlie was holding a fresh cup of coffee.

"Just the way you like it. Piping hot with a shot of Bailey's," he said.

"Bailey's! Where did you get that?" Léa reached for the cup.

"You like Bailey's. Cindy likes Amaretto. I figured I'd get extra credit if I came properly prepared."

"Good call." Léa took a sip of her coffee and handed the cup back to Charlie. "Perfect. Keep this warm for me. I'll be there in a few minutes."

As Charlie turned to leave, Léa crawled out of her sleeping bag and started doing pushups. But the pushups weren't what caught Charlie's eye.

"Not that I mind the view," he said, "but it's pretty cold out here. After last night's adventure on the roof, maybe you should get dressed so you don't get sick."

"Don't worry about me. I do this every morning, and our house has never been all that warm." Léa breathed heavily between words.

When she finished her pushups, she rolled over and started doing stomach crunches. After she counted out twenty, she rolled back over for more pushups.

"Get going," she said between reps. "You're enjoying yourself too much."

"Sorry. Didn't think you'd mind." Charlie backed out of the tent.

Léa glanced up at the empty tent flap and shook her head. After a few more pushups, she rolled over and began another round of crunches.

"What's cooking?" Cindy asked as she entered the room.

"Coffee, bangers, and scrambled eggs," said Charlie.

Cindy reached for a coffee cup, but Charlie stopped her.

"Hang on." He grabbed one of the backpacks scattered around the camp stove and unzipped a side pocket. With a slight flourish, Charlie pulled out a mini bottle of Amaretto and tossed it to his sister.

"Nice," said Cindy.

She tore off the top and dumped it into her cup before filling it with coffee. She poured fast enough to mix the amaretto, without spilling.

"Did you bring Bailey's for Léa?" she asked.

"Sure did."

"Winning friends and influencing people," Cindy said, sipping her spiked coffee. "You're off to a good start this morning. So where is Smart Girl?"

Charlie pointed to the tent. "Hear that?"

The room fell silent, and Cindy heard the sound of heavy breathing coming from the tent. She raised one eyebrow at Charlie.

"It's her morning workout," he said. "And before you ask, she's no better dressed now than she was last night."

"As I recall, you weren't all that well dressed either."

Charlie shrugged. "Seemed like the right thing to do at the time."

"What was the right thing to do?" Pat appeared in the doorway.

"Morning," said Cindy.

She poured another cup of coffee and held it out for Pat. He took a big sip and looked over at the tent, listening to the heavy breathing.

"It's her morning workout," said Charlie.

During the pause in conversation, Léa's breathing began to taper off, and soon the room was silent. Everyone sat sipping their coffee and watching the tent flap. A few minutes later, Léa emerged, fully clothed and ready for anything.

"What's everyone looking at?" Léa snarled her nose and retrieved her coffee from the camp stove. After enjoying the aroma, she took a sip and looked up to see everyone still watching her.

"Charlie was just telling us about your workout style," said Pat.

Léa took another sip of coffee and sat down in one of the chairs. She stared back at her friends and let the silence hang over the room for a few minutes.

Finally, she said, "Really? We're going to do this?" She didn't hide the annoyance from her face. "We're not twelve. After everything that happened last night and everything that could happen today, I can't believe you guys are wasting time on what I do or don't sleep in."

"Sorry. Of course, you're right," Charlie said. "But you're also our friend, and we can't resist the chance to have some fun with you and ..."

Léa prodded. "And ..."

"And I just think you're really hot."

The others bit their tongues.

"Thank you," said Léa. "Nothing wrong with that. But it's morning and I'm starved."

"Me too," Cindy said, reaching for the camp plates and forks.

Charlie smiled at Léa and began serving breakfast.

"So what are we going to do about what we heard last night?" asked Cindy, polishing off her eggs. Charlie reached into his pocket and pulled out his recorder. "We don't need to hear it again," she said sharply.

Charlie slipped the recorder back into his pocket.

"Well, in the movies, this is when they decide if they're going to split up or stay together," said Pat.

"What movie is that, mate?" asked Charlie.

"Never mind," Léa said. "We're not splitting up. Whatever is going on here, we should all see it together."

The others agreed.

"Okay then." Léa gave a quick nod. "Let's finish up this great breakfast and see if we can figure out what we heard last night."

CHAPTER 7 - LUNCH

The Castle, 3 p.m.

"Am I the only one who's starving?" asked Léa.

"Nope," said Charlie. "Just the only one who's said anything."

"Let's head back to our room for some food. Then we can decide where we want to explore next."

Ten minutes later, a fresh pot of coffee was brewing on the camp stove, and everyone was munching on some hastily assembled sandwiches.

Between bites, Charlie skimmed through the pictures he'd snapped that morning. Cindy watched the camera screen over his shoulder. Pat was pouring coffee, and Léa was concentrating on her sandwich.

"Wait, go back one," said Cindy.

"This one?"

"Yeah. You guys. Check this out." Cindy waved the others over.

Everyone crowded around Charlie, and Cindy pointed at the small camera screen. "Anyone else notice these symbols carved next to all the doors around this place?".

"Yeah. They're everywhere," said Pat through a mouth full of sandwich.

"They're door signs. Sorta like a castle directory," said Léa.

Pat stepped just outside the room's doorway and pointed at the crown carving. "That's just like the one outside these rooms."

"We must be in the royal rooms," said Charlie.

Léa laughed. "Brilliant."

"I saw those crossed axes by the stairs to the roof," said Cindy.

"I didn't see that one." Léa pointed at one of the pictures.

"Me either," said Pat.

Charlie swallowed a hunk of sandwich. "That was by a door downstairs."

"Any place else?" asked Pat.

"Nope. It was by a door next to the big fireplace in the main hall."

"That's our next stop," Léa said, reaching for her backpack. "Someone turn off the coffee pot."

"Hang on," said Pat. "Some of us are still eating."

"Yeah," said Cindy and Charlie at the same time.

Léa slumped into a camp chair. "Okay, I guess I can be patient for a few more minutes."

When lunch was finished, everyone headed downstairs.

The main hall was big enough for multiple tennis courts and rows of spectators. There were several fireplaces, but the big one at the end of the hall was the one they were interested in. A door stood on either side of the fireplace.

"Not this one," said Pat, pointing to the carved stone next to the door on the right. "It has deer antlers and leads to what I think was the kitchen."

"So no one has seen a stone carving like this anywhere else?" Léa asked, examining the left hand door.

They all shook their heads.

Léa pushed open the old, wooden door and peered inside at a dusty, spiral staircase. Below, the steps disappeared into darkness. She reached into one of her backpack's many pockets and pulled out a flashlight.

"Let's go." Léa snapped on the light.

Pat and Charlie exchanged nervous glances before Pat followed Léa into the stairwell. Cindy paused by the door and shook her head.

"I really don't like this."

"Me either," Charlie said. "But we should probably stick together."

"I guess." Cindy's voice was meek, but she walked through the door.

Charlie followed his sister. The steps were steep. He unslung his backpack, pulled out a flashlight, and snapped it on. The light illuminated the stairway and the dust particles hanging in the air.

"Could the dust be any thicker?" asked Pat.

"How far down do you think it goes?" asked Cindy.

Léa's voice echoed. "A long way."

The group descended.

And kept descending.

"We must be under the castle and deep into the cliffs," said Pat.

"Any sign of the bottom?" asked Cindy.

"Actually, I think so," said Léa. "Everyone stop for a minute." The group paused, and Léa turned to face them. "Now don't freak out, but let's shut off the flashlights for a second."

"Are you crazy?" asked Charlie.

"Just for a second."

"It's okay, mate," Pat said. "Go ahead."

As the lights snapped off, the spiral staircase plunged into darkness. Once their eyes adjusted, a faint light appeared at the bottom of the stairs.

Léa's voice emerged from the darkness. "There's the bottom."

"That's a long way down," said Charlie.

Léa nodded, though no one could see. "I wonder how light is getting all the way down there?"

"I know one way to find out," said Pat.

He turned on his flashlight and took a step down the stone staircase. The four friends continued to make their way slowly down the stairs.

At the bottom, they saw that the light was coming from a long hallway. As they entered the stone hallway, Cindy's quiet voice called out from behind them.

"Am I the only one who thinks this isn't such a good idea?" She planted her feet on the last stone step. "I've got a bad feeling about this."

Charlie walked back to his twin sister. "Me too," he said.

"What are you now?" Pat said. "Luke and Leia from Star Wars?"

Charlie shot Pat an annoyed glance. "Laugh it up, fuzzball."

"Whenever I get a bad feeling, something bad usually happens," said Cindy.

Charlie flicked his glance between Pat and Léa. "And when we both get one at the same time, it's pretty much a guarantee."

They all looked to Léa, who was staring at the ground.

Pat sighed. "There go the wheels in her head again."

Léa shined her light down the long hallway—on the walls and down at the floor. She walked a few steps with the light directed at the stone floor. "I don't see any footprints. The dust on this floor hasn't been disturbed for a long time."

"You know what?" Cindy's voice rose. "I don't fucking care about the dust! We're a long way from home, we've heard really awful sounds coming from deep in this place, and something doesn't feel right."

Charlie put a hand on her shoulder. "What my little sister is trying to say is that if something bad is down here, we might not be able to get home."

Léa made a fast decision. Moving quickly, she slipped her backpack off her shoulders.

"Then you guys need to be cool about this," she said.

She unzipped a hidden pocket and pulled out a small, nine-millimeter semi-automatic handgun. No one said anything. No one moved.

"Like I said yesterday, I don't believe in ghosts. And like I said last night, I don't believe what's going on here will turn out to be all that dangerous." She pulled back the slide, loaded a bullet in the chamber, and cocked the gun. She then snapped on the safety and slipped the gun into her jacket pocket. "But I'm not about to take stupid chances that I'm wrong."

The room remained silent for a while.

Charlie opened his mouth slowly. "Okay ... Well ... Okay." He glanced at Cindy. "I guess I feel a little better. How about you?"

Cindy was still standing on the last step of the staircase. She thought a moment and stepped off the stairs. "Not really. But I'm with you."

"Okay then," said Léa.

She slipped her backpack over her shoulder and headed down the long hallway. Everyone else followed suit. Eventually, they were all walking side by side.

Charlie moved beside Léa. "Where did you pick that up?" he asked.

"My dad didn't want his little girl going out into the big, scary world without a way to take care of herself."

"Don't you need a permit for something like that?" asked Pat.

Léa shot him an sideways glance and kept walking.

Soon the floor began to slope downward, and the air became thick with dust.

"Hey guys," Léa said, "pick up your feet. The dust is getting a bit thick in here."

"Did you notice we're going downhill again?" asked Charlie.

Léa spoke quietly. "Yeah."

"But the light is getting brighter," said Cindy.

"It sure is. Let's stop for a second." Léa shut off her flashlight and slipped it into a side pocket of her backpack. She looked back at Cindy and tucked her right hand into her jacket pocket.

"Are we still okay?" Léa asked Cindy.

"Yeah, I guess."

"Let's keep going," said Pat.

As they walked, hallway brightened. Eventually, the corridor opened into a large room.

Charlie spoke quietly. "What the bloody hell is this place?"

"Told you I got a bad feeling," said Cindy.

The room was as big as a school gymnasium and was lined with burning torches. But it was the contents of the room that stopped everyone in their tracks. The objects were old and dusty. They seemed clipped from a medieval history book.

"Is that what I think it is?" Pat pointed.

"It sure is," said Léa. "That's a rack. Over there is an iron maiden, and I think they'd put people in those cages and hang them over a fire pit."

"Oh my God! Is that what I think it is?" Cindy pointed in the opposite direction.

The group approached what appeared to be four wooden crosses planted in the stone floor. The crosses were empty, except one. A human skeleton was nailed to the last cross in the row. As they studied the metal nails in the hands and feet of the skeleton, they remembered the metal *clank*s and the shrieks of pain they had heard last night. A heavy metal mallet leaned against the base of the cross.

Pat looked closely at the skeleton. "This poor bugger has been dead a real long time. What we heard last night couldn't have come from him."

"This isn't real," said Léa. "A real skeleton wouldn't hold together on a cross like this."

"So it's a fake?" asked Charlie.

Léa turned away from the skeleton. "A rather bad fake."

"But why a cross? Wasn't it was more of a Roman thing than a Scottish Island thing?" asked Pat.

"It's universally recognized as a religious symbol," answered Cindy.

"It's also universally recognized as a rather awful way to die," said Léa.

"So it's here to scare people?" asked Charlie.

"Didn't scare me. What's down there?" said Léa.

Charlie peered around the corner. "Looks like a hallway to the prison cells."

More fiery torches lined a hallway with over a dozen heavy, wooden doors. A big barrel sat near the entrance.

"It's full of water," said Pat.

He reached for a big spoon hanging on the wall. Pat dipped the spoon into the water and sniffed it. "Smells fresh." He dumped the water back into the barrel.

Léa started down the hallway, looking into the cells. Each room was lit from the outside and had a small stool and two empty buckets covered with dust.

"None of this makes sense," she said, turning back to the group.

"What doesn't make sense?" asked Charlie.

He never got his answer. Léa's eyes opened wide. She drew her gun and ran toward the room's entrance. "What happened to the door?"

Cindy, who was still staring at the skeleton on the cross, turned on her heels and ran for the door. But it wasn't there. A solid, stone wall blocked the exit.

"It was right here!" Léa patted the wall with her palm.

"Are you sure?" Charlie's voice shook with nerves.

"Look down. See our footprints?"

Everyone looked down and saw footprints in the dust.

Charlie pushed against the wall. "Don't just stand there, help me!"

All four of them pushed their weight against the stone wall, but it didn't budge.

Léa stopped pushing and turned her head. "Everyone be quiet."

A low hissing seemed to come from all around them.

"Cover your face!" yelled Léa as she pulled her shirt over her mouth and nose.

But it was too late.

Cindy, Charlie, and Pat fell to the floor. Léa staggered to the wall and fought to remain standing. She heard metal *clank* by her feet. Looking down, Léa saw that she dropped her gun.

Then everything went black.

CHAPTER 8 - TRAPPED IN A DUNGEON

The Castle, 7 p.m.

Léa felt a dull, throbbing pain in her head, arms, and shoulders. She was still groggy, but the pain helped her slowly crawl out of the unconscious fog. Her left arm was numb. She tried to move, but nothing happened. Her body was cold. When Léa tried to open her eyes, the blackness engulfed her again.

Suddenly, her whole body shivered. She barely opened her eyes. Léa lay on her left side. As her eyes began to focus, Léa looked up to see a wooden cell door.

It was closed.

Light from the hall torches streamed into the stone cell through the barred window in the door. Léa's left arm sent urgent messages of pain to her still-foggy brain, and she tried again to move. Nothing worked. Her brain seemed dull. She couldn't think of anything except the pain.

Léa focused on the stream of light. The air was heavy with dust particles twinkling like stars in the beam. Her mind crawled through the fog of unconsciousness.

Léa's left arm and shoulder throbbed. Then she remembered she had another arm. She could use her right arm to push herself over.

Brilliant! her foggy mind exclaimed.

Léa tried to to push herself off her left arm, but her right arm wouldn't move. She concentrated, but it still wouldn't move. Confused and exhausted, she fell asleep.

She woke a few minutes later. Or had it been a few hours? Léa couldn't tell. Her eyes popped open as another cold shiver rippled through her body. She eyed the window set in the wooden door.

Léa still couldn't move her right arm. As light streamed through the window, her mind slowly returned. She tried to wiggle the fingers of her right hand. She felt her fingers move, but she also felt them touching her back. Something hard tugged against her wrist. Another cold shiver rippled through her body.

It's time to figure out what's going on here.

Léa looked down at her body. Adrenaline surged through her. She was lying on her left side with her arms handcuffed behind her back. Her legs were shackled, a short chain locking her ankles within two feet of each other.

Not only had someone handcuffed and shackled her, but they had removed all of her clothes. A wave of panic swept over Léa as she struggled against the metal of the handcuffs, but they only dug deep into the flesh of her wrists.

After a few moments of fighting against the handcuffs, Léa struggled to sit up. After several attempts, she was finally successful. She coughed at the dust her movements had stirred. Grey, dusty dirt covered her body.

The room was empty except for two wooden buckets and a small, three-legged stool. The stone walls were bare, and the only source of light was the small, barred window.

Her left arm ached as blood circulated back to her numb hand. She flexed her fingers.

Once her arm and hands stopped throbbing, she looked down at her feet to examine the leg shackles.

"Wait a minute. These are new," she said aloud.

Her voice was rough from the thick dust, and she needed water. But it was nice to hear the sound of her own voice.

Léa twisted to try to get a look at the handcuffs. They were painfully tight, but she was able to see that they were modern, too.

"Not what you'd expect in an old dungeon," she said softly. "Let's see what's in those buckets."

Léa scooted over to the bucket, hoping she'd find water. The progress was slow. Every time she scooted forward, the handcuffs and leg shackles dug painfully into her wrists and ankles, and the dirt on the cell floor coated her body.

"As long as there's water in that bucket," she mumbled.

After what seemed like an hour of scooting across the floor, pain shooting through her arms and legs, Léa finally arrived at the bucket and peered inside.

"Success."

The word was barely out when another coughing fit came on. When the fit passed, Léa lowered her mouth into the bucket. Before her lips touched the water, she stopped.

She saw her reflection in the water. Her face was dirty, and her hair was matted. But what had surprised her was the big bandage covering the side of her forehead.

"That explains the headache."

She lowered her face once again into the bucket and took a long drink of water. It was the best tasting water she'd ever had.

After the ripples settled, Léa examined the bandage in her reflection. It was as dirty as her face, with a patch of blood in the middle. The bleeding seemed to have stopped now.

"Must have hit my head when I lost consciousness."

Her voice sounded a little better, and she took one more drink of water.

"That's much better." Her voice sounded almost normal.

She looked around the room again and noticed a smaller bucket near the stool. Léa decided to check out the cell door, but she didn't plan to scoot to it.

"Time to try to stand up."

She edged away from the bucket to make sure she wouldn't knock it over. She extended her legs in front of her, feeling the handcuffs and shackles binding her limbs. She looked down at her dirty toes.

"I can figure this out," she said softly.

As her mind began to work through the problem, the silence of the dungeon was shattered.

"Hey! Is anyone out there?" Charlie yelled from another cell.

"Charlie, are you okay?" she shouted back

"Not really. I'm handcuffed and shackled, and someone took all my clothes."

"Me too," yelled Léa.

"Charlie!" Cindy's voice emerged.

"Cindy, are you okay?" yelled Charlie.

"Charlie, help me!" Cindy's voice was panicked.

"I can't," he said. "Are you hurt?"

"No. But I'm all locked up and my clothes are gone."

"Same with us," yelled Léa.

"I'm so scared, Charlie." Cindy fought back tears of fear. "Get us out of here!"

"I think we'd all like to get out of here about now. Any ideas Léa?"

"Not yet. I was just trying to figure out how to get on my feet."

"Anyone heard from Pat?" yelled Charlie.

"No," said Léa.

"Pat!" Charlie shouted.

There was no response.

Léa tried. "Pat!"

Still no response.

"He must still be out from the gas," said Léa.

"Gas?" yelled Cindy.

"Remember that hissing sound before we all blacked out?" Léa said. "They had to be using some kind of knockout gas."

"They? Who is they? And what are they going to do with us?" Fear laced Cindy's voice.

"Calm down, Cindy," said Léa.

"Don't tell me to calm down!"

"It's going to be okay," yelled Léa.

Cindy kept crying.

"How do you know it's going to be okay?" Charlie shouted through the walls.

"Because I hit my head when the gas knocked me out. And whoever took my clothes and cuffed me also bandaged the wound."

"What? You're hurt? Are you okay?" asked Charlie.

"I'm fine. They stopped the bleeding and bandaged me up. So I don't think they're going to hurt us."

"You're fucking crazy!" yelled Cindy. "We're locked in a, old dungeon, handcuffed, shackled, and naked! But don't worry 'cause Smart Girl says they won't hurt us!"

"Take it easy, Sis. Léa's been right about this from the start."

"Bullshit!" yelled Cindy.

"Come on guys," Léa said. "Try to get on your feet."

"What for?" yelled Cindy.

"So we can check out our cell doors."

"Whatever." Cindy's sobbing echoed through the cells.

Léa shook her head and inched back to the water bucket for another drink. The yelling and the dust had made her voice scratchy again. As she sipped the water and glanced around the cell, her eyes caught on the three-legged stool.

That's it.

"Hey, Charlie. Do you have a small stool in your cell?" she yelled.

"Sure do."

"Use that to get on your feet."

"Sounds good," he yelled back.

Except for Cindy's fearful sobs, the dungeon was quiet. Léa scooted over to the stool. After thinking it through one more time, she leaned her right shoulder against the stool and pushed herself onto the seat. The rough wood left splinters in her arm. Once her shoulder and arm were on the stool, she rolled onto her chest.

Good thing I've got small boobs.

Léa surprised herself by laughing out loud. No, not laughing—giggling. Léa never giggled, but now she couldn't stop.

What is so funny? she thought.

Then she figured it out. It was the word *boobs*.

Léa said the word out loud and started giggling again.

"Amazing," she said out loud.

Léa figured she must have a lot of stress to burn off. Amazing how saying a silly word helped her focus. She filed away that bit of knowledge and concentrated on her current task.

Léa could still hear Cindy crying in her cell, and she felt bad for her. But she also felt a surge of pride at the fact that she was staying in control and might think her way out of all this.

"I hope," she said softly to herself.

Léa was able to pull her feet up toward the stool's seat and inch onto her toes. She spread her feet as wide as the short chain allowed and worked her way onto her feet.

As she slowly transferred her weight from the stool to her feet, she heard a crash and a cry of pain from Charlie.

"You okay?" she yelled.

Charlie moaned a few times.

"Charlie?"

"I'm fine. I got a little impatient and fell."

"Did you hit your head?" yelled Léa.

"Yeah. But not too bad."

"I'm almost there. Try again, and take it slow."

"Yeah, okay." Charlie said weakly.

Léa paused to catch her breath, then pushed more of her weight onto her toes, moving slowly to keep from falling like Charlie. A few more inches, and all of her weight was shifted to her feet. She leaned forward and began pushing herself up.

"Almost there ..."

She was nearly halfway up when she lost her balance. Thinking fast, she pushed harder with her left leg, pivoting her body to the right. She was falling, but she kept pushing with her left leg and aimed for the stool.

Léa closed her eyes and held her breath as she waited for the pain of hitting the floor. But the pain never came. She slowly opened her eyes and found herself sitting half on the stool.

"Yes!" Léa shifted her weight entirely onto the stool.

Léa was breathing heavily, and sweat flowed like dirty rivers down her body. Léa craved another drink of water, but she had to finish what she'd started.

After a few deep breaths, Léa planted her feet firmly on the ground and stood up.

"I made it!"

"Great!" yelled Charlie from his cell.

"Give it a try, Cindy," Léa said.

"Why bother?"

"Never mind the *why*, just concentrate on standing up."

Léa waited for a reply, but she got only silence.

She sighed and brought her focus back to her own cell.

Time to check out the door.

The chain between her ankles *clink*ed against the stone floor, stirring up dust. Walking to the door, she nearly lost her balance because the chain reduced her normal stride by more than half.

Walk more slowly. She did not want to pull that stool trick again.

Léa was too short to look through the small window in the door. From her angle, she could only see the ceiling of the hallway.

She noticed a small, wooden handle nailed to the door at shoulder height.

Why put a handle on the inside of a prison cell?

Light shone around parts of the door's edges, as though it wasn't completely closed. Turning slightly, Léa bumped her shoulder against the door.

It moved.

She bumped the door a little harder. It moved even more. Shuffling her feet, Léa leaned back and bumped the door as hard as she could. A sharp pain shot through her shoulder, but Léa was expecting it and kept her eye on the door. It definitely moved, but it was also clearly latched.

Léa rolled her shoulder to ease the pain, making the handcuffs tug at her already sore wrists. But that gave Léa an idea. Being careful not to step on the ankle chain, she turned her back to the door, leaned forward and tried to reach the handle with her hands.

"Not even close," she whispered.

Carefully facing the door, Léa looked up at the window and down at the gap between the door and the wall. Then she peered at the handle. She glanced over her shoulder at her cell.

"The stool!"

Reminding herself to walk carefully, Léa shuffled over to the stool. She carefully shoved the stool across the floor with one foot.

"What are you doing?" yelled Charlie.

"Pushing the stool over to the door so I can look out the window. How are things going for you?"

"Not so good. I can't seem to get on my feet."

"I pushed my chest up on the stool, then was able to use that for leverage to get my feet under me."

"Tried that. But it's not working out that well," yelled Charlie.

"Why not?"

"The stool keeps slipping out from under me."

Léa started to respond, but she hesitated. It had been a while since she'd heard anything from Cindy.

"Any ideas, Cindy?" she said.

"Leave me alone."

"Come on, girlfriend. We're trying to help Charlie get on his feet," yelled Léa cheerfully.

There was only silence. Léa shook her head and resumed shoving the stool toward the door. She almost kicked the stool over.

Take it easy.

After a few more shoves, she arrived at the door. Léa was breathing heavily again and was covered with even more dirt and sweat.

"I don't know about you. But running around in handcuffs and leg chains is turning out to be a great workout," she hollered.

She could hear Charlie laughing from his cell, and Léa smiled. She was glad to help keep Charlie's spirits up.

"Good thing they left you in your workout clothes," he yelled back.

Now it was Léa's turn to laugh out loud. Through her laughter, she thought she heard something. She fell silent and realized that Cindy had laughed, too.

"Do my ears deceive me, or are there signs of life from my girlfriend, Cindy?" Léa said.

"Thanks, I needed a bit of a laugh," said Cindy.

"Glad to hear your voice, little sister."

Léa sat on her stool, shifting back to lean against the door and rest. Léa smiled at the sound of Charlie and Cindy talking. When the conversation dropped off, Léa spoke up.

"So, any ideas about how to get Charlie on his feet?"

Everyone was silent again, but only for a few moments.

"Shove the stool against the wall so it won't move out from under you," yelled Cindy.

Charlie yelled back. "Good idea."

Léa heard Charlie moving his stool across the floor. She also thought she heard a second stool being shoved around. Cindy might be trying to stand up, too.

Léa leaned more of her weight against the door and felt it shift. She closed her eyes and thought about how much the door had moved. That didn't seem right. A jail cell door should not move that much.

One thing at a time.

After a few minutes, Charlie's stool stopped moving. After another minute, Charlie broke the silence.

"Success!"

"Good job," Léa said. "Now get your stool over to the door so we can see what we can see."

"On my way," he yelled.

When Léa opened her eyes, the first thing she noticed was dust hanging in the air. The sight of it made her thirsty for more water.

"Whoa!" yelled Charlie.

"What's wrong?"

"This damn leg chain almost put me back on my face."

"We're going to have to walk a lot slower till we get these things off," Léa said.

"You really think you'll be able to get them off?" said Cindy.

"Sure we will," Charlie chimed in. "We're with one of the smartest girls in town, remember?"

"Right, I'd forgotten," said Cindy.

Léa smiled and carefully stood up. She turned around and inched her legs as close to the stool as possible. Léa took a deep breath. Balancing on her left leg, she slowly raised her right foot. Before it reached the seat of the stool, it stopped. The chain was too short.

She pushed away the wave of frustration. This was only the first of what would surely be many obstacles to regaining her freedom. She needed to stay positive and patient.

Léa stepped back and breathed deeply, trying to clear her head. She'd come this far, and she wouldn't let a leg chain stop her.

Maybe she could hop onto the stool. She took a step back and shuffled her feet, squatted down, and jumped as high as she could. Léa quickly decided that wouldn't work. Her feet didn't come close to clearing the stool's height.

Léa approached the stool, pivoted, and sat down again. Leaning against the door, she closed her eyes and ran through solutions.

Léa felt another wave of frustration building, and she knew that was no good. Once frustration took over, anger and fear would soon follow, and those emotions would keep her locked in this cell.

Léa thumped her head against the door. Again, she felt the door move loosely in its frame, and that was enough to help her regain focus.

Léa opened her eyes, and the first thing she saw was the smaller, empty bucket. Léa decided it was a bathroom bucket. The half-smile returned to her face.

Good thing I haven't had to go yet.

She shuffled across the small cell and kicked the bucket over to the stool.

Léa was getting better at moving around her cell, but she constantly reminded herself to take it slow. Tripping over the leg chain would send her falling face-first onto the stone floor. With no free hands to break her fall, it could do some real damage.

Once the bucket was beside the stool, Léa flipped the bucket with her toes and nestled it against the stool's leg. Léa smiled and used the upside-down bucket to step onto the stool.

The stool was actually a little too tall, and Léa had to scrunch down to see through the window.

This is going to start hurting fast.

Looking through the barred window, a breeze blew against Léa's face. She closed her eyes and breathed deeply. The dust in her cell had made breathing a chore, but the air blowing through the window was cool and clean. Léa took several deep breaths and opened her eyes.

Once her eyes adjusted to the light, Léa saw that her cell was about halfway down the hallway. To the right, she could barely see the big water bucket Pat had found before they'd been taken prisoner.

Across the hallway, two of the cell doors were closed. The rest were open. To the left were more open cell doors and some benches.

The dust on the floor of the hallway had been stirred up quite a bit, and Léa saw a lot of footprints. Some of them were pretty big.

Charlie's face popped into the window across the hall. She smiled at first, but her happiness was replaced with concern. Half of Charlie's face was badly bruised and covered with blood.

"Hey, Charlie, are you okay?"

"Hey, Léa. I'm a little groggy, and it hurts to laugh. But I guess I'm okay."

"That fall really messed you up," said Léa.

"Looks like you had your own fall, too."

"I'm guessing it was when the gas knocked us out."

"So someone patched you up before locking us down?"

Léa nodded. "That's what I'm thinking."

They both resumed examining the hallway. Léa tried not to look at Charlie, but the blood and the bruising concerned her. She made a mental note to keep an eye on him, in case his injuries were worse than they seemed.

Léa thought she heard shuffling noises, and a minute later Cindy's head appeared in the window of the cell door next to Charlie's.

"Look who decided to join the party!" said Léa.

Cindy's face was as dirty as Charlie's. Her eyes were red, and her cheeks were streaked with dried tears and dirt.

"I heard you guys taking about someone patching your head up?" said Cindy.

"Yeah," Léa said. "That might be a clue about what they plan to do with us."

Cindy's face scrunched up. "What kind of a clue is that?"

"I'm thinking we're not in as much trouble as it looks like."

"I don't fucking believe you." Cindy's irritation was growing.

"Why not?" asked Léa.

"You think they stripped us down and chained us up for a few laughs? Well in case you and our 'just kidding' hosts haven't noticed, I'm not fucking laughing!" Cindy screamed.

"If they'd meant to really hurt us, why did they bandage Lea's head?" asked Charlie.

"If they didn't mean to hurt us, why are we locked in a dungeon dressed like porn stars?"

Léa laughed out loud.

"You think this is funny?" said Cindy.

"No. But I think you're funny." Léa was still laughing.

"Well, you don't see me laughing, do you?" said Cindy.

"No, I don't," said Léa. "And you may be right. There's still a lot about this that we don't know. But I'm not going to start freaking out, and I suggest you don't either."

"I'm not freaking out," Cindy bit back.

"No, you're not." Léa didn't pay much attention to Cindy's response. There was something else on her mind. "So, all the doors on your side of the hallway are open except for the cells you two are in. I can't see anything on my side of the hallway, and we haven't heard anything from Pat."

"I've been thinking about that," said Charlie. "But all the doors on your side of the hallway are open except yours."

"And that door at the end of the hall," said Cindy.

"What about it?" asked Léa.

"There's an opening, but no door."

Léa tilted her head. "*Hmm.*"

"So maybe Pat wasn't invited to this party?" said Charlie.

"Maybe they've taken him away for ..." Cindy let her thought trail away.

"We don't know a thing about that," said Léa. "So I suggest you don't go thinking about what *could* be happening."

"What else do you suggest I think about?"

Léa sighed. She didn't feel like arguing with Cindy anymore. And her legs and back were killing her.

"Look, I need to sit down for a few. You two keep looking around, and yell if you see or hear anything."

She started to step down off the stool when her hands brushed the wooden handle. Now was the perfect time to give her cell door a proper tug.

Inching back up against the door, Léa grabbed the handle and planted her feet firmly on the stool. She took a deep breath and tugged the door handle as hard as she could.

The spring-loaded latch responded with a quiet *clink*, then a louder *clunk*, and the door sprang open. It happened quickly and Léa didn't have time to let go of the handle. As the door swung open, it pulled her backwards off the stool and sent her sprawling into the hallway.

As she fell, Léa saw the fiery torches lining the hall.

Then the ceiling.

Then Charlie's surprised face watching her from his window.

She felt herself hit the floor.

Then she blacked out.

CHAPTER 9 - WAKING UP

The Castle, 10 p.m.

Léa saw Charlie's face smiling down at her.

"Welcome back," he said.

Léa was lying in the middle of the hallway outside the cells. The black leg shackles were still locked tightly around her ankles. Léa tugged at her wrists to check the handcuffs behind her back. As she tugged, an intense pain shot through her arms down to her fingers.

"Careful there," said Charlie. "When you fell, your back and head took most of the impact. The handcuffs left some pretty bad bruises, but I don't think anything is broken."

Charlie was sitting on a bench against the wall. Blood was caked around one of his ears, but he seemed to be in good shape.

Léa struggled to sit up. After a few attempts, she was successful. She looked up and down the hallway and smiled.

"What are you so happy about?" asked Charlie.

"We're out of the cells."

"Thanks to you," he said.

At the other end of the hallway, Cindy emerged from the end cell.

"You feeling better?" asked Cindy, somewhat cooly.

"I guess." Léa shifted around on the floor, trying to get a little more comfortable.

Cindy sat beside her brother on the bench. Her whole side was badly bruised.

Léa gave Charlie a questioning look.

"Cindy isn't handling the leg chains very well," he said.

Cindy fidgeted on the bench. She and Charlie sat on the edge of the seat to make room for their hands.

"These things fucking hurt," Cindy growled.

"At least we're out of the cells," said Léa.

Charlie perked up. "And just wait till you see what we've found at the end of the hallway."

"What?" asked Léa.

"It's a surprise." Charlie smiled.

"It's a fucking toilet and a water fountain," snarled Cindy.

"Brilliant." Léa's smile mirrored Charlie's.

She pulled her feet under her and inched toward the bench. Léa tried to use the bench to help her stand, but a wave of dizziness washed over her.

"Maybe later," she said.

"You smacked your head pretty hard," said Charlie.

"How long was I out?"

"More than an hour. I was starting to get worried that you might not wake up," he said.

Léa moved her shoulders back and forth and shuffled her feet. More sharp pain shot through her wrists and lower back, but she was determined to get to her feet. More dizziness washed over her, and she stopped moving.

"Cindy's right about one thing," said Léa.

Cindy stared straight ahead and didn't respond.

"Okay, I'll bite. What's my little sister right about?" said Charlie.

Léa inched up the bench again.

"These things fucking hurt," said Léa.

Charlie and Léa both laughed. Cindy continued her angry stare-down with the wall on the other side of the hallway.

"I know it must seem crazy for you to hear this," said Léa, "but it really will be a lot better if you'd lighten up a bit."

Cindy's eyes blazed with anger and fear.

Léa just smiled. "I know you're afraid. So am I. But you lose control when you let anger and fear take over."

"Control? What makes you think we're in any kind of control here?" said Cindy sharply.

Léa inched up the bench a bit more. Still dizzy, she took it slow, but focusing on Cindy was helping.

"Sorry, that's not what I meant. Of course we're not in control of this situation. But I am in control of myself, and that keeps my brain functioning. That's my best hope of getting out of here."

Cindy looked away from Léa. Charlie fidgeted on the edge of the bench. After a few more minutes, Cindy leaned forward.

"You're right, of course. But I'm just so afraid and angry ... and ... and ... humiliated."

"Why?" asked Léa.

Cindy shook her head. "*Why?*" Anger colored her voice. She leaned back, picked up her feet from the stone floor, and gave her leg chain a sharp yank. "Look what someone's done to us."

"I get that. Like I said, we're all scared. But why are you humiliated?" said Léa.

Cindy let out an impatient huff. She looked down at her naked body and back up at Léa. "Hello?"

"*You* didn't strip us down and slap us in handcuffs," said Léa. "Someone did this to us. I'm not humiliated so why are you?"

"Just because you have a great body and get your kicks running around like this doesn't mean the rest of us do." Cindy planted her gaze on the wall.

"Oh please, not that again. Last night on the roof was just a bit of fun, and what I dress like when I'm alone is my business."

"I'm just saying, some of us aren't as comfortable as you are right now," said Cindy.

Léa shook her head and inched up the bench a little more. She was nearly able to stand, but she was still very dizzy. Léa managed a brief smile at Cindy.

"You think I'm comfortable? This isn't my idea of a night out on the town either."

"You just seem to be dealing with this better. You're figuring things out," said Cindy.

Léa was breathing hard, but she was still making progress with the bench. "My muscles are cramping up just as bad as yours are. My head is killing me, and I'm still dizzy from that fall I took. And if you think I'm dealing with this well, then you should know that I'm just as frightened as you are."

"You? Frightened? Why?" asked Cindy.

Léa glanced at Charlie.

"Last night you asked about Tara. Don't take this the wrong way, but I really miss her and wish she was here right now. When we're together, we figure things out faster and better," she said.

By now, Léa had her feet beneath her. She smiled at Cindy and then at Charlie. With one big push, Léa stood, spun around, and sat down on the bench.

"Actually, you seem to be doing pretty good on your own," said Charlie.

"You said it last night. We've been friends since we were five. She catches things I miss. I catch things she misses. And she's my best friend," said Léa. "I'm frightened because I need my best friend with me right now. We were planning to explore this place together. But she's gone, and I'm just as afraid as you are, Cindy."

"But you're doing something," Cindy said. "You got us out of the cells."

"I'm figuring things out because I want to get these fucking chains off, take a shower, and put on something warm."

Cindy gave a small laugh.

"Now what's funny?" asked Léa.

"You. You hardly ever swear."

"You know what they all say back in town," said Léa. "'Profanity is merely the attempt of a weak mind to express itself forcefully.' What I say is, 'If you only use it occasionally, it can make friends laugh and maybe even make them feel better.'"

"Well if it's a shower you want, maybe it's time for us to take a little walk," said Charlie.

"A shower?" said Léa.

"Come on." He slowly got to his feet.

Cindy stood, as well.

Léa pushed off the bench, but as soon as she stood up, she began to waver and immediately sat back down.

"Maybe I should wait a little longer," she said.

"Was it as bad as when you tried to sit up on the bench?" asked Charlie.

She shook her head. "No."

"What do you think?" Charlie asked Cindy.

"If it's not as bad now, then maybe she's getting a little better."

"That's what I think, too. Let's give it a few," said Charlie.

Léa leaned against the wall, closed her eyes, and waited for her head to clear. Her head was splitting, and her arms, wrists, and back were sore. But she felt the fog lifting from her mind. After a few more minutes, Léa spoke up.

"Let's try this again."

Charlie and Cindy waited patiently as Léa leaned forward and slowly got to her feet. She took a few steps forward.

"Okay. Tell me about this shower and why you two are still a mess?" She smiled.

"We haven't figured out how to get it working," said Charlie.

"Sounds like a job for the smartest girl in town," said Cindy as they walked down the hallway.

The room at the end of the hall was the same size as the cells, but it didn't have a door. The walls were the same gray stone, but instead of stone, the floor was smooth concrete with a drain in the middle. A long, wooden bench ran along the right wall, and a stainless steel, prison-style toilet and sink stood on the left wall.

"It works, too," said Charlie as he nudged his sister.

"What?" asked Cindy.

"Let's give Léa a few minutes alone."

"Yeah, okay."

Cindy and Charlie turned to leave, and Léa called after them. "Thanks."

She quietly walked over and sat down on the stainless steel toilet.

This is so bizarre. But the timing couldn't be better.

Léa counted six shiny shower nozzles sticking out of the walls in the back of the cell—three on the right and three on the left.

A few minutes later, Léa stood up. "Okay guys, I'm done."

She walked over to examine the shower nozzles, stacked vertically on each wall. There were no shower controls, just the nozzles pointing toward the corner.

"So how do we get them working?" asked Charlie.

"Not sure," said Léa.

"We thought it might have some kind of proximity sensor if you stood in between the nozzles, but nothing happens," said Charlie.

Léa shuffled into the corner, and Charlie and Cindy followed, sitting on the wooden bench that ran the length of the far wall. Léa watched as they sat down. Her eyes ran the length of the bench, then up the walls to the other corner of the cell. Nothing but the same dirty stone walls.

"Wait a minute," said Léa quietly.

She edged over to the other back corner of the cell. Léa leaned over the bench to examine one of the stones in the wall. She took a deep breath and blew a puff of air at the wall, raising a small cloud of dust and revealing another symbol carved into the stone—a modern shower symbol.

Léa turned to Cindy and Charlie and smiled.

"Watch this," she said.

Léa pressed her shoulder against the stone with the symbol. The shower nozzles sputtered once, and six powerful jets of water splashed against the corner. Léa approached the streams and carefully raised her knee into one of the jets of water.

"It's even hot!"

Léa submerged herself in the streams and slowly turned, the hot water washing the dirt from her body. She moved her face under the water and opened her mouth for a few sips, then lowered her head into the stream. Léa spun in slow circles under the water until the jets suddenly shut off.

Léa shook the wet hair from her eyes.

"You gotta try this," she said.

She shuffled over to the bench and sat next to Cindy. She leaned against the stone wall and closed her eyes. When no one else moved, Léa turned her head slightly and opened one eye.

"Well, come on. You'll feel a lot better," she said.

"Go ahead," Charlie told Cindy.

Léa closed her eyes again and silently asked herself, *What's next?*

As she heard the shower start, Léa ran through everything that had happened since they had arrived in the dungeon. She kept returning to the same conclusion.

"None of this makes sense," she said quietly to herself.

"What doesn't make sense?" asked Charlie.

Léa opened her eyes and looked around the room.

"All of this. The dungeon. The handcuffs. The goofy skeleton on the cross. The cell doors. This nice bathroom."

"What's wrong with the skeleton?"

"It's so fake. It's like a bad Halloween decoration."

"Oh," said Charlie.

Cindy stood beneath the hot jets of water, her leg chain *clink*ing. Léa's eyes stopped on Cindy's bruised wrists, handcuffed behind her back. Then the water shut off, and Cindy returned to the bench.

"You're next, Charlie." said Cindy.

Charlie pressed the shower symbol to activate the water and walked into the six powerful jets, turning slowly just like Léa and Cindy had done.

Léa looked again to the shower symbol. Tilting her head, she closed her eyes and listened to the sound of the shower.

"I wish I could do that," said Cindy quietly.

"Do what?" asked Léa, her eyes still closed.

"What you're doing right now. You're figuring things out aren't you?"

Léa opened her eyes.

"I haven't figured anything out, yet. In fact, just the opposite."

Léa noticed Charlie had stopped turning and was holding his head and bloody ear under the water and twisting his shoulders in and out of the stream.

"What do you mean?" asked Cindy.

"There are just too many questions. Too many things that don't make sense."

"Like what?"

"If we really are someone's prisoners, why weren't the cell doors locked?"

"It's not like we can just hop on our bikes and ride down to the coffee shop," said Cindy.

Léa considered. "True."

The shower stopped, and Charlie shuffled back to the bench and sat next to Léa.

Cindy looked up at the ceiling. "This is so fucked up."

"That's just what I've been thinking," said Léa. "None of this makes sense."

"How do you mean?" said Charlie.

Léa glanced at the toilet, then at the shower in the corner. She looked down at her legs, lifted her feet off the floor, and looked at the leg shackles tightly locked around her ankles. She tugged on the chain a few times, then lowered her feet back to the floor.

Charlie let out a long sigh. "One thing's for sure. If we get out of this alive, we'll be in therapy for a year."

"I think we'll all get out of this just fine," Léa said.

"How can you be so fucking sure?" said Cindy.

"Well, like I've been saying," said Léa, "none of this makes sense."

"You've been saying that shit for a while now," said Cindy. "So how about you tell us why."

"Because shit happens for a reason," said Léa with a smile.

Charlie let out a small laugh. "So what's the reason?"

"Sorry, but I haven't figured that out just yet."

"Wonderful," said Cindy. "And that leaves us pretty much in the same spot we've been in all day."

"Like I said earlier, we're out of those cells," said Léa.

"Like I said earlier. It's not like we can just hop on our bikes and ride to town for coffee."

Léa nodded. "You're right about that."

"So what's next?" asked Charlie.

As if to answer him, the light from the torches dimmed. Cindy and Charlie started to stand.

"Hang on," said Léa. "Don't try to get up."

"Why?" asked Charlie.

"Shh ..."

"What are we listening for?" Cindy whispered.

"That."

"What?" asked Charlie.

"Hear that hissing sound?" said Léa.

"Yeah."

"Sounds like more knockout gas. Make yourselves comfortable, guys." Léa shifted on the bench.

"Why?" said Cindy.

"Lean back, and relax. Right now." Léa's voice was sharp.

Charlie and Cindy leaned back, but they didn't relax. Léa stretched out on the bench.

"Good night, guys. See you in the morning," said Léa.

A few seconds later, the knockout gas reached them.

They were asleep in less than a second.

CHAPTER 10 - THE NEXT MORNING

The Castle, Sunday, 8 a.m.

Léa felt something move under her.

"Not again," she whispered.

She remembered how difficult it had been to wake up from the first round of knockout gas, and she wasn't looking forward to another hangover. Léa fidgeted and felt the familiar pain in her arms and wrists from the handcuffs. She opened her eyes and found herself still on the bench in the bathroom cell, but the lights from the torches were burning brightly again.

"Good morning, I guess," she said.

Léa was lying on her right side, but she didn't feel the hard wood of the bench. Using her legs as leverage, she sat up and looked around.

Cindy had slumped from the end of the bench into the corner. Léa had fallen onto Cindy's legs, and Charlie had fallen off the bench and was lying on the floor.

Léa shook her head, and her hair fell into her eyes. Surprisingly, she wasn't hungover at all. In fact, she felt refreshed. She shuffled her feet, leaned forward, and stood up.

Not bad.

Her arms and shoulders ached from having her hands locked behind her back for so long, but she was pleased with herself for learning how to move around.

Léa realized she needed to pee. She tiptoed to the toiled and hoped no one would wake up before she was finished.

As Léa sat down, she noticed the dirt and dust that seemed to cover the castle was gone. There were no dusty footprints on the floor. Even the walls seemed to be clean. Léa's gaze moved around the room. Something else had changed.

When Léa had been looking through the window of her cell door, she had seen blood on Charlie's ear. The shower had washed away the blood, but now, a bandage covered Charlie's ear. Léa couldn't tell for sure, but she was almost certain that the bandage on her own head had been replaced.

Léa finished up and turned to face the stainless steel prison toilet. There was a button on one side and a foot pedal at the base. Glimpsing back at Charlie and Cindy, Léa hoped she wouldn't wake them quite yet.

She twisted her shoulders and hips to reach the button, which flushed the toilet. Cindy and Charlie remained asleep.

Léa smiled and moved to the sink. She pressed the foot pedal, and fresh, cool water spurted from the tap. Léa took a long drink, then moved her face into the stream. Bending down even more, she let the water soak her hair.

With one eye on Cindy and Charlie, she left the cell as quietly as the leg chain would allow.

In the hallway, Léa leaned over and shook her wet hair. In one practiced motion, she tossed her head back with just enough force to fling the wet hair from her eyes, over her shoulders, and down her back.

"Now, if only someone would have delivered coffee and breakfast," she said.

Glancing back in the room, she saw that Charlie and Cindy were still sleeping. Léa decided now was the perfect time to look around. Reminding herself to walk slowly and carefully, she started down the long hallway. Except for the absence of dirt and dust, nothing had changed since last night. All the cell doors were open.

Léa emerged from the hallway into the main dungeon area. Everything was just as it had been yesterday afternoon.

"At least it's cleaner," she said loudly.

She noticed that someone had topped off the big water barrel.

"Thanks for the water, but coffee and Bailey's would have been nice."

Léa looked around the empty room.

"Still giving me the silent treatment?" she taunted.

The room remained silent.

"Fine, have it your way."

She lifted one foot off the floor and rattled the leg chain.

"But, for the record, this is getting quite tiresome."

Léa decided to let Cindy and Charlie sleep a little longer. She would explore the old dungeon. Again reminding herself to walk carefully, Léa examined the room.

She started by circling the perimeter, scrutinizing the walls. She paused where the dungeon door had been. Two of the old, carved symbols were etched into stones of the wall. Nothing seemed to have changed since yesterday.

Léa moved on to the cages hanging over the fire pits, then to the old rack. After looking over the old torture equipment, she stopped in front the skeleton nailed to the wooden cross.

"So what do you have to say for yourself today?"

She stared at the skeleton. It stared back.

"Didn't think so," she said.

"Didn't think what?" said Cindy behind her.

Léa slowly turned and grinned. "Good morning!"

"You're in a good mood," said Cindy, looking Léa up and down. "And you've even managed to look good."

"Well, it's not my idea of a perfect morning," said Léa.

"What's your perfect morning?"

"I would have liked the use of my hands, arms, and legs for my morning workout," said Léa, her volume rising.

"I'm right here. You don't have to shout."

"Sorry, wasn't talking to you," said Léa confidently.

"Fine, Smart Girl. I can see that you've not only managed to look great this morning, but you've also figured something out."

Léa smiled at Cindy. "Maybe. But let's get your day started off on the right foot, too."

Léa headed back down the hallway, stopping after a few steps and turning back to Cindy, who hadn't moved.

"Come on," said Léa.

Cindy slowly shuffled down the hall. "You seem to be getting around without too much trouble."

"It's not too tough once you figure out how," said Léa over her shoulder.

"So what's the secret?"

"Just take shorter steps, and never, ever get in a hurry."

When they arrived at the end of the hallway, Léa turned and smiled at Cindy. "Let's get you cleaned up."

"What for?" Cindy grumbled.

Léa rattled the leg chain with her foot. "Because I think we're getting these things off today."

"Really? How do you figure?"

"Later," said Léa. "Let's get you feeling better first."

Léa walked into the bathroom cell, but Cindy didn't budge.

"Come on."

"Why?" said Cindy.

Léa smiled and nodded her head toward the sink. Cindy didn't move.

Léa gestured toward the sink and mouthed the word, *please*.

Cindy stared at Léa, who mouthed, *pretty please*.

"Oh, okay." Cindy shuffled over to the sink.

Léa whispered into Cindy's ear. "They've been watching us this whole time. I'm convinced this is a test of some sort. So let's show them we're not afraid and we're still totally hot."

Cindy pinched her eyebrows and huffed. "Whatever."

Léa pressed the sink's foot pedal. "Come on. Stick your face and hair in the water."

Cindy shook out her hair and dropped her face into the sink.

"That's a girl. Get your hair good and wet, too," said Léa.

Once Cindy's hair was sopping wet, she straightened up.

"Now shake out the water, and when you're almost through, toss your hair back over your shoulders," said Léa.

Cindy peered at Léa through her drenched hair. Then she turned slowly toward Charlie. A wicked smile appeared on her face. Cindy shuffled over to her brother and shook the water all over Charlie.

"Bloody hell!" yelled Charlie as Cindy tossed her wet hair over her shoulders.

"Way to go!" Léa laughed.

"Good morning, big brother!"

"Good morning. You two seem to be doing well this morning," said Charlie through a yawn.

"If you believe Smart Girl, here, we'll be getting out of this place today," said Cindy.

"Is that so?" Charlie struggled to his feet.

"That's what she says."

"Well, then," he said. "Let's get a move on. I'm anxious to meet our hosts."

"I still haven't figured out all the details," Léa said. "But it's starting to clear up."

"Sounds good. But if you two will excuse me, I'd like the bathroom to myself for a few minutes."

Cindy followed Léa to the door, shuffling her feet to keep from tripping.

Charlie said to Léa, "You're getting around pretty good."

Léa winked at Charlie and left the room.

When they were gone, Charlie walked over to the stainless steel prison toilet. He glanced toward the empty doorway, shook his head, and smiled.

A few minutes later, Charlie appeared at the door. Cindy was sitting on the bench near the big water barrel, and Léa was examining a cell door's lock. She turned when she heard Charlie.

"Pick up your feet," she told him. "Don't shuffle."

"I don't want to do another face plant," said Charlie.

"Take smaller steps. Just don't shuffle like convict," said Léa loudly.

At Léa's confident expression, Charlie stood taller and walked down the hall. His stride was short, but he walked otherwise normally, making Léa smile.

"Well done. Now sit down. We have to talk," she said.

Cindy shook her head and rolled her eyes. "No idea what has Smart Girl all excited this morning."

Charlie sat down on the bench. Léa sat between Cindy and Charlie. "Ever since we got here," she said, "I've been saying that something doesn't seem right. Right?"

Charlie looked over at his sister. "Right."

Cindy looked up at the ceiling and rolled her eyes again.

"Right," she said grudgingly.

"If we were truly prisoners, why would they only latch the cell doors and not lock them? We had water and shit buckets. So why let us out of the cells?"

Léa saw Cindy smile at the words "shit buckets."

"Right," said Cindy.

"That tells me that our hosts don't want us to just rot away. Right?" Léa was talking faster.

"Right," said Cindy and Charlie together.

"And another thing. They built all this." Léa gestured toward the ceiling and down the hall. "They built a nice bathroom complete with a working toilet and a shower with hot water. Then at bedtime, they knock us out and while we're sleeping, bandage Charlie's busted up ear, and change my bandage, too. Everyone with me?"

"With you," said Charlie with a smile.

"Right," said Cindy.

"Good." Léa began talking faster and faster. This was what she lived for. Figuring things out. Making things work. "All this. All this, is a test."

"A test!" said Cindy. "That's what you've come up with? How does being stripped down and chained up bring you to that conclusion?"

"Haven't the foggiest." Léa smiled.

"What the fuck! You made us listen to all that. Convinced me to toss my hair around like some brainless school-girl tart and you haven't the foggiest?"

"Oh, chill out, little sister."

"Don't call me *little sister*, and don't tell me to chill out. You don't strip people down, handcuff them, and lock them in some medieval dungeon to fucking test them!" Cindy's eyes blazed.

Charlie watched his sister with shock in his eyes. But Léa smiled even bigger.

"What are you so fucking happy about?" said Cindy.

"You."

"If I weren't fucking handcuffed, I swear I'd knock that smug smile right off your fucking face."

"You know, Tara, you're really hot when you're naked and handcuffed," said Léa. "But you're even hotter when you're angry."

Cindy's eyes were full of disgust. "Tara? I'm not Tara. I don't fucking believe you. Are you even in the same room with us?"

Léa looked straight ahead and cleared the cobwebs.

Where did that come from?

She thought for a minute, then shook her head again and tried to get the conversation back on track.

"Look. I never admitted to having all the answers. And despite me conjuring up Tara just now, I still think this is a test of some sort. I really do think we're close to figuring out how to get out of here."

She kept her expression calm, looking first at Charlie, then at Cindy. Charlie appeared, understandably, surprised, but Cindy looked straight ahead, her face blank. No one spoke.

Léa was annoyed that everyone's attention was so easily distracted by her absentminded slip of the tongue when they should be focused on escaping the dungeon.

"It's really not that big a deal, is it?" asked Léa.

"I guess not," said Charlie. "This is such a bizarre situation. But, it's a little weird that you'd bring Tara into this now."

Léa considered. Maybe it hadn't been an absentminded slip of the tongue, after all. What was it she had said?

You know, Tara, you're really hot when you're naked and handcuffed, but you're even hotter when you're angry.

Did that mean more than she missed and needed her best friend? Léa wanted to know right now, but she realized she wouldn't have that answer for quite a while. There were more important things to think about.

For now, she wanted to get free of the handcuffs, the shackles, and the dungeon. But she'd given her friends and herself a bit of a shock. She needed to snap everyone out of it. So Léa stood up, walked to the opposite wall, and turned to face Cindy and Charlie.

"I'm sure Sigmund Freud might have something interesting to say about what just happened. But I don't give a shit what old Siggy thinks right now," she said.

Both Charlie and Cindy looked surprised, but at least they were listening to her.

"I just really want to get out of here. Don't you?" said Léa.

Charlie nodded. "Yeah."

Cindy only stared at her.

"I just really want to get out of here. *Don't you?*" Léa said directly to Cindy.

Cindy hesitated. "Think you can stay in this universe?"

"I'll try," said Léa. "Before Tara appeared in the conversation, we were this close—" Léa pivoted on her legs to reveal her hands, cuffed behind her back. She held her fingers apart. "This close to figuring out how to get out of here." Léa spun back around and smiled. "Is everyone back with me?"

"With you," said Charlie.

After a pause, Cindy gave Léa an annoyed scowl. "Get on with it, Smart Girl."

"Before Tara came up, I was trying to convince you that this is all a test. I'd mentioned my bandage and the new bandage on Charlie's ear. Now, how about a few more things?"

Cindy and Charlie were once again listening to her every word.

"Did either of you notice how clean the cell block was this morning?"

Charlie and Cindy looked down the hall. They nodded. Léa smiled. She had them back.

"So, new bandages on wounds and a clean cell block. We have unlocked cell doors and what any prisoner would call a fairly nice bathroom. Add to all that, they knocked us out with something that made us sleep without giving us hangovers." Léa paused to let this sink in. "When I got up this morning, I took a walk around this goofy old torture chamber. Don't ask me how, but I'm convinced that I'm—"

Léa paused, pivoted and used her fingers to once again illustrate her point.

"This close to figuring our way out of here."

Everyone smiled.

"So what do you need from us?" asked Charlie.

"I don't know. I'm trying to figure out the next step."

They quieted down for a few minutes. Léa smiled. She'd gotten them to forget about her mental hiccup and concentrate on the problem.

Success!

"Okay, Smart Girl," said Cindy. "Tell us what you did and what you saw, from the moment you got up."

Léa took a step back and leaned against the far wall of the cell block. She described her morning, listening for a new facet of her story—anything that might help her think her way out of the dungeon.

They talked it through for what seemed like hours. Charlie asked Léa questions. Cindy asked Léa questions. Léa asked them both questions. Then the questions stopped.

"We still have a solid wall where the door used to be," said Cindy.

They all agreed, that was the way to freedom. They just didn't know how to open the door.

Léa shook her head. "I'll be back."

Léa headed to the bathroom cell.

"This is so fucked up," said Cindy.

"You said it." Charlie looked up at the ceiling.

"I don't know what bothers me more. The fact that I've spent this much time running around naked and chained up with my brother or that Smart Girl took a temporary detour from reality."

"We're all gonna need months of therapy after this." Charlie sighed.

"What the fuck, Charlie."

"What the fuck, Cindy."

A few quiet moments later, they heard a commotion at the end of the hallway and looked up to see Léa walking as fast as she could.

"Looks like Smart Girl just found the crown jewels," said Cindy.

"She better slow down or that chain will trip her."

"I'd love to see her do a big old face plant," said Cindy.

"That's kinda mean."

"Yeah. Whatever."

Léa walked past them. "Come on! I think I know how we're getting out of here."

"Here we go." Charlie lumbered to his feet.

"Yeah. Maybe." Cindy followed him.

They met Léa where the door had been. "Those symbols," she said breathlessly. "They're everywhere in this castle."

"Slow down. Catch your breath," said Charlie.

But Léa kept talking.

"They're everywhere. Right?"

"Yeah, they're everywhere," said Cindy.

"And right here, too." Léa nodded toward what had been the door to the dungeon, then gestured in the direction of the cell block. "But there are only two down here. In the shower and right here."

"How do you know?" asked Cindy.

"Because while you two were sleeping, I took a walk around this dodgy chamber of horrors and didn't see any symbols, except these."

"Okay. So there are only these two etchings. So what?" said Cindy.

"So, remember how the one in the shower works?"

"Yeah," said Charlie.

"Wanna bet these work the same way?" Léa smiled and approached one of the symbols. She leaned her shoulder toward the wall and pressed the stone block. Just like the one in the shower, the block with the symbol moved. But this time, nothing happened.

"Okay then. Charlie, you take the one on the right, I'll take this one," said Léa. "On the count of three."

Charlie nodded.

Léa counted down. "One, two, three."

Charlie and Léa pushed their shoulders against the carved symbols. Silently, the wall slid up to reveal the hallway they'd entered through the day before.

"You fucking bitch!" yelled Cindy.

Léa turned to see who was standing in the now-open doorway.

"You know, Léa. You're really hot when you're naked and handcuffed. But you're even hotter when you're the smartest girl in town," said Tara with a smirk. "Nice to see you, too, bitch," she said to Cindy.

Tara was dressed all in black. From the heavy-duty boots to the commando pants to the black bulletproof vest, Tara's appearance had changed drastically from the last time anyone had seen her.

But it wasn't just her clothes.

Tara carried an AK-47 assault rifle, pointed straight up in the air. A holstered handgun was strapped to her right leg, and a large commando-style knife hung upside-down from her vest.

Tara reached into a pocket of her commando pants and pulled out a small set of keys. She smiled briefly, winked at Léa, and pressed a button on the remote attached to the keychain.

To her left, what appeared to be a solid stone wall silently slid away to reveal another long hallway.

After replacing the keys in her pocket, Tara dropped the stock of the rifle to her left hand so that it pointed toward Léa, Cindy, and Charlie.

"Let's go," she said.

"Do you really need that?" asked Léa.

"No. But the boss likes us to make an impression."

"The boss?" asked Léa.

"Come on. You're about to meet him."

Léa's brain was working overtime. She was relieved to see Tara, but she was shocked at Tara's appearance and at the fact that her best friend was pointing a gun at her. Plus, hearing her own words repeated back to her was a little unsettling.

"You heard me? What I said, about you?" asked Léa.

"Aw, look at that," said Cindy. "Smart Girl and Tough Stuff are about to have a tender reunion."

Tara pointed her gun at her. "I never really liked you before, and I like you even less now."

"What? You gonna shoot me?" Cindy taunted her.

"Shut up, Cindy," Charlie whispered.

Without moving the rifle, Tara looked to Léa.

"Yeah, I heard, everything. There'll be time for us to talk later. Don't worry, you'll understand everything. It'll be okay."

"All right then," said Léa. "Let's meet this boss of yours."

She started through the doorway and into the hallway that had just appeared. Charlie and Cindy walked slowly behind her.

"I don't think Smart Girl saw any of this coming," Cindy said to Charlie.

"Just shut up, and keep walking," said Tara.

Cindy looked over her shoulder and smiled as they walked through the underground hallway.

CHAPTER 11 - THE OLD MAN

The Castle, 8:30 a.m.

An old finger touched a button on the console beside the worn desk. The old TV monitor on the desk came alive. When the picture stabilized, it showed a long hallway, with four tiny specks at the end. Over the next few minutes, the specks grew larger until they were identifiable as people.

The old man sighed and reached for another button.

"Yes, Commander Dennis," scratched a woman's voice over an old intercom.

"Tell your old man we'll need seating for our three new guests soon," said the old man.

"David is on his way and will be there momentarily," the woman's voice scratched back.

"Thank you, Pattie." The old man switched off the intercom.

As the four people walked down the hallway, the old man adjusted his reading glasses and sorted through the files on his desk. The one he needed had five stars on the outside of the folder. He opened it and examined the pictures that fell out, glancing occasionally at the monitor.

He let out a small laugh. The picture in his hand was of the same young woman now leading the pack down the hallway.

"Walking fearlessly into the unknown."

He replaced the picture in the file and slid all the files into a battered leather briefcase.

The group was still traversing the hallway when someone knocked on one of his three doors.

"Come in, David."

The door opened, and David McNally, the same man from the coffee shop in town, entered carrying three stainless steel stools. He was dressed like Tara, in black commando boots and pants and a black bulletproof vest.

A handgun was strapped to each of his legs.

He limped across the office and plugged each stool into a stainless steel hole in the floor. When he was finished, the stools sat in a row in front of the old man's desk.

"All ready, sir," said David McNally.

"Yes." The old man looked back to the monitor. The group was nearly to the end of the hallway.

"You know the one we're interested in?" said the old man.

"Yes, sir."

"There could be trouble with the other two. The other girl is quite angry, and I'd expect her brother won't react kindly if she gets out of hand."

"I'm sure you won't let things get out of hand," said McNally. "But we'll keep them locked down until we're sure they'll behave."

"Yes." The old man turned in his chair to pour a cup of freshly brewed coffee. "Help yourself." He pointed to an empty cup.

"Thank you, sir," said McNally.

But he didn't pour a cup for himself.

The old man watched the monitor until the group arrived at the door. "Here we go." He sat up straight in his chair.

The door opened, and Léa, Cindy, and Charlie entered, Tara following closely.

"Come in, come in," said the old man. "Captain, you might want to help our guests with their seats."

McNally smiled pleasantly. "Hello Léa, Cindy, and Charlie. Come in and sit down. Each of you please stand behind a stool. Leave your feet and leg chain behind the stool, then carefully take a step forward and sit down."

Léa was first to sit down. Charlie was next, then Cindy.

"Welcome," said the old man. "You three have been through quite an ordeal, and I'm sure you all have questions. You'll get a few answers right now. But before we begin, I want to assure you that you are among friends."

"Not too many of my friends strip me down, chain me up, and lock me in a dungeon," said Cindy.

"Yes, I'm sure you must find your present situation quite bizarre," said the old man. "But there was a reason."

Cindy huffed. "I can't wait to hear your reason."

"You were watching us the whole time?" asked Léa.

The old man nodded. "Yes."

"You could listen to us too?" asked Léa.

"Yes."

"You listened to everything I said?"

"Yes."

"Then my only real question is, was I right about all this?"

"Yes."

"So this was a test?"

"It was."

"Pretty fucked up test if you ask me," said Cindy.

"It's a pretty fucked up world, Miss Martin," said the old man.

"So what kind of test was it?" said Cindy. "Screening for a porn video?" She rattled the leg chain against the stainless steel stool and stared defiantly at the old man.

The old man looked up at McNally and laughed. "That's a good one, isn't it, Captain?" he said.

"A good one, sir."

"And it's one we've heard before, right Miss Wells?" said the old man to Tara.

Tara looked at the ground and smiled. "Yes, sir."

"Yes, hardly original. Your friend Miss Wells said almost the exact same thing nearly a year ago."

All three looked up at Tara, who continued staring at the ground.

"But back to your question, Miss Taylor," said the old man. "Yes, this was indeed a test."

"Back to my original statement. It's a pretty fucked up test," said Cindy.

"Back to my original reply to your original statement, Miss Martin. It's a pretty fucked up world."

"Did we at least pass your fucked up test?" asked Cindy.

"You and your brother could have done better, but you still passed." The old man turned to Léa. "But you, Miss Taylor. You are doing quite well."

"It's not over?" said Léa.

"It is for you Cindy and Charlie. Captain, I'm sure the Martins would like to freshen up a bit and have a spot of lunch. Is everything ready?"

"Yes sir," said McNally.

He opened one of the three doors in the bare office. Two more men dressed in black entered, followed by a nurse carrying white bathrobes.

"Cindy, Charlie, please stand up carefully, and take a step back from your stools," said McNally pleasantly.

The two men dressed in black helped Cindy and Charlie to their feet. The nurse draped bathrobes over their shoulders.

"All right then," said the nurse with a smile. "Come on."

"Where are you taking us?" Charlie glanced back to Léa.

"You're going to our small hospital," said the old man. "They'll take a look at that ear of yours. Then you'll be off to a hot shower, some clean clothes, and a comfortable bed."

"But, you said we didn't do so well on your test. That can't be good for us." Charlie's nerves echoed through his voice.

"You didn't fail the test," said the old man. "You just didn't do as well as we'd hoped. You and your sister are in no danger, Charlie. I need to continue with Miss Taylor right now. We'll all visit again soon."

Charlie looked down at Léa. "Are you going to be okay?" he asked.

Léa looked directly into the old man's eyes.

"I'll be fine."

"Come on, you two," said the nurse. "Let's get you to your rooms. Then we can get those cuffs off."

The two men dressed in black firmly took hold of Charlie's and Cindy's arms and walked them toward the door.

"Léa!" cried Cindy.

"You'll be okay, Cindy. Go with them."

Léa didn't break eye contact with the old man. Once Charlie and Cindy were gone, she cocked her head slightly, and her eyes narrowed.

"I sure hope I didn't just lie to them," she said.

"You didn't."

"So I'm still being tested?"

"Just a few more details," he said. "As your friend Miss Martin said, this was a pretty fucked up test. Do you have an idea why nice people like us would subject a nice girl like you to something so bizarre?"

"Maybe you're not so nice," said Léa.

"Oh, I think we're nice enough."

Léa looked over to Tara and at the gun strapped to her leg.

"I'll have to trust you on that one."

"Nice of you. So what did you think about our test?"

"I had a great time."

Tara looked down as a single half laugh, half snort popped out of her nose.

"Well that's a first," said the old man.

"Definitely a first," said David.

"Not many people have as much fun with our little test. Aside from making sure you had a good time, why do you think we came up with it?"

Léa thought a moment.

"I'd have to say this was a test to see how we'd react to an extreme situation," said Léa.

"Good start."

"Judging from all the guns in the room, I'd say you play some rough games. So you came up with a rough test."

"Good so far," said the old man. "But keep going."

"But mostly, I'd have to say this was a problem-solving test."

"Almost there."

Léa thought for a few moments.

"Problem solving in a bizarre situation?"

"Yes. But I'm looking for just one more thing."

Léa looked up at Tara again, then back at the old man. She replayed the events of the past few days and smiled.

"And successfully escaping from the bizarre situation?"

"Bravo," said the old man. "Captain, would you take those silly things off now?"

"Let me?" asked Tara.

"Be my guest," said McNally.

Tara reached into her pocket and pulled out her key ring. Standing behind Léa, Tara unlocked her handcuffs, then her leg shackles.

Léa slowly moved her arms in front of her and flexed her hands. She stretched her arms and legs one at a time. "That's better." Léa nodded at the man's coffee cup. "Now may I please have some of that coffee?"

"Of course," said the old man.

He poured a cup of coffee and slid it over the desk toward Léa.

Léa stood and reached across the desk for the cup, but it slid out of her weak fingers. She flexed her sore hands and gripped the mug more tightly, slowly picking up the cup and returning to her stool.

She held the mug to her nose and took a deep whiff. Closing her eyes, Léa sipped the coffee. "*Mmm*, almost perfect."

"Almost?" said the old man.

Tara smiled before Léa spoke. "Got any Bailey's?"

"Not down here," said the old man.

Léa took a few more sips of coffee and set the mug on the empty stool beside her. She rubbed her sore and bruised wrists and decided the old man wasn't all that bad. After all, Tara seemed to trust him. Léa knew she was out of danger.

She sensed that the test might not be over, but she didn't care about that. She wasn't as angry as Cindy, but Léa felt some paybacks were due. She wanted to own the room.

"So, this was a test to see how I'd behave in a bizarre, stressful situation and to see if I'd find a way to escape from that situation."

"Yes," said the old man.

"But your little test isn't over, is it?"

"Why do you say that?"

"You haven't offered me a hot shower, clean clothes, and a comfortable bed yet," said Léa.

"Would you like your hot shower, clean clothes, and comfortable bed now?"

Léa picked up her cup of coffee and smiled at the old man. "I'm fine."

She took a sip of coffee.

"So what's next?" asked Léa.

"Don't you have any more questions?"

"Dozens." Léa began to feel the coffee's effects and enjoyed the rush of energy. But she also enjoyed the fact that she was gaining control.

"You're pretty sure of yourself, aren't you?" said the old man.

"Yes." Léa said with a smile. "I am."

"Would you mind telling me why?"

Léa looked up at Tara with a confident grin. "Because that's my best friend. If I were in trouble, she'd know, and that means I'd know. And as you said, I've practically passed your silly little test."

Léa finished her coffee.

"I can see, Miss Wells, that everything you've told us about Miss Taylor is true. You have indeed passed your test. Would you like your hot shower, clean clothes, and comfortable bed now?"

"I'm fine. How about you?" said Léa.

"Me?"

"You. After all, you're the old man with a naked young woman in his office."

Léa slid her empty cup across the desk and looked into the old man's eyes.

"So pour me another cup of that weak-ass coffee. Then you can tell me who you are and what this is all about."

The old man reached for the coffee pot.

"Well. It all started over fifty years ago," said Alan Dennis.

PART 2: HOW IT ALL BEGAN

CHAPTER 12 - THE DAILY SENTINEL

London, 1965

The gray, dirty building sat on a gray, dirty street corner in one of London's gray, dirty neighborhoods. The home of the *London Daily Sentinel* had survived several bomb hits during the London Blitz, along with many years of hard times. It looked like it could crumble into a pile of rocks at any minute.

In this old part of town was an old diner, an old men's clothing store, and several old law firms. Across the street, an old food mart and an old accounting firm sat between vacant storefronts.

Between the food mart and the accounting firm were two sets of shiny metal and glass double doors. The doors seemed completely out of place in a neighborhood of traditional brick and wood.

Above the doors, a red circle cut by a blue bar announced the presence of the London Underground. The addition of the small "tube" station was this neighborhood's only attempt at modernization over the course of a hundred years.

One of the shiny doors swung open, and a single person exited the station. The man was tall and skinny. Not slim. Not trim. Just skinny. His clothes were rumpled.

As the door closed behind him, Alan Dennis reached into his pocket for a cigarette. Light rain started to fall, and he stepped under the tube sign, attempting to shield his lighter and cigarette.

After he lit his cigarette, Alan stood under the sign, quietly surveying the old newspaper building. He put away his cigarette case and pulled a battered flask from another pocket.

In one fluid movement, he replaced the cigarette at his mouth with the flask, swallowed a long drink, then replaced the cigarette.

Alan took a long drag and looked sadly through the smoke at the old newspaper building. At ten in the morning, Alan had already emptied half the scotch in the flask.

Twenty-eight-year-old Alan Dennis enjoyed a little success, but more than his share of failure. A few awards decorated his desk, and Alan had scooped plenty of stories. But whenever times were tough, he was always the first reporter laid off.

After several minutes of standing in the rain, something caught Alan's attention. A line of trucks pulled out of the underground garage. Alan checked his watch. It was only 10:15 in the morning. A fleet of trucks that early meant only one thing: A special edition was hitting the streets.

Alan crossed the street and climbed the five steps to the main entrance. He paused to look over his shoulder as the last of the delivery trucks disappeared into the thick London fog. He pitched his cigarette onto the sidewalk and walked into the building.

"Mister Dennis, thank God you're here. The Reds are on the march this time for sure." Mary-Jane Hawkins looked most agitated.

"How awful," Alan said. "I might have to give up scotch for vodka."

"Oh, get on in there. Sir Richard has been asking for you all morning." Mary-Jane waved him into the newsroom.

Alan moved to the center of the newsroom. Beneath a huge chalk board, the city desk editor glanced up from his phone call. He jabbed his cigarette in Alan's direction, then jabbed the cigarette toward the owner's office.

Ignoring the editor, Alan studied the chalkboard filled with stories and the names of reporters assigned to cover them. After only a few moments, Alan realized what was going on. Shaking his head, he headed toward his own desk. The city editor cupped his hand over the phone.

"Get your ass in there now, Dennis," he shouted.

Alan ignored the city editor and continued toward his desk. A copy of the special edition had been tossed on top of the pile of older papers. A single headline dominated the top half of the newspaper:

RED NUKE SUB SPOTTED OFF ENGLISH COAST

The series of stories that followed included a few Alan had written about the Soviet military and the poor state of diplomatic relations with Moscow.

As he skimmed the special edition, Alan glanced over his cluttered desk and around the newsroom. Nearly everyone was running around with what Alan called *their hair on fire*. After his first few years in the news business,

Alan had learned that it was never necessary to rush around like an idiot.

He read the special edition from cover to cover. When he was finished, he crumpled it up and tossed it toward the trash can.

"Not exactly front page news to you, is it?" said a quiet voice.

Alan's boss, Sir Richard Carter, the owner and managing editor of the *London Daily Sentinel* smiled down at him.

"No, sir. I'm afraid not."

"If I have my dates right, you've known about this for right around six months," said Sir Richard.

"That sounds about right. What blew up to cause all this?" Alan waved at the chaos around them.

"A late night visit from some government fool. Apparently, now was a convenient time to leak the story."

There it is, thought Alan.

The government had deliberately delayed Alan's exclusive story six months. As Alan considered this latest development, Mary-Jane quietly approached Sir Richard. She whispered in his ear and produced a single sheet of paper for him to sign.

As Sir Richard scratched out his illegible signature, Alan tried to figure out why it was so important to delay his story six months. He studied the chalkboard of stories.

He knew without a doubt that there was no national-security reason to kill the story. He had gotten it from a trusted source at the Admiralty who would never have talked otherwise. With the possibility of a threat to national security eliminated, Alan reached two simple conclusions.

Either someone screwed up, or someone wanted to sell something. Alan turned back to Sir Richard.

"The only reason I'm not staging a silly meltdown is because I'm guessing you're just as disgusted about this as I am."

Sir Richard smiled. "Plus, you've been in this business long enough to know that silly meltdowns don't solve anything and usually result in ulcers."

"Actually, I just don't care that much anymore." Alan sighed. "But it's not like you to take this lying down. I'm guessing you have a few ideas that those who forced us to sit on the story won't like."

"Oh yes, indeed."

"So what do you want to do?"

"I'm not going to do anything." Sir Richard. turned toward his office and spoke over his shoulder. "But you're going on holiday. Come along."

Alan gazed around the frantic newsroom and down at his ridiculously cluttered desk. Sir Richard stood in the door of his office, smiling.

Alan slowly followed.

CHAPTER 13 - HANDBOOK NUMBER 10

Sir Richard's Office

"Close the door, and pull down that shade," said Sir Richard.

Alan eyed Sir Richard for a moment before closing the door and dropping the shade, making the paneled office even darker. Like the old newspaper, Sir Richard's office had that musty, old-world smell. An ancient radio played classical music, and the only sources of light were two green-shaded desk lamps.

"I think we'll be more comfortable over here," said Sir Richard.

He sat in one of a pair of overstuffed leather chairs with the old radio between them. The chair squeaked as he leaned to one side, producing a set of keys from his pocket.

"Sit down, old boy. This'll just take a moment." Sir Richard pointed to the other chair.

He turned to the radio and pressed his finger against the fabric grill covering the speaker. A small panel under the volume control popped open to reveal a shiny keyhole. Sir Richard turned a key in the slot, and a larger panel popped open, revealing another metal door with another key hole. Sir Richard selected another key and opened a hidden safe.

"Very clever," said Alan.

Sir Richard put two fingers to his lips, smiled, and shook his head. He turned up the radio's volume and changed the channel to a rock and roll station before beginning to sort through the items in the safe.

"I simply can't stand this new, modern music." Sir Richard grimaced. "But it should prevent anyone from listening in."

Alan sat up in his chair and leaned closer to his boss. "We should also talk much more quietly," Alan said. "A loud radio helps, but the best bugs can still pick up loud voices."

"Indeed."

Sir Richard pulled a small pamphlet from the safe. Then he firmly shut the inner door, locked it, and closed the outer panel.

Sir Richard leaned back in his chair with the pamphlet on his lap. He peered over his reading glasses at Alan and patted the pamphlet with his palm.

"This is why we sat on your story for nearly half a year," he said.

Alan's eyes dropped to Sir Richard's hands covering the pamphlet.

"Alan, look at me."

He looked up.

"You've no doubt heard of the Official Secrets Act," he said sternly.

Alan nodded.

"Over the next few days, you will learn many secrets. Far beyond the Official Secrets Act. You must give me your word, upon your honor, that you will not betray the trust I am about to place in you." Sir Richard looked deeply into Alan's eyes, his face deadly serious. "If you betray my trust, I can promise that you will not only disappear from the face of the earth, but you will disappear in a most unpleasant way. There will be no appeal, no reprieve. There must be absolute trust between us."

He paused as Alan glanced again at the covered pamphlet. Alan reached into his pocket for his flask. "I gather what you're about to tell me won't be appearing in the paper."

Sir Richard only stared.

"I'm just a washed up, mostly drunk reporter. Why tell me something I can't report on?"

Sir Richard's expression softened. He set the pamphlet on a side table, out of Alan's view.

"True, you do drink a bit too much, and you smoke way too much. But we're going to change all that."

"Who's 'we?'" asked Alan.

"So I can trust you? I can count on you one hundred percent? You understand the penalty for betraying my trust?"

Alan nodded.

Sir Richard watched Alan for a long time before reaching for the pamphlet. He passed it to Alan with hesitation. "From this day forward, you are no longer a washed up, mostly drunk reporter. Put that silly thing away, and read this."

Alan stuffed the flask back in his pocket and took the pamphlet from Sir Richard. The government publication was only about twenty pages. The cover was dominated by a mushroom cloud, and the title was printed in red, block letters.

CIVIL DEFENCE HANDBOOK NO. 10:
Advising the Householder on Protection Against Nuclear Attack

Alan opened the pamphlet and began reading the table of contents:

BASIC FACTS: What Happens When an H-Bomb Explodes
PREPARING THE HOUSE: Guard Against Fire
WHAT TO DO IF IT HAPPENS: Warnings

And the last chapter ...

LIFE UNDER FALL-OUT CONDITIONS: The First Days and How to Manage Later

Alan turned the pages slowly. As he read more of the small pamphlet, his expression changed from mild amusement to outright disbelief.

Sir Richard watched Alan read, remembering the day he had first laid eyes on Her Majesty's Government's best attempt to help the average family protect themselves from the unimaginable. As Alan read the last pages, Sir Richard reached for a heavy crystal decanter and two glasses. He poured two stiff drinks as Alan closed the pamphlet.

"Well, it doesn't get any more fucked up than this," said Alan.

Sir Richard handed Alan a drink and smiled patiently.

"Typically, I believe foul language is merely the effort of a weak mind to express itself forcefully. But in this case ... well said."

Alan smiled back at Sir Richard as they sipped their drinks. He reread the pamphlet's title as he swirled the amber liquid in the heavy glass and began to fit the puzzle pieces together.

Most reporters concentrate on the first four of the five Ws of reporting. It's easy to ask who, what, when, and where. Some eventually ask the last W. But most stop at those first four.

Alan had never been content with the first four Ws. He always wanted to understand the *why*. After years, Alan had learned that the *why* was almost always more important than the other four Ws.

Why this ridiculous waste of time, effort, and paper? thought Alan.

Sir Richard sipped his drink.

"I think you've had enough time to mull it over. Let's hear some of that famous Alan Dennis instant analysis."

Alan set down his drink and reached into his pocket. He fished out his cigarettes, and Sir Richard reached over and snatched them from his hands, tossing them into the trash.

"You won't be allowed to smoke where you're going. So you might as well stop right now."

"Where I'm going?" asked Alan.

"You'll learn that soon enough." Sir Richard leaned back in his chair and pointed to the pamphlet. "Come on, now. Get to it."

With a wistful look toward the trash can, Alan leafed through the pamphlet. He paused every now and then to read over a page, glancing up to see Sir Richard watching him. When he reached the back cover, Alan closed the book, took a drink, and smiled at Sir Richard.

"They're using the news about the Russian sub as a diversion." Alan waved the book in the air and continued. "This is shit, I mean complete nonsense. If they hit us with nuclear weapons, pretty much everyone will be dead within weeks. The authors of this pamphlet know that, and they're hoping to use the Soviet sub news to divert attention from the fact that nothing, *nothing* will do a damn bit of good once bombs start dropping."

"And now the most important part. Why would they do this?"

"Because there's nothing else they can do," Alan replied.

"Quite right. Well done, as always."

Sir Richard emptied his glass and stood. "Finish your drink, you're leaving," he said.

Alan downed his drink as Sir Richard opened his desk drawer and tossed an envelope toward Alan.

"You're to go home and pack," Sir Richard said. "You'll be gone for more than a few months. Bring plenty of warm clothes."

"Warm clothes? So this won't be a tropical beach vacation?"

"I'm afraid not." Sir Richard smiled and pointed to the envelope.

"In there you'll find a letter. Sign it, and leave it with Mrs. Hawkins. It'll ensure that your rent and other bills remain paid while you're away. You'll also find train tickets, a few passes, and instructions." Sir Richard pulled out his pocket watch. He tapped it and wound it a few times. "You'd better get a move on. Your train leaves in less than two hours and you're not known for your punctuality."

Alan waved the envelope and turned to leave. As he reached for the door handle, Sir Richard called after him.

"You know how some people dream of getting a second chance? A new life? This is more than that. This is your chance to do what every reporter out there dreams of."

"What's that?" asked Alan.

"Make a difference."

Alan stood in the doorway, hoping to hear more about this second chance and making a difference. But Sir Richard only smiled.

"Off you go," he said.

CHAPTER 14 - LIGHTS, CAMERA, ACTION!

An Old Movie Studio, Scotland, 4 p.m.

"Quiet on the set!" yelled the assistant director.

The noise on the sound stage disappeared as a short, overweight man held a bullhorn to his mouth.

"Lights," he shouted.

Suddenly, the room was blazing in white light. The temperature on the already warm stage began to rise.

"Camera," shouted the overweight man into his bullhorn.

"Speed," shouted another similarly built man with an unlit cigar hanging from his lips.

The assistant director waddled to an even shorter man sitting by the camera and handed him the bullhorn.

"Mark the film," yelled the assistant director.

"Scene 27-A. Take two. Mark." A man snapped down the top of a clapper board and quickly ran off the set.

"Action!" yelled the man by the camera.

"I'm going to explain to you the system of warning signals that will be used in this country in the event of a nuclear attack." The actor was seated at small, wooden desk on a set designed to look like a country police station. He was dressed as a local police official, and he wore a stern but friendly expression, speaking slowly and seriously.

"An exact knowledge of the signals and what to do when you hear them, could save your life."

"Cut!" yelled the director.

"How was that?" The actor's stern voice had softened.

"Fine, fine." The director looked over his shoulder. "Makeup. Can we please, for the love of God, do something about that unholy glow on Steven's forehead?"

A man with a makeup kit in his hand and several towels tossed over his shoulder ran on set and dabbed the perspiration from the actor's forehead. He hurriedly applied some powder and ran back behind the camera.

"Let's try again. Quickly everyone!"

The man with the clapper board took his place. "Scene 27-A. Take three. Mark."

"And ... action!"

The actor repeated the same lines as before.

"Cut! Wonderful, Steven. Take a break."

The assistant director looked at his watch and whispered to the director.

"Right-O. Call it." The director handed the bullhorn back to the assistant.

"All right, you lot. Cut the lights, cut the sound, and open up the doors."

He passed the bullhorn back to the director.

"Tea time!"

Alan stood near the back wall. To gain access to the sound stage, he'd shown his pass at the door and waited while security made a phone call. A teenager had escorted him inside and pointed to the spot by the back wall, where he now stood.

"Please stand back here, sir. When they call 'quiet on the set' you must maintain absolute silence."

Alan had started to respond, but the kid had taken off before he could.

Alan was amazed at the number of people just standing around. He inched toward a rickety old table piled with paper. He glanced down at the top sheet.

CIVIL DEFENCE BULLETINS 1-8
SHOOTING SCRIPT/SCHEDULE

Alan picked up a packet and leafed through the pages. He realized immediately why Sir Richard wanted him to see this.

"And who are you, sir?" A big man in a suit appeared in front of him.

Alan spoke quietly. "I have a pass."

The man snatched the script out of Alan's hands. "Why don't you show me that pass?"

Alan smiled as he recognized the guy as security. As a reporter, Alan had spent more time dealing with security than actually reporting. He'd learned long ago to keep his passes handy and to kill them with kindness.

"*Daily Sentinel*, huh? The boss doesn't like reporters, and neither do I."

The man scrutinized the pass, and Alan kept smiling. Eventually the man tossed the pass and the script to the floor and walked away without another word.

"Thank you, officer."

Alan picked up the pass and the script and continued reading, looking up every now and then to see what was happening on the set.

Nothing more exciting that watching a bunch of people taking a break.

The room was filled with technicians, carpenters, and older guys dressed in suits. Everyone looked like they belonged. Except the two people standing in the corner near Alan.

"Tea and biscuits, love?" said the woman pushing a refreshment trolley around the room.

"Yes, thanks." Alan took a cup of tea and a few biscuits. Sipping his tea, Alan casually approached the man and woman in the corner.

"Enjoying the show?" he said casually.

"Oh yes, thank you," said the woman.

The man said nothing.

Seconds ticked by. Alan took another sip of tea.

"You two don't appear to be a part of this lot. Neither am I," he said.

They looked Alan over, and the man winked at the woman.

"You two together?" asked Alan. They ignored him. After a few moments of silence, Alan took another sip of tea. "Well then. Lovely conversation. Enjoyed meeting you both."

Alan walked back to the script table to finish his tea. He glanced occasionally to the corner, where the man and woman talked quietly together.

"Ten minutes," the assistant director yelled.

No one seemed to care. Alan finished his tea and continued watching people stand around. The woman managing the tea trolley collected cups and napkins.

"Five minutes," yelled the assistant director.

Alan pulled from his pocket the envelope full of tickets, passes, and instructions. He had train tickets to Liverpool the next morning, several hundred pounds of bank notes, and a single-page itinerary. His instructions upon arriving at the film studio were to watch the production and wait.

"One minute till we close the doors," yelled the assistant director.

Alan searched for more instructions. Nothing else, just wait.

"All right then. Quiet down," yelled the assistant director.

The director took the bullhorn and waited for everyone to quiet down. The woman with the tea trolley disappeared just as the big door began to close. A few more people shuffled in and out of the studio.

"We need to go back and shoot Scene 1-A. Seems there was some noise on the tape," said the director.

The actor picked up his script and flipped through pages. A loud buzzer sounded, and the studio doors slammed shut.

"How about it, Steven? Ready to give it a go?" said the director.

"All set." The actor tossed his script on the floor.

"Let's see if we can get this moving a little faster than normal. I'd like to wrap this afternoon," said the director.

"Yes, sir," said the assistant director.

Alan watched the process start again like an old, lumbering machine sputtering to life. Same thing, time after time. Same instructions. Only the lines recited by the actor were different.

"Scene 1-A. Reshoot. Take one. Mark," yelled the man with the clapper board.

"Action," yelled the director.

"The government has decided that in the present state of international tension, you should know how best to protect yourself from the dangerous effects of nuclear attack. If this tension should lead to war—"

A commotion erupted at the main studio door, and the entry buzzer sounded loudly.

"Cut. Dammit all!" yelled the director as everyone looked back at the door.

"Thank you so much!" said an older man over his shoulder as he blundered into the studio, all eyes on him. "So sorry to be a bother," he said pleasantly.

Everyone stared as the older man shuffled deeper into the studio. His fine clothes were mismatched. The pants and coat were parts of different suits. His gray hair was barely combed. He looked like an unmade bed.

He walked to the center of the room and waved to the crowd watching him.

"Good afternoon, everyone," he said.

Alan recognized him and smiled. The director was stomping toward the old man, but his expression changed dramatically when he recognized him.

"Nicholas, Nicholas. So sorry to interrupt your little show," said the old man. "As usual, the train was on time, but the taxi driver clearly didn't understand my request for haste."

"Sir Richard. So good of you to come."

"I trust you'll be joining us for dinner tonight?" asked Sir Richard.

"If I can keep the show on schedule," said Nicholas.

"Then I won't keep you."

Sir Richard spotted Alan and headed in his direction when several old guys in suits politely intercepted. Sir Richard glanced at Alan with a pained expression. Alan smiled back. He'd seen that expression on Sir Richard's face before.

"Quiet on the set. That includes you lot." The assistant director glared at the suits chattering away with Sir Richard.

Sir Richard patted one of the suits on the back and started toward Alan, waving over the couple in the corner, as well.

"Glad you all could make it," Sir Richard whispered.

"Please, Sir Richard," yelled Nicholas the director.

"Right you are." Sir Richard smiled back.

He shook Alan's hand and whispered in his ear. "Let's sneak out."

Sir Richard gestured for them to follow as he made for the door.

The entry buzzer sounded loudly again.

"Please, Sir Richard!"

"See you tonight, Nicholas." Sir Richard and the group barely made it out the door before it slammed shut.

The director smiled at the door, before noticing he had the room's attention. He wiped the smile from his face and replaced it with tired irritation.

"Right. Now that the *royals* have left, maybe we can finish this up. Take it from the top."

CHAPTER 15 - DINNER AND SOME SECRETS

A Small Scottish Pub, 8 p.m.

"Thank you, my dear. Now if you could just leave that bottle and close the door on your way out," said Sir Richard.

"Certainly." The young woman smiled as she pushed the cart loaded with dirty dishes out of the room.

Sir Richard watched the door close and reached for his scotch.

"Everyone all topped off?" He didn't wait for a response. "Good, good. You know, I've been waiting a long time for this dinner."

"I remember you talking about this back in forty-nine," said Nicholas the director.

"And here we all are," said Sir Richard. "Alan, here, is new to this lot. But I think you'll find we're fairly friendly once you get to know us."

Alan and Sir Richard had been joined by the movie director and the couple from the studio.

"Excuse me, Sir Richard," said the man.

"Yes, David."

"With all due respect, sir, why is someone like him here? A reporter could be a bad risk."

"Quite," said Sir Richard. "But I think he'll fit into our plans quite well. Plus, he's from outside the family, and that will add a whole new perspective, don't you think?"

"I guess." The man was clearly not enthused about the Alan being in the room.

"Family? I don't see much family resemblance around this table," said Alan.

"Not literal family. We all worked together during the war," said Sir Richard.

"I see. And how will my perspective fit in nicely?" Alan took a drink of his scotch.

"Always cutting to the last chapter. That's good and part of that new perspective that I think will serve us well. But first, a little history might help."

"Sounds good." Alan sat back in his chair.

Sir Richard took another sip of scotch and began speaking slowly, but as the story unfolded, his words moved faster. He clearly enjoyed telling this story.

"Do you know how we won the war against Hitler?" asked Sir Richard.

"In the end," said Alan, "I'd have to say it was because a lot of things came together at the right time and in the right place."

"Quite right," said Sir Richard, turning to Nicholas. "Put it another way, Nick."

"It was a combination of military might, excellent intelligence, an ace or two up our sleeves, luck, and a little something that we all were a part of."

"And what was that little something you were all a part of?" asked Alan.

"A very special part of military intelligence," said Sir Richard. "Our boss at the time liked to refer to it as 'corkscrew thinking.'"

"You had a boss?" asked Alan.

"I wasn't always an old man with a title." Sir Richard fidgeted in his chair. "As I said, we were all in what you'd call military intelligence. Our job was to hatch plans to divert Jerry's attention. We were rather successful at it, too."

"You see," said Nicholas, "the German military mind is brilliant and dedicated. But it's always marching in a straight line. Once a plan is agreed upon, it was very hard for Jerry to make changes in direction. Our group was assembled to exploit that weakness."

"And we did it quite effectively," said the woman.

"With—what did you call it—corkscrew thinking?" said Alan.

"Yes," said Sir Richard. "Our boss, Sir John Godfrey, sought out the most unconventional and brilliant minds of our time."

"Most effectively," said the woman.

"You haven't formally met Pattie and her husband, David," said Sir Richard.

"They seem a bit young to have been a part of military intelligence during the war," said Alan.

"We were orphans of the Blitz," said David. "Lots of kids lost families and homes."

"There were so many that a few slipped through the cracks," said Sir Richard. "These two were left to fend for themselves on the streets of London."

"When I ran into them," said Nicholas, "they were working as a team, and, unknown to me, actually lifted my wallet."

Sir Richard chuckled. "We only caught them because I saw the whole thing when I was running to catch up with Nick. Pattie was the diversion. She caught Nick's eye and bumped him on one side while David snatched his wallet on the other."

"The next day, they arranged to have us arrested and thrown in jail," said Pattie.

"They let us cool our heels for a few days," said David. "Then Sir Richard shows up with that fatherly smile, and we ended up with a new home."

"They were just trying to survive," said Sir Richard, "but they went about it most cleverly."

"So, a happy ending for these two?" asked Alan.

"Sort of. Actually, I'm lucky they're still talking to me," said Sir Richard.

"Nonsense," said Pattie.

"Nothing you could have done about it," said David.

"You see, they were just kids," said Nicholas, "but they had incredible survival skills. Plus, they were orphans, and they were available. So we sent them into harm's way."

"Harm's way?" asked Alan.

Sir Richard looked down at the table. "We dropped them into Germany to pass messages, right under the Nazis' noses."

"Who would suspect children?" said Nicholas.

"We were quite successful, too." Pride was obvious in Pattie's voice.

"Apparently we carried some very important information and plans," said David. "We didn't win the war, but we certainly helped it along."

The whole table paused to drink their scotch.

"Berlin was literally hours from falling when a rather nasty Nazi colonel recognized us," said Pattie.

David continued. "He had us arrested and taken out of the city."

"We thought he was trying to help us," said Pattie. "Until we arrived at the barn."

The table went silent again. Pattie and David sipped their scotch. Nicholas gulped his. Sir Richard ran a finger around the rim of his glass.

"What happened to these two wasn't pretty," said Nicholas . "They were carved up pretty badly. But that Nazi bastard didn't kill them."

"We were lucky to find them in time. But we did, and I am grateful they don't hold the ordeal against me," said Sir Richard.

"Nonsense," said Pattie. "We knew all too well the cruelty in the world. We learned that when our families were killed."

"But we also knew good things happen, too," said David. "We'd both been orphaned the same day. Yet we found each other and learned to survive together."

Pattie nodded. "Once we learned to survive. We ran into this lot, and we got the chance to make a difference. Get some payback, you might say."

"So what did that colonel do to you?" asked Alan.

"Things more horrible than I hope you can imagine," said David.

"What's important is that we had a choice," said Pattie. "We could let what that man took ruin the rest of our lives, or we could accept it and move on."

"We moved on," said David.

"So what happened to that colonel?" asked Alan.

"We found him in Switzerland," said Pattie slowly.

Another silence swept the room.

"And?" asked Alan.

"Sir Richard gave us the opportunity to settle the score," said David.

Another silence.

"And?"

"They decided against it," said Sir Richard proudly.

"We didn't want to let that man's evil into our hearts. So instead of going on a mission of revenge, David asked me to marry him."

"What takes most a lifetime to learn, these two already knew," said Nicholas.

"When you set out on a course of revenge," said Alan, "you first dig two graves. You taught me that lesson, Sir Richard."

"That was your first day on the job. The things you're able to remember."

"I just listen well," said Alan.

Sir Richard laughed. "Now you know part of the reason why he's here. This one, despite all his faults, not only listens, he learns and he learns faster than anyone I've ever known."

"That's unusual," said Nicholas.

"Precisely," said Sir Richard.

The silence descended on the room again as everyone sipped their scotch. Sir Richard passed the bottle around the table. Alan surprised himself by deciding not to refill his glass.

"Your story is truly amazing," he said. "As a reporter, it's one I'd dearly love to tell. But I don't think that's why I'm here." He looked over at Sir Richard. "Is it?"

"No," said Sir Richard. He shifted in his seat with a glance toward Nicholas. "Tell me, Alan. What did you think about today's performance at the studio?"

"With apologies to you, sir," he said to Nicholas, "I thought it was complete bullshit."

"Watch your language," said Pattie and Sir Richard together.

"Oh please, spare me the 'strong language and weak minds' line," said Alan.

"We'll spare it when you learn it," said Pattie with a smile.

Alan grinned and shook his head. "Earlier this morning, I was shown a book that your actor mentioned. Handbook Number 10 was all about how the typical British homeowner could protect his family against a nuclear attack. But we all know the instructions in that book and in your movie won't do a bit of good."

"Why do you say that?" asked Nicholas.

"When the mushrooms start sprouting, nothing will do a damn bit of good. And don't go saying 'strong language and weak minds' again because that book and your film are both bullshit. I suspect everyone at this table knows it." Alan paused. "And that's why we're all here, right?"

"Right." Sir Richard looked around the table. "So what do you all think?"

"I like him," said Nicholas.

"He's not a member of the family," said David.

"He has no idea what life is like living in the shadows," said Pattie.

"And," David began, "it's not easy trusting someone none of us know."

"All good points," said Sir Richard.

Everyone was watching Alan, who still wasn't sure exactly what was going on. But he remembered what Sir Richard had told him early that morning.

"Earlier today, someone I trust and admire told me I had not only the opportunity to get a second chance at life, but a chance to make a difference." Alan looked to Sir Richard. "I'm not sure exactly what all this means. But a second chance and the possibility of making a difference is too good to pass up."

Alan stopped talking. Too many times, he'd heard people keep speaking long after they'd made their points.

"Nice." David shifted in his seat. "But you've never been trapped. Backed into a corner, knowing that you're a few seconds away from death. I'm not sure that makes you the best person to be in charge."

"In charge? In charge of what?"

"We've come up with a rather clever name for it all," said Sir Richard. "It's something we're calling *The Growlers*."

"The Growlers," repeated Alan.

"The Growlers. But I think that's enough for tonight. The train leaves at eight thirty. See you all tomorrow." Sir Richard stood up from the table.

"Now, just a minute," said Alan as everyone got up to leave.

"Good night," said Nicholas with a big smile.

"You'll probably become our boss. So I'm sure you'll understand if we enjoy leaving you in the dark tonight," said David.

"Good night, Mr. Dennis." Pattie smiled as she and her husband limped out of the room.

Alan picked up the nearly empty bottle of scotch and gazed at the door.

"So that's the way it's going to be," he said to the empty room.

He looked down at the bottle, then set it back on the table. As he started to leave, he paused at the door.

Alan turned and glanced back at the empty room.
He smiled and left.

CHAPTER 16 - THE TRAIN TO LIVERPOOL

A Cold Train Platform, The Next Morning

"I just love the beginning of a journey," said Sir Richard.

Everyone was standing on the train platform as they waited to board the train to Liverpool. Nicholas was cradling a paper cup full of coffee. Pattie and David were standing close and trying to stay warm.

Alan arrived last. "Good morning," he said cheerfully.

"What are you so happy about?" said Sir Richard.

"Well, you said that I'll not only be given a second chance at life, but I'll also be able to make a difference. Then you said I'd be put in charge of something. Even though I don't have all the details, I'd say I'm entitled to feel pretty good this morning."

"You're not in charge of anything yet," said Sir Richard.

"No, but I don't think I'd be here if something rather amazing wasn't about to happen. So if it's all the same to you, I'll keep feeling pretty good, thank you."

"Fair enough," said Sir Richard.

"All aboard!" yelled the conductor as the gates to the train platform opened.

"Shall we go?" said Alan, leading the way down the platform.

"Amazing," said Sir Richard.

"What's amazing?" asked Nicholas.

"Alan Dennis has never been first in line to do anything, let alone get on a train."

"Looks to me like you've created a monster," said Pattie.

"Probably," said Sir Richard. "But this could be just the monster we need."

Pattie whispered to David and gestured toward Sir Richard. "Can't be any worse than the monster we've already got."

David snorted in agreement.

"Come on, you lot," yelled Alan from the end of the platform.

"Oh, I'm sure things could get a lot worse," said David, as he and Pattie limped down the platform.

"They may be right, you know," said Nicholas quietly.

Sir Richard smiled. "I'm counting on it."

As the train pulled out of the station, everyone watched Alan. But he didn't notice. He was enjoying the view from the train's big windows. The town disappeared behind the train.

Alan had already decided to give up smoking, and he only drank one glass of scotch last night. Sir Richard smiled. A new man had been reborn from the wreckage of the old one.

"If I were you," said Nicholas, "I'd be going out of my mind with questions about Growlers and such."

"Actually, I am. But since you all were perfectly happy to leave me with nothing but questions last night, I've decided not to let it bother me." Alan smiled confidently and looked around the coach. "Since I'll be in charge of all this at some point, I'm sure I'll have all the answers eventually. So instead of tying myself in knots, I'm content to practice a little patience and enjoy the countryside. But most importantly, I'm not giving you lot any satisfaction."

Alan turned back to the window and away from the group's surprised faces. Sir Richard laughed out loud.

"That's my Alan," he said.

"Bravo, Mr. Dennis," said Pattie.

"Nicely done," said Nicholas.

David looked silently out the window.

"What's on your mind, David?" asked Sir Richard.

"It's what I said last night, sir. He's not a part of the family. Worse, he's a reporter."

He spat out the word 'reporter' like it was dirty, like it tasted bitter.

"You see, David—"

Alan interrupted Sir Richard. "You don't like reporters, Mr. McNally?"

"No, I don't. And it's Commander McNally."

"Of course, Commander. But you do realize I was invited here by Sir Richard?"

"Which is the only reason I haven't thrown you off the train."

"David," said Sir Richard.

"It's all right, sir." Alan held up a hand. "I can see I'll have to earn your trust. Till then, will you at least tolerate having me around?"

David glanced at Pattie. "Sure," he said, "why not?"

"Good." Alan kept his gaze on David for a few moments, then turned to Sir Richard. "Can we talk here, or do we need to wait for somewhere more private?"

"I think this is as good as any," said Sir Richard.

"Except for The Castle," said Nicholas.

"Castle?" said Alan.

"You'll be there soon enough," said Sir Richard.

"Well then," said Alan. "Since we can talk now, how about I start, and you can tell me where I've gone wrong."

"You all are in for a treat," said Sir Richard. "It's a sight to see Alan's brain fully engaged."

"Fine then. Impress me," said David.

"Yesterday morning," began Alan, "Sir Richard showed me what was probably one of the most worthless government booklets I've even seen. It was called *Civil Defence Handbook Number 10: Advising the Householder on Protection Against Nuclear Attack.*" He looked to Sir Richard. "Did I get that right?"

"To the letter."

"A few hours later, I'm at a movie studio where an actor plays a government official and quotes that same, worthless booklet." Alan took a breath. "Then, I'm at dinner with people claiming to have worked together in military intelligence during the war, and now we're on a train, which I've just learned is bound for a castle." He looked again to Sir Richard. "You said something about Growlers, and it's been mentioned that I'm to be the head of these Growlers. Yesterday, you said I'd not only have a second chance at life, but also get to make a difference. So my big guess is that you Growlers think you're going to end nuclear war."

"Yes and no," said Sir Richard. "Yes, we're The Growlers, but no, I don't believe anyone to be capable of stuffing the nuclear genie back into the bottle. That being said, we think we might be able to make the world a bit safer."

Alan paused to let this last bit of information sink in. He ran through the possibilities. A group of ex-military-intelligence people who thought they could end the threat of nuclear war, and they called themselves The Growlers.

Before going to bed the night before, Alan had stopped off at a local book shop with its lights on. After holding up some money to the glass door, the owner let him in. Alan had found the dictionaries and looked up *Growlers.*

The third definition he'd found had gotten his attention. *Growler* was an old nautical term used to describe an iceberg that floated just below the waterline. They were incredibly hard to spot and did major damage to ships.

Hiding just below the surface of the water and capable of doing major damage.

He'd tossed some more money at the confused bookstore clerk, tucked the dictionary under his arm, and hurried off to his hotel room.

In the train compartment, Alan was fitting more puzzle pieces together. He spoke about the iceberg definition with a grin.

Nicholas, Pattie, and David were surprised, but Sir Richard beamed with pride.

"And how do you think this band of—" Sir Richard paused, carefully forming the word. "—Growlers might actually stop the threat of nuclear war?"

"Because you have one of your own. Probably a nasty one, too. Sort of a *my gun's bigger than your gun* kind of thing," Alan answered.

"Holy shit!" said David. "If this fool of a reporter can figure us out, what's to stop someone with actual connections and intelligence from connecting the dots?"

"Language, dear," said Pattie.

David shook his head in annoyance.

"My language aside, Sir Richard. If this bloke could hit the nail on the head, how will we stop old Ivan or the bloody Yanks from figuring it out?"

"The bloody Yanks and old Ivan aren't as smart as Alan. Plus, he did have a few more clues than they're ever going to get," said Sir Richard.

"It's that second part that's the key, Commander. You left clues scattered all over the place for me to put together."

"Indeed," said Sir Richard.

"Still pretty impressive," said Nicholas.

"I take it we're doing all this without government approval?" asked Alan.

"No official government approval. But I do have personal approval from the Royal Family and the Prime Minister," said Sir Richard carefully.

"And we have a few friends scattered around the world," said Nicholas.

"Can you say who?" asked Alan.

"A few in America, France, and Sweden," said Sir Richard.

"Don't forget Moscow," added Nicholas.

"Oh yes, Her, too," said Sir Richard.

"Her?" asked Alan.

"Just wait till you meet—Her," said Sir. Richard.

As suddenly as the conversation had begun, it stopped. Everyone seemed content to gaze out the window at the passing countryside.

"This all probably costs a little bit of money," said Alan after a few minutes of silence. "Did you pass the hat or something?"

"That was our job," said Pattie. "We were still on the payroll, so to speak. Before leaving, we arranged for a few diversions of funding and resources from other projects."

"*Were* on the payroll?" asked Alan.

"We retired last week," said David.

"But not before making a few *special* financial transactions," said Pattie.

"You took the money and ran?"

"Sort of." She smiled.

"That also had Royal approval," said Sir Richard. "But only for the initial funding. We'll have to arrange for our own paychecks in the future."

"How soon before the money runs out?" asked Alan.

"No need to worry about that. We have a plan," said Sir Richard.

"I see." Alan turned back to the window.

As the old train lumbered along, so did the conversation. Alan interrupted the silence with occasional strings of questions.

He learned that Sir Richard had spent the early years of the war working for Sir John Godfrey, the legendary head of Section 17M. The unit was so secret that fewer than twenty people knew of its existence.

From an obscure, tobacco-stained office deep in the Admiralty, a small group of unique people had conceived plots and plans designed to misinform and misdirect the enemy. Sir Godfrey had surrounded himself with distinctly creative minds capable of dreaming up the diabolical plots that would give the Allies the edge.

Sir John Godfrey had called it *corkscrew thinking*.

For the next three years, Sir Richard had been surrounded by widest range of people society had to offer: scientists and mathematicians, professors and safe-crackers, chess players and con artists. Some were so devious that they would have been in prison if not for the war.

At his small desk in the corner of Section 17M, Sir Richard had realized the world would need people like this in the future. Once the war was over, the group would most likely disband, and Sir Richard had seen that as a horrible waste.

As the Allies surrounded Berlin, Sir Richard had taken it upon himself to somehow keep together this group of extraordinarily brilliant and deviously criminal people.

Then the war ended, and everyone went home. Sir Richard's home was the old *Sentinel*, and it had been there, in his dimly lit corner office, that he had conceived of a plan that would take most of his life to execute.

"So what's next?" asked Alan.

"Next?" said Sir Richard.

"We're coming to the station. Where do we go from here?"

"Ah, yes," said Sir Richard. "We'll need a cab."

"Where to?" asked Alan.

"To the docks."

CHAPTER 17 - THE BOAT TO DUBLIN

The Liverpool Docks, 1 p.m.

"Captain Taylor. You have a visitor, sir," said the young officer, his hand covering the phone.

"Who is it?" asked the old captain over his shoulder.

"Someone named Richard Carter," said the young officer.

The old captain turned and smiled at his junior officer.

"That's *Sir* Richard Carter to you, Watkins. My compliments, and ask Sir Richard to join me on the bridge for tea once we've departed."

"Yes, sir." The young officer began speaking quietly into the phone.

Captain Taylor turned back to the front windows of the ferry boat bridge. Thick fog had rolled into the channel, blanketing the Irish Sea from Liverpool to Dublin.

"Perfect weather," he said.

"Hardly, sir. We won't make good time in this lot," said his first officer behind him.

"In a hurry, James?"

"No, sir. But some of our passengers might be."

"We'll get them there in one piece. Once we're underway, have the chief engineer pop up to the bridge, will you?" said the captain.

"Yes, sir," said the first officer.

"All secure on the auto deck, sir," said the young officer with the phone.

"Excellent. James, why don't you take us across this trip?"

"Yes, sir. Thank you, sir."

"Not too fast. I wouldn't want to run into anything," cautioned Captain Taylor.

"Of course, sir." The first officer headed toward the starboard wing of the bridge. "Stand by to cast off. Stand by to make turns for three knots."

"Excellent," the captain said. "Have Sir Richard join me on the port wing and send for a fresh pot of tea."

"Yes, sir," said the young officer.

"And have Mister Wells join us on the wing, too," said the Captain as he walked into the fog.

"Yes, sir."

Captain Taylor looked over the bridge rail as the old ferry boat came to life and edged away from the dock. He watched with satisfaction as the first officer expertly merged the old boat with the other traffic in the River Mersey.

"Left half rudder, steer west-south-west, two, nine, zero degrees," yelled the first officer from the starboard bridge wing.

The captain sat back on the chair of the port bridge wing and listened to his crew handling his ship. He smiled with satisfaction as the port, the town, and the shore disappeared into the thick fog.

"Make turns for five knots," yelled the first officer.

The bells of the engine telegraph sounded as the order for more speed was relayed below decks. The old boat vibrated as the speed picked up.

"My dear Captain Taylor. So good to see you again," said Sir Richard from the bridge doorway.

"My dear Sir Richard. Welcome aboard." Captain Taylor rose and offered his seat to his old friend.

"Oh, I'm fine, thanks. But I could do with a spot of tea," said Sir Richard.

"Oh, how inconvenient," said the old Captain. "We were running a bit behind schedule. So I'm afraid we had to leave port without stocking up."

"What? No tea?"

"Tea, sir," said a young steward from the doorway.

"Ah, good. Just put that tray down over here." Captain Taylor smiled.

The young steward gently placed the tray on the small table near the captain's chair.

"You always did like to conjure up minor catastrophes. Like being out of tea," said Sir Richard.

"It's all in good fun. That'll be all, steward." The young man left as the captain began pouring tea. "You'd better drink up." He handed a full cup to Sir Richard. "We'll be there in about fifteen minutes."

"Everything all set?"

"Of course," said the Captain.

A few minutes later, a big man in greasy clothing appeared in the doorway.

"You sent for me, sir?" said the engineer.

"Good. Mister Wells. You remember Sir Richard Carter," said the Captain.

"That I do, sir. It's been a while, though."

"Yes, it has," said Sir Richard, reaching out to shake his hand.

"You'll forgive me, sir." The engineer held up his greasy hands. "It takes a lot of tender loving care and even more grease to keep this old tub running smoothly."

"Is everything set for Sir Richard and his friends?" asked the Captain.

"Yes, sir," said the engineer.

"Very good then." The old captain stood up. "Drink up, Sir Richard. It's almost time for you lot to disappear."

Sir Richard drained his tea and shook the captain's hand. "You'll be joining us later this year?"

"Next summer," said Captain Taylor. He glanced at his watch. "But you two do need to get moving."

"Till next summer, then," said Sir Richard as he turned to the engineer. "Lead the way."

Captain Taylor watched Sir Richard and the engineer leave the bridge. He checked his watch again. "Any minute now."

As if to answer, the old boat shook as it struck something floating in the water.

"What was that?" asked the young officer manning the phone.

"All stop. Check the hull for damage," said Captain Taylor calmly.

Bells from the bridge telegraph signaled the command to stop the boat.

"Lookouts, report sightings to the bridge," said the captain.

He watched as his orders were smoothly carried out. The first officer walked over to stand beside him.

"It seemed to hit the starboard side," said the first officer quietly.

"Why don't you run along and see if you can spot it."

"Yes, sir."

The captain looked at his watch again. A few minutes later, reports began flowing into the bridge.

"Engineer reports the hull sound, sir," said the young man with the phone.

"Very good," said the captain.

"Looks like an old crate," yelled the first officer from the starboard bridge wing.

"Thank you, good work. You all keep an eye out for more debris on the starboard side. Make turns for half a knot. Steer two, seven, zero."

Captain Taylor checked his watch again and hoped Sir Richard had collected his friends and arrived at their destination. He walked onto the port bridge wing and looked into the fog until he spotted what he was looking for.

"Give me another point to port."

"One more point to port," called the quartermaster.

On the port side of the old ferry boat, someone had opened a cargo doorway near the waterline. A few moments later, the engineer waved.

Two more big crates hit the starboard side of the boat.

"Slow it down just a little more, and give me another point to port," said the captain.

His whole crew was watching the starboard side of the boat. The captain smiled and looked ahead as an old, derelict barge slowly emerged from the fog.

A few more crates hit the starboard side, but the captain remained focused on the old barge.

"One more point to port, then steady as you go."

"One point to port and steady as we go, sir," called the quartermaster.

Captain Taylor smiled as the old barge passed within inches of his boat. Looking back, he saw his engineer step onto the barge. He helped five others step off the slow ferry.

The engineer stepped back onto the boat. He waved at the five people on the barge. Then he waved up to the bridge and quietly closed the cargo door.

A few more crates hit the starboard side of the old ferry as it continued into the fog. Captain Taylor looked back one more time as the barge with its five new passengers disappeared. Then he focused on the bridge as his officers and crew continued watching for crates.

The old captain smiled and sipped his tea.

CHAPTER 18 - AN UNDERWATER SURPRISE

The Irish Sea, 2 p.m.

"Everyone all right?" asked Sir Richard.

"Yes, sir," said Nicholas.

"That was fun," said David, holding on to Pattie.

"Oh yes. Fun. That's what it was," she said.

"Something you don't do every day," said Alan, wearing a big smile. He walked over to the side of the barge, draped with long, rusty chains. "We appear to be rather tightly held in place."

"We didn't want it to drift around too far," said Sir Richard, "or else it would have been harder for us to leave the ferry boat."

"I trust those loud *thud*s we heard against the boat's hull were meant to divert attention from us?" asked Alan.

"Quite right," said Nicholas.

"Also," said Alan, "there appear to be more than we five involved in this group of Growlers."

Sir Richard looked into the fog. "There are about a hundred of us now."

The ferry boat had long since disappeared in the fog. Several old, wooden crates bobbed up and down in the waves.

Alan still stood next to the mooring chains holding the barge in place. Sir Richard checked his pocket watch and walked over to Nicholas.

"This could be entertaining," he said quietly.

"I wish I had my camera," said Nicholas.

Alan heard the two men talking behind him. Something was about to happen. He looked up and down the length of the barge, sure that the surprise wouldn't be dangerous.

Minutes ticked by in silence.

Waves softly splashed the side of the old barge. After a few minutes, the splashing sound changed slightly, and Alan heard dripping water.

Alan determined to react calmly and not to give the others the satisfaction of seeing him surprised. He looked out into the fog, waiting.

A few bubbles rose to the surface, then the water began boiling. The intensity increased as dark gray metal broke the water beside the barge. When the sea stopped boiling, Alan studied the submarine that had emerged. A rather old submarine.

"That's an old Nazi sub," he said.

"Quite right." Sir Richard approached the edge of the barge.

A man appeared at the top of the conning tower. He looked down and waved.

"Good afternoon, Sir Richard," he said.

"Good afternoon, George. How was your voyage?"

"No problems at all, sir."

The man scanned the foggy horizon and shouted a few commands down the open hatch. "Drop us down a bit so they can get on board a little easier."

"Yes, sir," called a voice from deep inside the sub.

Soon, the water around the sub began to boil, and the sub sank until the deck was level with the barge.

"Gangway crew topside," said the man, who was clearly the sub's captain.

Six more men appeared on deck and moved a gangplank into place between the sub and the barge.

"If you'll all come aboard, we'd like to get underway as quickly as possible," said the captain.

"Right you are," said Sir Richard loudly.

"And we are running silent, so no excessive noise, please," said the captain.

"Right you are, Captain," said Sir Richard more quietly.

He boarded the sub and disappeared down the hatch. Pattie, David, and Nicholas followed, with Alan bringing up the rear. Pattie and David had trouble getting down the submarine's hatch. Alan remembered Nicholas's words from the night before.

They were carved up pretty badly.

Watching Pattie and David struggle with the narrow ladder, Alan's concept of the phrase *carved up* expanded significantly.

Alan knew David had a problem with him because he wasn't a member of their intelligence family. But watching Pattie and David struggle, he decided that one of his first priorities would be to win their respect.

No. Not respect.

Alan was younger, and compared to Pattie and David he'd had a fairytale life. Despite years of smoking and heavy drinking, Alan was in much better shape.

As David finally disappeared into the submarine, Alan decided he'd never earn their respect. The best he could hope for was their acceptance, and that would probably take years.

Alan gazed down the length of the submarine and into the fog. He thought of Sir Richard's promise of a new life and the chance to make a difference. Alan realized this was a chance few would ever have.

Alan loved being a reporter. He had trained hard and had become one of the best. But something had always been missing.

The best reporters were observers, never participants. Sure, their words and photos could bring about subtle changes. Sometimes, their stories actually changed people's lives. But those were rare moments indeed, and Alan longed for something more. He watched the deck crew stow the gangway.

These people are doing something.

He was tired of being an observer. He wanted to be a participant. Now, he had that chance, and he might also impact the world on a scale few could ever imagine.

Nicholas disappeared into the sub. The deck crew had finished stowing the gangplank and were lined up to climb down the hatch.

"After you, sir," said one of the crew.

"Please, a minute," said Alan.

The crewman looked up at the captain, who nodded.

"Not too many minutes sir," said the crewman as he turned to his gangway crew. "All right, you lot. Down you go."

"Prepare to dive," said the captain.

Alan heard orders passed through the submarine and the sound of electric motors spinning up.

Then Alan heard a change in the sound of water splashing against the sub's rusty hull. Alan tilted his head, closed his eyes, and listened. It wasn't his imagination. The sound of the waves was different. As he opened his eyes, he saw the captain had left the conning tower and was standing next to him.

"I remember when I took my first command. Something changes in you," said the captain.

"You must know what they want me to do," said Alan.

"Of course. Sir Richard hates keeping things secret."

"Really?"

"Odd, isn't it? For a man who grew up in the wartime secret service, you'd think he'd be all about secrets." The captain paused. "I hate them, too. You've no doubt heard Sir Richard's admonition about profanity?"

"Many times." Alan smiled.

"'Profanity is nothing more than a weak mind trying to express itself forcefully.' That's also the thing about secrets."

"How so?"

"Most secrets are unnecessary," said the captain. "I call it the effort of a weak commander to maintain control."

As a reporter, nearly every time Alan had discovered a secret, he'd learned it was hardly worth being kept.

"Brilliant," said Alan.

"Quite so."

As the two men stood on the deck of the old submarine, Alan listened to the sound of the waves and decided it was time to trust himself.

"Someone's out there," he said.

"Yes. And they mean to stop us."

"I'm holding things up," said Alan, walking toward the hatch.

"Not to worry, sir." The captain smiled and headed toward the conning tower.

"Why is that?"

The captain reached the ladder and began to climb, speaking down to Alan.

"Sir Richard says you're the best of the best. But more so, he tells us you're the one man he knows can make all this happen, and I'd say that's good news for us."

Alan pointed into the fog. "There's someone out there, and you just said they mean to stop us. How can I help with that?"

The captain ducked under the rail and looked down at Alan. "You can't. That's my job, and that's the good news for you."

Alan started down the hatch. Just before disappearing into the sub, he looked up at the captain.

"Why is that?" he asked.

"Because I'm the best of the best at what I do." The captain disappeared from the conning tower. The last thing Alan heard as he climbed down the sub's hatch was the captain's voice.

"Dive the boat."

CHAPTER 19 - SILENT RUNNING

The Bottom of the Irish Sea, 3 p.m.

The hatch clanked shut above his head, and Alan heard the sound of pressurized air and bubbles all around him. The deck below his feet began to move, and he felt the whole boat sinking. A crewman tapped Alan's shoulder and pointed down a long corridor.

"Your friends are down that way, sir."

"Thanks," said Alan.

He bumped his head on a few of the low pipes as he made his way aft. Alan passed by a small area that was nicely paneled before he found himself in the old sub's control room. The captain smiled at Alan and nodded to an open doorway.

"Pressure in the boat," said a crewman.

"Very good. Ahead slow. Make your depth six-zero feet. Steer course three, four, zero degrees." The captain watched as his handpicked crew carried out his orders smoothly.

The first officer appeared in the doorway Alan just walked through. "Our guests are enjoying tea in the ward room, sir."

"Very good, F.O. Tell them I'll be along in a few minutes, and remind them we're maintaining as much silence as possible."

"Yes, sir."

"Let them know they'll feel a little bump soon. I intend to put her on the bottom in a few minutes to wait out anyone who might be trying to follow us."

"Any idea who that might be?" asked the first officer.

"Not yet, but one of our new passengers heard someone lying off our starboard beam." The captain nodded toward the ward room.

"Really? I didn't think there was a sailor in that lot," said the first officer.

"There isn't. Let them know I'll be along in a minute."

"Yes, sir."

The first officer turned to leave. The captain looked at the ship's clock, then down at the chart. He did some fast calculations.

"Chief of the Boat," said the captain. "Maintain slow ahead for another ten minutes. Then, as quietly as you can, put her on the bottom, and maintain absolute silence."

"Aye, sir," said the chief of the boat.

The captain ducked through one of the pressure-tight doors into the sonar room, manned by a sailor much older than the captain.

The sailor held up a hand to the captain. His other held an old set of headphones to his ear. He pointed to one of the dials on his sonar set and held up two fingers.

"Any idea what it might be?" asked the captain quietly.

"Dual screws, lightweight. I'd guess they're some sort of coastal patrol boat."

"Are they pinging?"

"No, sir," said the old man. "But I'm sure they've got underwater ears just like we have. Probably better than this old rig, too."

"I'll take this old rig and your ears over anything they have. Pass any changes along to me in the ward room."

"Aye, sir," said the old man, still listening to the water.

As the captain made his way back to the ward room, he felt the old sub slow down. He smiled to himself as he walked down the rusty corridor. His chief of the boat was slowly cutting back on power as they headed for the bottom of the river, hoping to set down the sub with as little noise as possible.

Turning the corner into the officers' ward, the captain found his five new passengers scrunched into the small seats, enjoying their tea.

"Welcome aboard," he said, pouring his own cup of tea. "Everyone settling in okay?"

"Quite well," Sir Richard said.

The captain sized up his passengers. He knew Sir Richard, but the others were strangers. One was studying the metal side of the sub. The man ran his fingers along the wet metal.

"Not to worry. That's not sea water," said the captain.

Nicholas touched his fingers to his lips. "But it's salty."

"That's condensation. We have a crew of about thirty men, and these old tubs didn't come with a dehumidifier."

"I see you had no trouble rounding up a crew," said Sir Richard.

"Of course not. It was just as you expected. They were all retired and bored. Everyone jumped at the chance to get back to sea."

"Retired?" said Alan.

"These men are all retired Royal Navy submariners who won't be missed," said Sir Richard.

"They were put out to pasture years ago," said the captain. "Not much excitement in retirement. So our little plot was a welcome change."

Alan began to realize he had found himself in a machine that had been years in the making.

"How long have you been scheming all this?" he asked.

"Many, many years," said Sir Richard.

The captain felt the sub's power diminish a bit more. He checked his watch and took a sip of tea. "As you all know, we've been running silent to avoid drawing attention to ourselves." The captain nodded toward Alan. "As you mentioned on deck, we do suspect someone has taken an interest in us. At present, we think there may be up to three surface craft nosing about."

"Any idea who?" asked Alan.

"More importantly, can you get away from them?" said Sir Richard.

"I think so. In a few minutes, you'll all feel a slight bump as I take her to the bottom. We'll wait about an hour, then see if we can give them the slip."

"The bottom? How far down are we?" asked Nicholas.

"Only about sixty feet," said the captain. "The river reaches a hundred feet not too far from here. I'm hoping to set her down at around eighty feet."

"Why not try to get to the deeper spot?" asked Sir Richard.

"Because that's where our friends would expect us to go. If I've timed it right, we'll pass over the deepest part of the river and set down on the other side. Hopefully, our friends will be concentrating their search behind us."

"Brilliant," said Alan.

"But what happens in an hour?" asked David. "They may be behind us, but surely they'll hear us when we leave."

"In about an hour, the ferry boats will be running again," said the captain. "Plus, I'm expecting some late afternoon barge traffic. All those boats should mask the sound of our departure."

The conversation paused, and a slight vibration began to build under their feet—and suddenly stopped. Alan's shoulder bumped against Nicholas. Across the table, Pattie bumped into David, who bumped into Sir Richard.

"We've stopped," said Alan.

The captain smiled and reached for a phone. He pushed a button and waited a few seconds.

"Nicely done, Chief. We'll stay here fifty-two minutes, then get back underway." He listened for a few moments. "Yes, have everyone take a break. Have the steward quietly pass around tea and biscuits." He listened for a few more moments. "No, don't worry about that. We can let old Bob decide when he needs to listen in. He knows the score." One more pause. "Right-O," he said, hanging up the phone and turning back to his passengers.

"As you heard, we'll break here, for now. Fifty-one minutes. The river traffic should pick up by then, and we might just slip away."

The captain noticed that one of his passengers was clearly nervous about being on a submarine. The couple seemed to have seen enough danger that they weren't worried about being on the bottom of a river in an aging German submarine.

"More tea, Sir Richard?" the captain asked.

"Yes, thanks. Then if you could point me to what I believe you in the Navy refer to as the head?"

"Actually, we're maintaining silence now, and the facilities are shut down. If you can give it an hour or so, we should be in the clear."

Sir Richard swallowed hard and pulled his tea cup away from the captain.

"I'll pass on that second cup of tea, then," he said weakly.

The others quietly pushed their tea cups away, too. The captain checked his watch again. Forty-nine minutes to go.

The passengers sat silently around the table. Every so often, one would fidget a bit, trying to get more comfortable, and they all stole glances at watches and at the wall clock. The captain smiled and decided to take pity on them.

"In my thirty years in subs, there has been nothing harder than learning how to patiently wait out someone who's looking for you," he said.

"What's the secret?" asked Nicholas.

"There isn't one. You just have to get through it the best you can."

"Well then," said Nicholas. "How do you get through it?"

"Sooner or later, the waiting always comes to an end," said the captain.

"Anything else?" asked Nicholas.

"The longer we wait, the better it usually is for those of us doing the waiting."

The phone clicked a few times. The captain reached for the handset and said, "Captain here."

He listened only a few seconds before issuing orders.

"All fans off. Absolute silence throughout the boat. I'll be there in a minute."

After quietly replacing the handset, he leaned forward and whispered to his passengers.

"We believe there is a hostile right above us. I'll have to leave you now and must insist on absolute silence. No talking at all. No shuffling your feet or anything that can cause noise."

The captain carefully moved his chair back, reached down, and removed his shoes. As he stood up, he smiled reassuringly at his passengers.

"Just a slight change of plans, that's all," he whispered.

As the captain turned to leave, everyone heard a dull, metallic *click*

108

outside the hull. The explosion that followed shook the submarine violently. Pipes burst, and the nuts and bolts shot like bullets around the small wardroom. Then all the lights went out.

Alan felt David's powerful hands grab his arm and shove him to the floor. His forehead smacked the corner of the hardwood table, and Alan felt warm blood flowing over his eyes and into his mouth.

"Sorry about that," whispered David. "But I've seen what those flying bolts can do when you're taking depth charges."

"Is that what exploded?" whispered Alan.

"Yes, and that's only the first."

As if to answer David, two more explosions shook the old submarine. More pipes burst. More nuts and bolts flew through the air.

About a minute later, the lights came back on.

Alan reached for a linen napkin and pressed it against his forehead. Everyone was hunkered under the table. Everyone except Sir Richard, who sat calmly in his seat as though nothing were happening.

Alan nudged David and pointed toward Sir Richard. David waved at Nicholas, then pointed up at Sir Richard.

"Get him down here," hissed David.

Nicholas reached up and tugged on Sir Richard's arm as another explosion shook the sub.

"Sir Richard, please get down here," said Nicholas.

He didn't move. Alan spotted a small drop of blood trickling down Sir Richard's temple.

"He's in trouble," whispered Alan to David.

David stood up as another explosion rocked the sub, and nuts and bolts, propelled by the high pressure of the water outside the sub, zoomed around the small cabin. David leaned over the table and pushed Sir Richard off his chair and onto the floor.

Alan reached out and grabbed Sir Richard's shoulder. When he rolled him over, Alan realized his mentor and friend had been killed.

Alan's head fell to his chest, and he closed his eyes for a few seconds. When he opened them, he looked over at David. His expression confirmed Alan's worst fears.

Sir Richard's lifeless eyes stared up at the underside of the table. A large bolt had drilled itself into the center of his forehead. Alan looked at David.

"Now what do we do?" he said quietly.

"We get you and this sub to Stromness."

PART 3: SPY SCHOOL

CHAPTER 20 - THE FIRST DAY

Léa's New Room, 6:30 a.m.

The iPad on the nightstand began playing gentle music.

It started with a piano.

Then some horns.

Then Van Morrison sang his 1995 song, "Days Like This."

Léa opened her eyes to the glow of blue floor-lighting in her windowless room. She didn't move as she listened to the song.

"When all the parts of the puzzle start to look like they fit," sang Van Morrison.

Léa smiled. Someone was sending her a message, and she guessed that someone was her best friend, Tara. Léa closed her eyes as the song played on.

"When everyone is up front and they're not playing tricks," sang Van Morrison.

The message was pretty clear. Today, Léa would get answers to questions she'd had for most of her life. As the song began to fade, Léa opened her eyes.

The iPad next to her bed read 6:30 a.m. Léa heard a hissing sound behind her. She smiled as she smelled brewing coffee.

The scent was enough to make Léa ready to start her day. But when she tried to sit up, she couldn't. Soreness from her day-and-a-half dungeon test shot through her body.

Léa lay on her back and raised her knees until her feet were planted flat on the bed. She hooked her hands behind her thighs and rocked back. Then in one movement, she stretched out her legs, and rolled forward to sit up.

Léa's muscles screamed in protest, but at least she was sitting up. The room's motion detector slowly brightened the lights.

Her counterweight maneuver had pulled off the single bed sheet covering her, and Léa could see how badly beaten up she was from the dungeon test. Cuts and bruises covered her body.

The worst damage was from the cuffs. Her wrists and ankles were badly bruised, and the stainless steel had left small cuts. Léa gently rubbed her wrists and ankles and surveyed her surroundings.

The room was larger than a dorm room. To her right, a combination dresser-closet sat beside a small door leading to a private bathroom with the nicest shower Léa had ever seen. It was modern and was made of cut stone and stainless steel. The first of its two settings gently sprinkled water from directly overhead.

The second setting was the stuff of dreams. A simple flip of a lever sent pulsing jets of hot water from each of the shower's four corners, giving Léa the best shower massage of her life. After the ordeal in the dungeon, Léa spent almost an hour in the hot shower, letting the pulsing jets massage her sore body.

To the left of the bed, the contents of Léa's backpack were neatly spread on a desk. Her laptop and phone were plugged in. A nearly empty bookshelf was bolted to the wall above the desk. The light on an AirPort Extreme Wi-Fi box glowed green from the corner.

She looked over her shoulder as she reached under the pillow and pulled out her 9mm semi-automatic handgun. Léa blinked and shook her head sharply, still barely able to believe the gun was back in her possession.

When she had arrived in her room the night before, she had been pleasantly surprised to find her laptop and phone on the desk and her backpack in the corner, but Léa had looked twice to make sure her eyes weren't playing ticks on her when she noticed the small, black pistol resting between her Mac and her iPhone. The fully loaded magazine had been pulled from the grip and laid next to the gun.

After her hour-long shower, Léa stepped over to the desk and picked up the gun. She examined it closely. Everything seemed normal. Thumbing the eight bullets out of the magazine, she inserted it into the grip and snapped it into place.

Léa pulled the slide all the way back, then let it go. It locked open because the magazine was empty. Léa forcefully thumbed the slide stop, letting it snap into place.

Turning toward the wall opposite her bed, Léa gripped the gun and aimed at an invisible target. She took a breath, let half the air out, moved her finger into the trigger guard, and gently squeezed the trigger. The empty gun gave a metallic *click*—it seemed to work.

The bullets appeared to be the same ones she'd loaded into the gun before the weekend. She reloaded the clip, inserted it into the grip, snapped on the safety, and carefully slid the gun under her pillow. Just before she dozed off, Léa's hand inched under the pillow and came to a rest on the gun.

The coffee pot hissed loudly, and the aroma of fresh coffee coaxed Léa awake. She inhaled deeply, gathering strength to move off the bed.

After carefully setting the gun beside her, Léa inched to the edge of the mattress. The pain from sitting up was fresh in her memory so Léa carefully swung her legs down to the floor and stood. A few muscles complained, but they didn't scream like before. Léa started toward the simmering coffee pot.

After one step, she leaned backward and reached for the gun. A sharp pain reminded her to move more slowly, and she stood carefully and eased toward the desk and that important first cup of coffee.

"Wait a minute ..." Léa stopped in her tracks.

That coffee pot hadn't been there when she'd gone to sleep last night. Neither had the coffee mug or the small bowl of Bailey's mini bottles. Also new, a blue plastic folder lay next to the coffee pot.

Someone had been in her room while she was sleeping. Léa thought about it for a minute and decided it was probably no big deal.

"Thanks for the coffee," she said to the empty room.

"You're welcome," said a voice from a small speaker next to the desk's light switch. "You've got an hour before breakfast, and you might want to look over the schedule in the blue folder."

Léa looked down at the folder, then at the coffee pot, then back up at the speaker.

"Okay, anything else?" she asked.

"Nope. Everything you need for today will be in that folder."

"Thanks," said Léa.

She set the gun on the desk and pulled out the chair, adjusting the towel she'd used to cover the seat the night before. She sat down and emptied a mini bottle of Bailey's into the mug, then poured her first cup of coffee. Inhaling the aroma, Léa took her first sip and examined the room again.

Except for the coffee pot and folder, nothing seemed out of place. She took a second sip and kicked up her feet on the corner of the desk.

As Léa sipped her coffee, she ran her fingers along the barrel of her gun. Then she reached over and flipped open the blue folder. It contained only three items: a blank legal pad, a pen, and a single sheet of paper. Léa tugged out the paper and read over her coffee mug.

SCHEDULE FOR: Léa Taylor
8 a.m. - Breakfast
9 a.m. - Intro to Spy School (don't be late)
10:30 a.m. - Tour of The Castle
Noon - Lunch

1:30 p.m. - Personal Survival/Electronic Safety
2:30 p.m. - Range
4:30 p.m. - Obstacle Course
6 p.m. - Dinner
7:15 p.m. - Movie Night
9:30 p.m. - Deep in the Cliffs Pub
10:30 p.m. - Lights Out

"Intro to Spy School," she said to herself in disbelief.

Time to clear the cobwebs. Léa blinked her eyes and snapped her head from side to side, dropping the sheet of paper to her lap. She took another sip of coffee and glanced down at her gun.

The iPad beeped, and a soft voice said, "You have one hour until breakfast."

Léa took a gulp of coffee, picked up the paper, and continued reading.

ITEMS NEEDED TODAY:
Blue Folder
The iPad by your bed
Your Mac & iPhone
Your Weapon (clip loaded, chamber empty, safety on)
Your Backpack
CLOTHING:
Physical Training Gear: shorts, shirt, socks, & running shoes
An extra towel from your bathroom

The schedule had clearly been prepared on a computer and printed just for her. But at the bottom of the page, someone had hand written a personal note.

Léa - clothing IS required today. Sorry. :-)

Léa's eyes closed again, and her head snapped from side to side. But she was smiling. The events of the past forty-eight hours were truly bizarre. But through it all, Léa had never felt like she was in any real danger. She looked up at the bookshelf. In the corner sat two objects she had requested during her strange meeting the night before. Léa sipped her coffee and smiled as her thoughts returned to the small office and the old man. A few moments before that meeting ended, Alan Dennis welcomed Léa into the organization he had spent the last fifty years building.

"Last year, I welcomed your friend Tara into our little circus. And now I want to extend the same welcome to you. We've had our eyes on you both for years and have the highest hopes and expectations of you."

"You've had your eyes on us?" Léa repeated.

"We have."

"Well, now you're getting a much better view of at least one of us," said Léa sweetly.

Halfway through the meeting, Léa had been offered a white, terrycloth bathrobe like the ones Cindy and Charlie had worn out of the small office. Léa had smiled and said she was fine.

"Why is that my dear?" Alan had asked.

"I think it helps level the playing field a bit."

"My dear, if you think your present attire has any effect on me, think again. I'm almost ninety years old."

"Whatever. Men will always be men, no matter how old they are."

"As are women," Alan had said, looking up at Tara. "I can see that you were right about her."

"Of course, I was," Tara had said with some of her annoying attitude.

Léa had noticed the attitude when Tara spoke to Alan. But when Tara looked at Léa, there were unfamiliar emotions in her eyes.

Fear and uncertainty.

That's not normal for Tara, Léa thought.

Alan yawned. "It really is getting late, and we can continue tomorrow."

As Léa stood up to leave the small office, she stopped at the door and turned back to the old man seated at the desk.

"Can I have those?" asked Léa.

"Excuse me?"

Léa pointed to the handcuffs and leg shackles. They'd been left on his desk after being removed from her wrists and ankles.

"Those," she said with a smile. Léa walked from the office door to the desk and picked up the handcuffs and leg chains. She looked over her shoulder and smiled at the old man as she left the room.

"Just a little souvenir thanks. Sweet dreams."

The next morning, sitting in her new room, Léa was pleased with herself. She was sore and bruised, and she still didn't have all the answers about her new surroundings. But one thing was for sure: All of the men she'd encountered in the past forty-eight hours had probably found it more difficult to sleep than she had. She thought that was true for some of the women she'd passed on the long walk to her new room, as well.

Looking at the blood-stained handcuffs and leg chains on the bookshelf, Léa thought back over the past weekend. After the initial panic of waking up handcuffed, shackled, and naked in an old dungeon cell, Léa had never lost control.

The reason was simple.

Somehow, she had known she was never in real danger. Once the initial panic had passed, Léa had focused on solving problems.

Beyond that, Léa realized that she had actually enjoyed the dungeon test. She admitted it to herself. It was a thrill. It was fun.

Léa spun the chair to face a full-length mirror on the wall by the door. She stood up, brushed the hair out of her eyes, and examined herself. Léa thought she was in pretty good shape except for the cuts and bruises, but they'd heal in no time.

The iPad beeped again and announced, "You have forty-five minutes until breakfast."

Léa drained the rest of her coffee and started toward the bathroom. The iPad buzzed again. Léa walked back to the bed and read the message on the screen: *Your mama may have never told you there'd be days like this. But today will be one of those days.*

Van Morrison began singing again as a picture of the old castle at sunrise slowly emerged on the iPad's screen. It was one of those amazing, one-in-a-million pictures that Léa was always on the lookout for.

She smiled at the image of the sunrise over The Castle. More text appeared: *This is going to be one of those days you'll remember for the rest of your life.*

Then one more word slowly focused, overlaying the picture.

Enjoy!

A single letter appeared near the bottom of the screen:

t

The song, the coffee, and the picture were all from Tara.

Léa smiled. No matter what happened, Léa knew it would be okay.

CHAPTER 21 - WELCOME TO SPY SCHOOL

The Castle Auditorium, 9 a.m.

The modern lecture hall was big enough for two hundred stadium seats. Ten surround-sound speakers lined the walls. Spotlights waited in the back of the auditorium, and a multimedia platform hung high overhead.

"Looks like they can put on quite a show," said Charlie.

"I count five projectors up there," said Pat, "and I'm pretty sure there are three more in the booth."

"Great," said Cindy. "Now we can all go to the movies, assuming they let us out of our prison cells."

"I haven't seen any prison cells," said Charlie.

"My room's rather nice," said Pat.

"It's still a fucking prison, even if the rooms are nice." Cindy rubbed her bruised wrists. "And let's not forget the kinky way we spent our first weekend with these perverts."

"There's a lot more going on here than meets the eye," said Léa. "Maybe you should hold off on judging this situation for a while."

"So that's your take on all this. Why am I not surprised?" Cindy fired back.

"Take it easy," said Charlie.

"No, I don't think I will take it easy."

"Well, Léa didn't arrange all this," said Pat. "So you could at least stop being so snotty to her."

"No, I don't think I'll do that either." Cindy gave Pat her best hatchet eyes before shooting Léa a look of utter disgust. "From what I could tell, Smart Girl here was having a high old time prancing about in that dirty old dungeon." Cindy's voice filled with anger. "So much fun that I hear you continued with your own little strip-tease parade through this prison last night. Well it may come as a nasty shock to you, but not all of us think spending a weekend stripped, handcuffed, and shackled in a dodgy dungeon while dirty old men watch us on television is good time."

Cindy looked straight ahead, pain replacing the anger in her voice.

"And it might come as an even bigger shock to all of you to learn that not all of us have a killer body like Smart Girl here, and some found the whole experience frightening and humiliating. So I'll thank all of you to stop expecting me to fucking laugh it off."

The four sat in silence, alone in the huge auditorium. Cindy wiped a few tears from her eyes, but she continued to stare straight ahead. After a few moments, Léa nudged Pat and motioned for him to trade seats. She sat down next to Cindy and took her hand.

"I am so sorry that I've made you feel this bad. You are completely right. What happened to us was really quite awful." Cindy didn't turn. "And you're right about me," said Léa. "I really was having fun with the whole thing. I'm sorry."

"You weren't scared?" asked Pat.

"Of course I was, at first. But eventually, I realized that if they meant to harm us, they would have already done it."

"You weren't there, mate," said Charlie. "She really was amazing to watch. Everything was like a puzzle for her to solve."

"I wish I had been there," said Pat.

He flexed the fingers sticking out of the cast on his arm. During the first round of knockout gas, Pat had fallen on his left arm and broken it in two places. One of the bones had broken through the skin, making it a compound fracture. The decision to pull him out of the dungeon test had been easy.

Cindy sniffed. "I guess I may have been taking all this out on you. And like Charlie said, you really are amazing to watch, Smart Girl."

"Thanks. But there is one part of the record we really do need to correct."

"What's that?" asked Cindy.

"I don't believe I was ever 'prancing' about."

Cindy shook her head and smiled. "Okay, Smart Girl. I'll give you that one."

"How does one actually prance about?" asked Pat.

"You thinking of taking lessons, mate?" asked Charlie.

"I'm just asking."

"Maybe they have special prancing classes here." Charlie reached for his backpack.

"I was just asking," said Pat.

Charlie pulled out a printed schedule. "No. No prancing classes on the schedule today."

Pat looked over at Cindy.

"Would you do something about your annoying brother?" he said.

"You're on your own. He's been annoying me a lot longer."

Léa checked the time on her iPhone. Three minutes to nine. She glanced at Charlie's schedule. This was the right place. Léa looked around the empty auditorium.

"For a punctual place," she said, "this room is strangely empty."

As if to answer Léa, everyone's iPads began buzzing with a reminder message: *Intro to Spy School begins in two minutes in the main auditorium.*

The lights blinked a few times, and people began filing into the room. In less than a minute, nearly every seat was taken.

A minute later, the old man from last night walked slowly to the stage. Even though he walked with a cane, he easily climbed the three steps leading to the stage. The lights dimmed as he faced the audience.

"Good morning. I see none of you wanted to miss another one of Mr. Austin's welcome extravaganzas. At this time, I'd like to introduce you to our four newest members, Cindy, Charlie, Pat, and I'm sure by now you all know Léa. Although you might not recognize her fully dressed."

Everyone in the room laughed.

"Sorry, my dear. That was a cheap shot. But you do make an impression."

After another round of laughter, the room quieted, and the old man continued.

"You may be surprised to know that we've been watching each of you for a very long time. Today, you'll each learn a great deal about your new home, as well as some surprising things about yourselves."

He paused and looked directly at Cindy.

"Now then. I know some of you are not that pleased to be here. In fact, one of you is quite angry with us about the ordeal over the weekend."

He smiled at Cindy. The entire room was watching her.

"If I may, allow me to ask two things of you. First, I would ask that you try to set aside your anger for the next few hours. A mind clouded by anger will have great difficulty learning who and what we are. And who and what you are."

The old man walked to the side of the stage, keeping his eyes on Cindy.

"The second thing I'll ask is that in setting aside your anger, you never forget what you're angry about. Yes, that's right. Your strong sense of right and wrong is why you're angry now. Eventually, you'll see how critical that sense will be. Not only for this group, but for me personally."

He reached the side of the stage and addressed the entire audience.

"This is a serious place. The work we do has serious consequences. So serious, that more often than we'd prefer, lives are taken. And sometimes, innocent lives are lost."

The old man looked down at his feet.

"Our successes will never be publicly celebrated, and our losses are only privately suffered."

He raised his eyes.

"But what we do matters a great deal. The work done by people in this room has literally saved the world."

He spoke to the four newcomers.

"You were selected long ago to be a part of this extraordinary group of people. You're not here by your own choice. But once you learn who and what we are, I think you'll be more than happy to stay."

The old man straightened up and smiled.

"So, we're a serious lot with serious jobs to do. But we also know that you can't be serious all the time. In fact, over the years we've learned to toss all that serious stuff aside and have as much fun as we can."

He descended the steps.

"Yes, I said fun. You see, if you're having fun, then you're learning in ways you never thought possible. You can even learn the most serious of lessons while having fun."

He sat down in the front row.

"So why don't we have some fun right now? Cindy, Charlie, Pat, and Léa. Welcome to Spy School!"

The room plunged into complete darkness and silence. Everyone seemed to be holding their breath in anticipation. Léa felt her heart racing.

They didn't have to wait long, and no one was disappointed.

A series of spotlights flashed across the stage, showing a man crossing from right to left.

The speakers pulsed with the famous Monty Norman signature theme signaling the beginning of every James Bond movie.

Once the man reached center stage, he drew a handgun and fired one shot into the audience.

As the gun fired, flames engulfed the stage. A wave of hot air gusted over the audience. As the flames and smoke cleared, The Castle appeared on stage, small, as it may have appeared to a ship at sea.

A cold breeze blew toward the audience, and the temperature fell rapidly. As The Castle emerged from the smoke, waves from the sea began to appear. The waves rose as though the audience was sinking under the water.

The music's volume decreased as the water rose.

The Castle was still visible through the waves. Just below the water, a dark, solid chunk of ice drifted into view. Then a deep, soft voice spoke slowly.

"They hide just below the surface. They're more deadly to a ship than an iceberg because you can't see them until it's too late. That's what we are. We're more deadly to our opponents because you never see us. Until it's too late. We are ... Growlers."

The music faded, leaving the sound of the waves and the ringing of a distant buoy bell.

The silent auditorium came alive with cheers and applause.

CHAPTER 22 - TOUR OF THE CASTLE

Main Classroom - 10:30 am

"All right then Professor, you've had them long enough." A short, man burst into the lecture hall and jogged down the stairs. The little man was Dick Boxx. He had suddenly appeared during the day's first class, Intro to Spy School, which had turned out to be quite the entertaining extravaganza. That was until the short, obnoxious man had proved to the newcomers why he was unaffectionately known as "Little Dick." As he ran down the aisle, Dick Boxx briefly focused on Cindy, Charlie, Pat, and Léa. After letting his eyes linger on Léa, he looked up at the man on the stage.

"As usual, you're running late, and I still have to take these cream puffs on their Tour of The Castle," said Dick

"This isn't going to be good," whispered Pat to Charlie as Little Dick bounded onto the stage.

"A sorry lot you have here, Professor. But I'll fix them up in a hurry."

As Little Dick looked over the group, Léa noticed some the audience leaving their seats and lining up along the wall. A few stretched, obviously preparing for a workout.

"Let me have your attention, cream puffs," said Little Dick.

The room quieted down. Little Dick shuffled around the stage. He had a full head of gray hair, and his nose had the appearance of someone who drank a little too much. Otherwise he appeared to be in fairly good shape.

As Léa watched people line up along the wall, she saw Tara standing by herself, dressed completely in black. But she wasn't wearing her heavy metal bracelets or a collar. Tara's eyes were fixed on Little Dick. Just as Léa was about to turn away, Tara looked her way and smiled.

Except for their brief meeting outside the dungeon the night before, Tara hadn't smiled at anyone in months, and now it was pretty clear why. Tara had been recruited the year before. And, while Léa knew Tara had had to keep things secret, there was still pain in her heart from feeling the loss of her best friend.

Little Dick cleared his throat.

Léa looked up at Tara, tilted her head slightly, and gave her a half smile. The silent message was clear: *We're still friends, but we have some stuff to talk over.*

Charlie nudged Léa and nodded toward the stage, leaning over to whisper in her ear. "Looks like we're about to get a fatherly talking to. I'm thinking 'no pain, no gain' and 'develop the right mental attitude.'"

"More like, 'You're all unworthy to be in my magnificent presence. But as long as you're here, you should at least try to make something out of your miserable selves,'" said Pat.

"We're all totally fucked." Cindy scowled.

Little Dick silently surveyed the room, waiting for all the whispered conversations to end.

"How about you, Smart Girl? You're strangely silent," said Cindy.

"I think we're all about to find out," said Léa.

Half an hour later, what had been listed simply as *Tour of The Castle* on the day's printed schedule had turned out to be worse than the weekend in chains.

"When you're tired, push harder," shouted the short, obnoxious man.

Over twenty people were running up the stone steps of the castle's north turret. They had already run up the south turret and twice around the inner courtyard.

"Come on, you lot! We've still got to do the west turret, and it's almost lunchtime."

"Oh fuck me," said Cindy between heavy breaths as she huffed up the stone steps.

"We haven't got time for that right now, but I do like your thinking, missy." The man smirked as he ran past her effortlessly. "Come on, you lot. Hurry it up. My lunch is getting cold."

Ten minutes later, Little Dick made good on all his promises to the group before leaving for the Tour of The Castle. Muscles screamed, and heart rates soared as the group reached the top of the north turret.

As everyone arrived at the top of the turret, Little Dick jumped onto the stone stairwell cap. "You're all weak and puny! I'd kill the whole lot of you if I ran you up the west turret."

Everyone was breathing too hard to celebrate the news that they'd be spared running up the final turret.

Little Dick jumped off stairwell cap and started down the stairs. "I couldn't take you up there anyway. It'd be an insult to Sir Richard," he shouted.

CHAPTER 23 - GUNS AND THE 'NET

The Castle's Shooting Range, 2:30 p.m.

Cindy, Charlie, Pat, and Léa found themselves outside a small classroom. A blue sign next to the door sternly read:

NO LIVE AMMUNITION
(NO EXCEPTIONS, EVER)

Keys dangled from lockers outside the door.

"I guess that means me," said Léa.

She unzipped the nearly hidden side pocket of her backpack. Her right hand disappeared inside the pocket and reappeared holding her 9mm gun.

"They let you keep that?" asked Charlie.

"And these, too."

Léa pointed the gun at the wall as her thumb slid along the grip. Pressing the small button, she released the clip, catching it as it sprang out of the gun. After setting the clip on top of the lockers, Léa pulled the slide and looked at Charlie.

"Check me," she said.

Charlie stared at her as she showed him the gun.

"Clear and empty, right?" said Léa.

"I guess," said Charlie.

Léa smiled and pointed to the empty chamber.

"Dad taught me that when you're handling guns around others, it's good to have someone confirm that it really is empty."

"It's empty," said Charlie.

"Thanks," she said.

She released the slide, moved her finger inside the trigger guard, and pulled the trigger. The gun made a dull *click* as she released the hammer. She slid it back into its hiding place. When Léa's hand emerged from the backpack's hidden pocket, it was holding an additional clip loaded with bullets. Cindy and Pat also watched her in amazement.

"Dad taught me to shoot a long time ago," she said. "He didn't want his little girl going out into the world without a way to protect herself."

"How long have you had that thing hidden in your backpack?" asked Cindy.

"Just over ten years."

Charlie and Cindy looked at each other as Léa opened one of the empty lockers and gently set both clips inside. As she closed the door and turned the key, the classroom door popped open, and Little Dick peered out.

"Class was supposed to start at three. You're all thirty seconds late," he shouted.

"Sorry, Mr. Boxx." Léa walked through the door, gesturing to the *No Ammunition* sign with her locker key. "Just following instructions."

"That's Sergeant-Major Boxx to you lot," said Little Dick. They filed into the small classroom, with only ten seats for students. One wall was lined with pictures of guns and hand-to-hand self-defense moves.

The other side was filled with computers, tablets, and phones. A black plastic box rested on each seat in the front row. Each box was labeled with a name.

"Well now, look who's here," said Charlie.

Tara sat slouched in the last row, typing on her laptop. She had changed out of the morning's running gear, back to her all-black commando-style clothes. Her black boots rested on the seat in front of her, and a pistol was holstered halfway down her thigh.

Léa looked down as Tara looked up.

"Hey," said Tara, a little unsure of herself.

"Hey."

"How's it going?"

"A surprise a minute," said Léa.

"More on the way."

"Bring 'em on."

Léa walked past Tara and sat beside the plastic box with her name on it.

"The two best friends don't seem all that friendly," Cindy whispered to Charlie.

"They'll be okay." Charlie took his seat and reached for the box.

"Why don't you leave those alone for now," said Little Dick. "Everyone settled?"

After a little fidgeting in the seats and some shuffling of backpacks, the room became quiet.

Little Dick smiled down at the students and put his hands behind his back. This wasn't the same annoying little man who had taken the stage earlier. He spoke quietly and seriously. He began by reintroducing himself.

"Sergeant-Major Richard Boxx, formerly of Her Majesty's Royal Marines. I was recruited fifteen years ago to help with physical training, hand-to-hand combat, and firearms instruction," he said. "Every afternoon, at precisely 2:30 p.m., I expect you in your seats ready to learn." He smiled at the group. "We took care of the first part of today's training when I ran your sorry asses up and down the stairs. Now, you're here for firearms and hand-to-hand combat training, which we call *personal safety*."

Little Dick gestured to the back of the room.

"Miss Wells is here to help with a whole new kind of personal safety, which we'll get to in short order."

Charlie winced as Little Dick referred to Tara as "Miss Wells." He had made that mistake once and was immediately corrected. Léa's eyebrows lifted.

Charle looked back at Tara. She hardly looked up from her typing, but he knew her well enough to notice the pace of her typing pick up. He caught Léa's eye, who had glanced at Tara, as well. Léa shook her head as they both looked back to the front of the class.

Little Dick paused until he was sure he had everyone's attention. As he began talking again, he slowly paced the small classroom stage.

"I was brought in because I can train up a platoon of men faster and better that anyone. But … I am not here to train you to be Royal Marines. While there's nothing a Royal Marine can't do, your work calls for a different kind of training."

He paused.

"Basically I'm here to teach you how to take care of yourselves in the cold, dangerous world." He pointed at the pictures lining the wall. "You'll learn all that and a little more. Now open those boxes, but do not touch what's inside."

Tara stopped typing to watch as they opened the boxes, revealing new handguns. She remembered her own reaction when she had opened her box. Even though she had regularly gotten to fire Léa's small gun, Tara had still been surprised.

Léa.

That was a scary topic for Tara. She suspected Léa wasn't too happy with her for hiding her first trip to The Castle. Tara knew she'd have a chance to explain soon, and she hoped Léa would understand that the Growlers hadn't given her much of a choice.

"Whoa," said Pat as he opened his box.

Everyone's reactions were about what Tara had predicted.

Even though the walls were lined with pictures of guns, the instructor was wearing a gun, and the black box was clearly labeled *Smith & Wesson*, everyone reacted with predictable shock at the new 9mm handguns.

Everyone but Léa, of course.

Without touching it, Léa carefully examined her new gun. It was the big brother of the smaller gun hidden in her backpack. They were almost identical. Léa also noticed a small plastic bag full of green "practice" bullets and two empty magazines.

"Ladies and gentlemen," said Little Dick, "let me introduce you to your new best friend. You are now the proud owners of new Smith & Wesson M&P nine millimeter handguns. The M stands for military, and the P stands for police. From this point forward, you are responsible for your gun's care. You are also responsible for every bullet it fires."

Little Dick explained basics of firearms safety. Then he had the students stand near the computers and face the opposite wall, where they began handling the guns, learning how they worked and how to properly clean them.

Tara looked down at her own gun and remembered her training in this classroom. She had been alone. She went through the Growlers' Spy School by herself, and she had scored an A in almost every one of her classes. Her only bad grade had been in a waste-of-time class called Verbal Manipulation.

"More like kissing ass to get people to do what you want," Tara had called it.

The class required tact, charm, and the ability to be nice to strangers, and Tara had little time for those characteristics. Then again, she hadn't been recruited for her nice-girl appearance and charm.

"Miss Wells," said Little Dick a little louder.

Tara refocused on the class. "Yeah."

"I said, why don't you give them your little talk now? And then we'll head over to the range."

"Yeah. Right." Tara snapped her laptop shut and walked to the front of the class.

Turning to face her four friends, Tara remembered sitting with them in the coffee shop a few days ago. Now, everything had changed, and she wondered how they'd accept her.

She set her laptop on the table and looked down at her black boots.

"I was recruited last year. As you heard from the show this morning, these guys have been around since the sixties. Fast-forward fifty years, and let's just say their knowledge of modern computers and the 'Net is nearly nonexistent. The one person they had who knew anything vanished into thin air just over a year ago. That's why I'm here."

"So changing schools and the bitchier than usual attitude was just an act?" asked Charlie.

"Yeah. Whatever. We can do kiss and make up later. Right now, I've got to make sure you don't do anything stupid online that'll tip off anyone about who you are and who we are."

She reached for her laptop, opened it, and pressed a few keys. A few moments later, cellphones, laptops, and iPads in everyone's backpacks began buzzing.

"I need each of you to take out your phone, Mac, and iPad and accept the updates I just sent you."

"What are you doing?" asked Pat as he reached for his backpack. "Using some kind of Net nanny to keep an eye on us?"

"No. This isn't 1984 and Big Brother isn't here to watch you. He is here to help you remain anonymous on the web and, more importantly, to give you a fast and foolproof way to call for help."

"What about all our social stuff?" asked Pat.

"It wouldn't look good if we all just disappeared, would it?" said Léa.

"You're right. It wouldn't look good at all. But you're all going to have to remove some stuff and watch what you post online." Tara spoke to Léa. "And you're going to have to do some editing on your webpage."

"You have a webpage?" asked Charlie.

Léa's eyes shot toward Tara.

"It's nothing," she said.

"Why didn't you tell us?" asked Pat.

"It's actually a nice little photographer's gallery and blog," said Tara. "But you're going to have to remove all the 'about me' stuff and most of the blog posts."

Charlie tapped on his iPad. "Where is it?"

Léa asked Tara, "Wouldn't it be better if I just shut it down?"

"Like you just said, you can't simply disappear."

"So what is it?" asked Pat.

"F-stop espresso dot com," said Léa.

"Perfect name for you, Coffee Girl," said Charlie.

A few seconds later, everyone had Léa's photographs on their screens. Even Little Dick looked over Pat's shoulder at the pictures.

"They're all so gray and dreary," said Charlie.

"It's all clouds, raindrops, and snow," said Cindy.

Léa shrugged.

"Sorry about that gray and dreary crack," said Charlie, "I mean, they really are amazing pictures."

"I figured you for more of a puppies, flowers, and city lights type," said Cindy.

"Okay, we can do that later along with kiss and make up," said Tara, looking down at her laptop. "No one has accepted the updates yet, and you all need to do that right now."

Everyone accepted the updates on their devices.

"So how does it work?" asked Charlie.

"Open your Facebook app, and write something stupid like *I'm a secret agent*. Then hit the post button only once," said Tara.

Fingers flew over the iPads and keyboards and paused after hitting the post button. Everyone looked back up at Tara.

"It stopped, right?"

Everyone nodded.

"Now, notice the color of the clock has changed to red. Touch the time, and hold it a few seconds."

Everyone held their finger or pointer over the red time display. Small boxes popped up with exclamation points and cancel/continue options.

"Every time you send something, the app checks to make sure it won't give anything away. If you hit cancel, it clears the post. If you hit continue, it will post it," said Tara.

"What if I hit post a second time?" asked Pat.

"It would bypass the safety check and post it. But it would also flag the online security system. We made that possible in case you were being watched by someone."

"Sounds simple enough." Léa stuffed her iPad and iPhone back into her backpack and snapped her gun case closed. She stretched and yawned. "Come on guys, this is getting boring."

Everyone looked at Léa.

"I wanna go shoot."

Ten minutes later, Cindy, Charlie, Pat, and Léa stood in a line, facing a set of targets ten feet away. Moments before the new kids opened fire, Tara whispered in Little Dick's ear. "Watch this."

When Little Dick gave them the order to open fire, Cindy and Charlie awkwardly drew their new pistols. They raised the pistols, aimed at the target, and fired off several shots each, which all hit the ground in front of them.

Pat didn't shoot the ground, but nearly every shot entirely missed the target.

Long before the others fired their first rounds, Léa emptied her gun with five fast, dead-center shots. She dropped the empty clip, catching it as it fell, and simultaneously holstered her weapon.

Tara leaned down to whisper in Little Dick's ear again.

"Even you've got to admit it. That's fucking awesome shooting," she said with more of her old attitude.

Little Dick ignored Léa's shooting and focused on Cindy's and Charlie's dismal performances.

"What did I tell you about having your target in your sights before you pull the trigger?"

Stunned by their own complete lack of shooting skill and by Léa's impressive performance, Cindy, Charlie, and Pat remained frozen with their empty guns still pointed downrange.

"Don't feel too bad." Little Dick smirked as he looked at the ground in front of Cindy and Charlie. "As you can see from the missing chunks of concrete, you're not the first shooters to find a bullseye on the ground."

But none of them were interested in the missing chunks of concrete.

They weren't listening to Little Dick. They were all looking at Léa's target.

"Drop your clips, and holster your weapons," said Little Dick.

No one moved.

Tara looked down at her shoes as a rare smile appeared on her face.

"Drop your bloody clips, and holster your fucking weapons!" shouted Little Dick.

Léa smiled at her friends and nodded her head toward Little Dick. They snapped back to reality. Three clips dropped to the ground, and three new guns were clumsily holstered.

"Now then. Pick up your clips, and let's see if you can remember what you learned less than an hour ago," said Little Dick.

CHAPTER 24 - MOVIE NIGHT

The Castle Auditorium, 7:15 p.m.

Cindy, Charlie, Léa, and Pat returned to the auditorium a little after seven and found the room empty. Again.

They stood in the back and stared at the stage.

"Okay, I'll be the one to ask," said Charlie. "Are we in the right place?"

Pat read from his printed schedule. "Yep. Movie night, 7:15 p.m. in the main auditorium."

Cindy shook her head. "Movie night. Un-fucking believable."

Léa checked the time on her iPhone.

"We're six minutes early," she said.

"So in five minutes and change, this whole place will magically fill up, and the show will start," said Pat.

"They do seem to keep a tight schedule," said Léa.

"The tighter the better." Tara appeared behind them.

"I was wondering if we'd see you here tonight," said Charlie.

Cindy grumbled, "I was pretty sure she'd be lurking around."

Tara ignored Cindy and walked toward the stage. "Most ops run on split-second timing. So showing up exactly on time for something like movie night is great training." Tara dropped into a seat halfway down the aisle. "Come on," she said. "These are the best seats in the house."

"Not the center?" asked Charlie.

"Aisle seats are better," said Tara, "in case you have to get up or want a snack."

Soon, all five friends were seated together near the middle of the auditorium. No one said anything for quite a while until Cindy broke the silence.

"So you knew about all this for a whole fucking year and never said shit."

"Sounds about right," said Tara, staring at the stage.

"Seems to me a true friend might have said something," said Cindy. "Instead, you let us walk right into a trap."

"The sooner you stop being mad at the world and start looking at the bigger picture, the sooner your life gets a whole lot easier," said Tara.

"I'm just saying that a good friend might have taken a little better care of her friends."

"We were never that a good of friends. And if you're too stupid to wake up and see how good things have gotten for you, then I'm not really interested in wasting any more time with you," said Tara.

Léa cleared the cobwebs. "Enough. Both you."

"Thank you," said Pat.

"It's been a really long day," said Léa. "We're all tired, and we would rather not listen to you two carry on."

After a few moments of silence, Tara said, "She started it."

Léa gave a quick laugh. Actually, it was more of a snort. Charlie looked at Cindy, still staring straight ahead.

Pat smiled and looked at Tara. "Wait a minute. When did you develop a sense of humor?"

"There's a lot you don't know about me," said Tara.

"I guess," said Charlie.

Léa checked the time. "One minute to go."

"Watch this," said Tara.

Almost immediately, the room began to fill with people moving quickly and quietly. Within thirty seconds, almost every seat was taken. As the last people took their seats, the old man with a cane started down the aisle.

"What's his story?" Léa whispered to Tara.

"That's Alan Dennis. He's been in charge since day one. Before all this, he was a has-been newspaper reporter."

"How did he end up here?" asked Pat.

"Long story," said Tara. "And it's a good one."

The auditorium quieted as the old man stopped in front of the stage. Alan Dennis faced the crowd and smiled.

"I'm sure we all remember our first day here. Earlier, we welcomed four new members to our little gang of thieves. So how's your first day going?"

After a brief hesitation, Léa spoke up. "A day we'll never forget."

"And how about you, Miss Martin? Maybe a little less angry with us?"

"A little," said Cindy.

"Well, like I said this morning, keep your mind open, but don't forget why you're angry."

"Not a chance," said Cindy, with a little less bitterness in her voice.

Alan leaned his cane against the stage and searched his pockets, producing his pipe and a bag of tobacco. Several members of the audience smiled and nudged their neighbors. Alan began filling the pipe.

"As you no doubt read on your schedules, it's movie night here at The Castle. Actually, we do movie night every Monday, Wednesday, and Saturday. As you might have guessed, our favorite movies are spy movies. But it's not all fun and games. You see, over the years, we've learned a lot from movies."

He looked down at his pipe, dumped the tobacco back into the bag, and tapped the empty pipe against the stage. Alan blew on the stem a few times, then began refilling the pipe.

"It was back in the seventies. Or was it the eighties? I can't remember. This tall, skinny man came to our attention."

The tall, skinny man sat in the middle seat of the front row. He had a full head of graying hair and held a complicated remote control. "It was 1981, sir," he said.

"So I was close either way." Alan smiled and continued filling the pipe. "For our new friends, this is Thomas Austin. You might say he's our movie-night maître d' ... among other things."

Alan stuck the pipe in his mouth and patted his pockets.

"You see, Thomas here wrote the book on special effects in the movies. What got our attention was a story he told about a little gadget James Bond used. It looked so convincing that the Royal Navy rang up the producers to ask how it worked. Imagine their surprise when they learned that it really was just a movie prop," said Alan with a sly smile.

The audience laughed. A few people clapped. Others said "Way to go, James" and "Show us how it's done."

"True story," said the old man as he continued to search his pockets. "So we invited old Thomas here to join us as sort of a special instructor of the cinema. He searches high and low for brilliant ideas we might use in our real-world jobs. He also provides us with more than a few laughs at the expense of some big-time movie stars."

That brought another polite round of applause from the audience.

"Thomas created that little show for you this morning, and you can bet he has some more special effects planned for you tonight. He tells me that tonight's show comes from 1968 and that it's a great example of creating what we like to call 'a false reality to manipulate the behavior of a target.'"

Alan looked down at Thomas.

"Did I say that right?"

"Yes, sir."

Tara whispered to Léa. "Remember that. It's a big deal here."

Léa nodded.

"It's just a short TV show tonight. As always, it'll be followed up with drinks and discussion at Deep in the Cliffs," said Alan. He seemed to give up searching his pockets. "Oh, for God's sake, Thomas, I haven't smoked this thing in years. Do you have match?"

"Of course, sir."

Thomas stood up and smiled at the audience. Reaching into his pocket, he produced a rather large match. He bent down and struck it along the front of the stage. The lights in the room dimmed as he lit Alan's pipe. As Thomas sat down, he slowly moved the match in front of his face. Then he stretched his arm to the side and held the match high.

"Everyone ready?" he asked.

The crowd gave a scattered, "Yes."

"Anytime you are, Governor," said someone in the audience.

"Get the show on the road," said someone in the back.

Thomas smiled and lifted his other hand, still holding the big remote. He gently pushed a button.

The lights dipped to black. The match in Thomas's hand ignited what appeared to be a huge fuse on the stage. The speakers sprang to life playing Lalo Schifrin's unmistakable theme from the old TV series *Mission: Impossible*.

The holographic fuse burned across the stage before it meandered over the audience. After a few figure eights, the flame sizzled back toward the stage. The famous TV theme built up to its explosive end as the sparks on the stage grew. As the song ended, the stage erupted in flames, and the room went completely dark.

Cheers of approval and enthusiastic applause erupted from the audience. A spotlight illuminated a podium in the corner of the stage. Thomas appeared at the podium and opened a small notebook.

"This episode of *Mission: Impossible* originally aired in November of 1968. It's called 'The Execution,' and it's a good example of what our group of impossible-mission spies did so well. They created a false reality to manipulate the behavior of their target."

He looked down at his notes. Then Thomas spoke directly to the newcomers.

"You will learn that the best scam is when the people you're trying to scam don't know they're being scammed."

"Absolutely," said someone in the audience.

"In tonight's show, the I.M. Force went to great lengths to create the false reality. Now, their scams get a little complex for our tastes. Here in the real world, we've learned to keep it as simple as possible," said Thomas.

"Too bloody right," said another voice in the audience.

"You see, the more complex the scam, the greater the chance of it blowing up in your face."

"Right you are, mate," called someone from the back of the room.

"In fact, if you'll all permit me. For the benefit of our newcomers, some of the best scams happen on the spur of the moment. The magic, so to speak, happens when you're able to take advantage of natural cover."

"Two more biggies to remember," whispered Tara. "Spur of the moment and natural cover."

"Spur of the moment. Natural cover. Got it," said Léa quietly.

"So enjoy the show, and we'll all meet at Deep in the Cliffs for a pint after." Thomas punched a few more buttons on his remote. The lights dimmed, and the screen came to life.

Peter Graves' face filled the big screen as a voice boomed from the speakers.

"Good morning, Mr. Phelps."

Everyone in the room applauded and cheered.

CHAPTER 25 - JANET AUSTIN

Deep in the Cliffs Pub, 8:30 p.m.

"What can I get you, miss?" asked David McNally.

The pub was a strange mix of two different worlds. One side of the room looked like any of the hundreds of smoky old pubs lining the country lanes of Great Britain.

Old-style Guinness and Murphy's Irish Stout pumps were two of thirty taps lining the back of the dark wooden bar. Above it, spotless old-world glasses hung upside down. Dark wooden booths lined the wall, and a few old tables and chairs were scattered in front of the bar.

Halfway across the room, the old world stopped, and the new world started.

"Anything from the taps, Miss Martin?" David McNally asked again.

Charlie nudged Léa. "Watch this."

He edged up to Cindy and gave her shoulder a sharp jab.

"Hey Sis, want some booze?"

Cindy snapped into the present. She punched Charlie on the shoulder. "How many times have I told you *not* to call me Sis?"

Charlie smiled and pointed to David. "Something to drink?"

Cindy looked over the taps lining the back wall. After scanning the taps two or three times she finally spotted something she recognized.

"Bass."

David went to pour her pint, and Cindy turned toward the far side of the room again. One wall was filled with flat-screen monitors of various sizes, and more monitors covered half of the adjacent wall.

The screens closest to the door were playing news channels, and the ones halfway along the wall played sports. But the monitors flowing into and around the corner captured everyone's eyes. They showed a wide panorama from the top turret of The Castle and the stormy sea outside.

A medium-sized cargo ship was heading south against the building seas. Each wave that broke over the bow seemed bigger than the last. Anyone who had ever been to sea knew exactly what was happening onboard that ship. Any coffee cup that hadn't been properly stowed was broken. Any tools not put away could become flying bullets with the power to break bones or damage vital gear. And anyone without an iron stomach had lost their dinner, lunch, and probably breakfast long ago.

"Here you go, miss," said David jovially.

Cindy looked into David McNally's smiling face. She was having trouble connecting the dots between the quiet man who cooked at the coffee shop, the tough as nails, heavily armed commando who everyone called Captain McNally, and the smiling barkeep who just poured her a pint of Bass Ale.

"Thanks." Cindy took her drink to an empty table in the corner. She sat down and watched the ship battle the building seas. The place was packed, and Cindy picked out conversations as she sipped her ale.

An older man sat with a group of three couples. "Remember what von Clausewitz said."

"Oh, God. Get ready for another chorus of 'war is merely the continuation of politics by other means.'"

"Well, I was actually going to go with 'the enemy of a good plan is the dream of a perfect plan.'"

The table erupted in laughter.

Another table seemed to be having just as much fun.

"Oh, give me a break," said a woman who was clearly exasperated. "The whole point of that episode was to titillate the audience with a little death penalty porn."

"What the bloody hell kind of porn is that?"

"Probably the kind she's got stashed back in her room right now."

The table erupted in a bray of obnoxiously loud laughter.

Cindy turned back to the panorama of the sea and tuned out the conversations around her. The past seventy-two hours had nearly brought her to the breaking point.

Setting aside the humiliation she felt from her weekend in these perverts' dungeon, Cindy was getting tired of all the mixed messages. Particularly the mixed messages she had gotten from the old man himself.

First, she was supposed to set aside her anger. Then she was supposed to remember what she was angry about.

What the fuck?

Cindy gulped the amber ale and carefully set the glass back on the table. She ran her finger around the lip of the glass.

Cindy knew she had a short fuse, and sometimes it was all she could do to keep from exploding with the fury of a thousand suns. Her parents had taught her how to pour water on the fuse before she exploded. But it wasn't easy.

"When you explode, you lose control, and things invariably get worse," her mum had said all those years ago.

Young Cindy had cried. "But it just builds up inside me to the point that it hurts."

"You use that as your reminder," her father had said. "Whenever you feel that kind of pain building up, you know it's time to stop yourself before you explode."

"How?"

"Practice and patience," her parents had said together.

Now Cindy sat alone, surrounded by people who had hurt her. Worse, Cindy knew these people were breaking more than a few laws. Even worse, her friends couldn't see that, and had decided to go along with these ... with these ...

Even in the privacy of her thoughts, Cindy couldn't find words to describe the people who had done these horrible things to her. Cindy reached for her glass of ale as a woman sat down at her table.

She was about forty years old, with black hair and a few lines around her eyes. She looked a little Asian and a little European. She had obviously decided long ago to stay in shape, and it showed.

"Janet Austin," said the woman with a slight smile.

"Austin? Like the movie guy?"

"Like the movie guy." Janet sighed.

Cindy sipped her ale and stared at Janet. She wanted to be left alone, and she really didn't want to get chummy with anyone. After staring at Janet long enough to make her point, Cindy turned back to the panorama.

The ship she'd been watching had sailed almost out of frame.

"All these years, and I never get tired of that view," said Janet as she watched the ship battle the waves.

Cindy looked back at Janet with her best *leave me alone* stare.

"You know, you're not the first person to be really pissed on their first day here."

Cindy gave Janet another death stare and looked away.

After a few minutes of silence, Cindy finished her pint. She was so angry that it hurt, and the pain was her reminder. Drawing on years of practice and her parents' advice, she decided it was time to put her anger aside. Cindy pointed to Janet's empty glass.

"What are you drinking?"

"Same as you," said Janet. She looked toward the bar and held up two fingers.

A few minutes later, two full pints of Bass Ale were delivered to the table. Cindy and Janet sat in silence for a few minutes, sipping their drinks.

"So how many more surprises do I have coming?" Cindy asked.

"Quite a few."

"Any you'd care to clue me in on?"

"Well, I'm pretty sure you know you were adopted as a kid," said Janet.

"No shit. Charlie and I are obviously Asian, and our parents are about as Scottish as you can get." Cindy took a big drink of ale. "You're going to need to do a little better than that."

Janet nodded toward the table where Alan Dennis was sitting.

"He arranged your adoption."

"He did? Why?"

"You got some of the basic history of this place. It was started before the Cold War, and everyone came from MI6 or from the military."

"Guys like Dick Boxx," said Cindy.

"Perfect example."

Janet leaned toward Cindy and lowered her voice. "Learn everything you can from that one. But never, ever trust him."

"I'll bet he's a bit of a backstabber."

"Not a *bit* of one. They don't call him 'Little Dick' for nothing."

"Thanks for that." Cindy sipped her ale. "Charlie and I aren't the only kids here who were adopted, are we?"

"Most of us are."

"Because orphans make the best spies," Cindy stated.

"Right. There's no one to miss us. And since we're alone in the world, this becomes our family," said Janet.

"You too?"

"Me too."

"Even Léa and Pat?"

"Léa is from France, Pat is from Russia, and your pal Tara is from Romania."

"She's not my pal," said Cindy.

"Tara's not that bad. Like most brilliant people, she just has no social skills."

"And no sense of loyalty to her so-called friends."

"Exactly what was she supposed to do? You're a smart girl. Use your brain."

Cindy looked away from Janet and remembered what her parents had taught her. Whenever you're faced with a problem, take a step back, and try to think it through without your feelings getting in the way. But for Cindy, emotions were as hard to keep in check as her hot temper.

"Okay, I get it," said Cindy. "She didn't have a choice."

"Now take that a step further, and think about all the people here who you're mad at."

"He had a choice." Cindy nodded toward Alan Dennis.

"Yeah, I guess he did. Then again, I'd rather this lot be here than not."

Cindy looked at Janet with disgust. "A bunch of rogue commandos playing James Bond? There are laws, and I'm pretty sure this is all wrong."

"There are a few people who might agree with you. But who do you think gets in an insane dictator's face and makes him stand down when he's ready to blow up half the world?"

"The government. Diplomats. The military."

"Don't be so thick. You're smarter than that," said Janet.

Cindy took a big swig of her ale and pointed to her nearly empty pint glass.

"That's my second ale."

"So?" Janet smiled.

"So. Don't expect me to reconcile all the evils of the world and then throw in some half-baked justification for a group of rogue spies on two pints of Bass."

She picked up her glass and swallowed the last drops. Then Cindy slammed the glass back on the table and let out a loud belch.

"Bravo! Well said."

Cindy nodded and held up two fingers toward the bar. A few minutes later, two fresh pints of Bass arrived at the table.

"Careful," said Janet. "You're clearly not used to all this booze."

Cindy swigged her fresh pint of ale.

"Don't worry. I tend to be a quiet, mellow drunk. Helps me not be so angry."

"You've got a full day tomorrow. I'd hate to go on Little Dick's Tour of The Castle with a hangover."

Cindy let out another loud belch and wiped her mouth with the back of her hand.

"So you guys. You guys go out, kidnap orphans, and then what? How did you know Tara would be, well, Tara? And how did you know Léa would be so fucking smart?" Cindy paused. "And what the fuck am I doing here? I'm not a hot chick or super smart."

Janet finished off her first pint and laughed. "I could explain, but you're getting pretty drunk, and we'll actually be going over some of this in class tomorrow."

"Class? You mean you're one of our teachers?" slurred Cindy.

"Among other things."

She took her fresh glass of ale and stood up from the table.

"What class?" asked Cindy.

"It'll be right up your ally. Basically, it's good and evil in the land of spies."

Cindy looked back at the panorama, which had darkened with the setting sun.

"Don't be too surprised if I'm not easily convinced."

Janet laughed. "Don't be too disappointed when you find out you're not the first to say that."

Cindy stared at the panorama. "Whatever."

Janet smiled. "By the way. You're also not the first person to show up to the bar on their first night with their nine millimeter stuffed in their pants."

Janet looked over her shoulder and raised her shirt to reveal her own gun stuffed in the waistband of her jeans.

"You just need to learn how to hide it better," said Janet.

"Whatever," said Cindy

"The sooner you realize that you're among friends, the easier it gets."

CHAPTER 26 - ARE WE STILL FRIENDS?

Léa's Room, 10 p.m.

The shower felt so good.

Once Léa finished with the soap and shampoo, she reached for the lever that changed the gentle stream of water into the powerful, pulsing jets of the shower message.

"Finally," said Léa to herself as she flipped the lever.

She'd been waiting for this moment all day. The gentle stream of hot water falling from the center of the stone shower stopped for only a second before the powerful jets in each corner took aim at Léa's body.

"*Aahh …*" There was both pain and pleasure in Léa's voice.

She had forgotten how strong the jets were, and they nearly pushed her against the wall. Léa shuffled her feet to keep her balance and began turning in a slow circle. The strong jets were just what Léa needed. On top of her soreness from her weekend dungeon ordeal, Léa had a whole new set of sore muscles.

Léa smiled as she twisted her aching body in the powerful jets. The Tour of The Castle run had been hard, and Little Dick was, well, a complete dick. But it had been a great workout.

Léa let the water pound the soreness from her aching muscles. She adjusted the water temperature, nudging it hotter.

What an amazing day, she thought.

Léa thought she heard a knock at her door, but the hot shower felt too good to leave. She wasn't sure she'd heard a knock, anyway, so she decided to enjoy the hot water a little longer.

Not much longer.

The knock turned to a pounding at the door. Léa sighed.

What now?

She cleared the cobwebs and shut off the jets. She stepped out of the stone shower and grabbed a towel.

Léa was tired and sore, and she had been going since the early morning. She wanted some time to herself, and whoever was banging on her door was not welcome. Still dripping wet, Léa reached for the button, and the door slid open to reveal the one person she actually wanted to see.

"Hey," said Tara.

"Hey."

Tara held up a bottle of wine and two glasses. "Your favorite."

Behind Tara, a guy in a white lab coat walked by. He smiled at Tara, but tripped over his own feet and nearly fell when he saw Léa.

"How's it going?" Léa smiled.

Tara looked down at her bare feet as a half-smile crept onto the corner of her mouth. She looked off to one side as the guy stumbled down the hallway. When he was gone, Tara looked nervously back to Léa.

"Come on in." Léa stepped aside to let Tara enter.

Tara set the glasses on the desk and opened the wine. Léa dried off in front of the full-length mirror. She tossed the wet towel into the corner and looked over the bruises and cuts covering her body.

"I don't think I've seen anyone with more bruises than you," said Tara.

"Been checking out people with bruises have you?"

"No." Tara laughed nervously.

Léa straightened the towel she had left on the desk chair and sat down. She nodded toward the wine. "Don't worry about letting it breath. It's getting late."

Tara poured two glasses, handed one to Léa, and sat down on the bed. They each sipped their wine, and the room became uncomfortably quiet.

"So, how pissed are you?" asked Tara.

Léa leaned back in her chair and propped her feet on the edge of the bed.

"It's kind of hard to be pissed knowing that you didn't have much of a choice."

"You sure?" said Tara. "You seemed kinda pissed earlier today."

"It was easy to get my head around what's happened. But my heart took a little time to catch up."

"That's fair," said Tara.

Silence descended over the room. Léa pulled her feet off the bed and balanced them on the edge of her chair. Tara watched her toes.

"I really can get my head around all this just fine," said Léa. "I can even understand why you couldn't say anything to me. Makes perfect sense." She took a sip of wine and set her glass on the desk. Leaning forward, she hugged her knees and looked down at the floor. "But having said that, I still feel like something's changed. Like maybe we've lost something. I don't know."

"Trust?"

"No. I know I can still trust you with my life. It's something else."

"A lot changed for me a year ago," said Tara. "And I suspect a lot changed for you this weekend."

Léa looked down at her bruised knees and lifted one arm to examine her cut and bruised wrist. "Did you get this torn up?"

"Yeah. Everyone who spends a weekend in the dungeon gets pretty messed up."

"Oh." Léa hugged her legs more tightly. She rested her chin on her knees. "Glad to hear it."

"What?"

"That you went through the test too."

"Why?" asked Tara.

"Because I need to figure something out about it."

"What's that?"

Léa's eyes flitted from Tara to the iPad by her bed.

"Earlier today, Cindy said she thought I enjoyed the whole ordeal. I've been thinking about it, and I'm not so sure I like the conclusion I reached." She paused. "I did enjoy it."

Léa looked down at her feet and nodded a few times. Without looking up, she repeated her last words, with more conviction.

"I did enjoy it."

More silence. A few more sips of wine. Finally, Léa looked back at Tara.

"Did you enjoy it?" she asked.

"No. It was no fun at all."

"That's what I thought. No one else did either. So what does this make me, some kind of kinky dungeon girl?"

Tara laughed. "I've known you my whole life, and there's no way you're a kinky dungeon girl."

"Even after what Cindy called my 'strip tease parade?'"

"I'm guessing you had your reasons."

Léa smiled and nodded. "I did."

Tara could see the wheels spinning in her friend's head. When Léa paused like this, she was usually about to say something brilliant, memorable, or hilarious.

"Several reasons. Mostly, I wanted them to know that even after stripping me down and chaining me up, I never lost control. And in the end, I beat them at their own game. I guess it all boils down to a little payback."

"Payback?" asked Tara.

"Sure. I knew what Cindy called my little 'strip tease parade' would keep most of the men and a few of the women up that night. Payback," said Léa with a sly smile.

"And it cost you absolutely nothing."

"What do you mean?"

Tara sipped her wine. "I grew up with you. If there is one thing I know about you, it's that you like to get naked. You've been into working out ever since you were a kid so you're more in touch with your body than most. You're just more comfortable with yourself. So your little 'parade' cost you nothing."

Léa looked down at herself, then up at Tara.

"I hope I haven't made you uncomfortable."

"I'm used to it. It's just you."

Léa gulped her wine. As she set her glass on the desk, she looked away from Tara.

"Thing is, I do get a bit of thrill out of it."

"Of course you do," said Tara. "We all do. You're just a lot more willing to share than the rest of us."

"That doesn't make me some kind of slut, does it?"

"No. Maybe a bit of an exhibitionist, but not a slut."

"Cindy doesn't seem to think so."

"And do we really care what she thinks?"

Léa hesitated. "No."

"Good. Just try to grow out of it by the time you're seventy."

"Not a chance." Léa smiled.

After a brief pause, they both erupted in laughter. They reached for their wine glasses, *clink*ed them together, and yelled, "Cheers!"

After the laughter died away, Léa looked down at her toes again. "There's something else."

Tara waited quietly. She had been monitoring the test—watching, listening. She knew what was coming.

Léa spoke softly. "Something else happened down there, and I don't know what to think about it."

"You made a comment and started wondering if you wanted more from me than friendship."

Léa looked up at Tara.

"You were listening?"

"Yeah."

Léa took another drink of wine. "I don't know where it came from. It just made me wonder about ... about what we are and what I want."

"So what are we, and what do you want?" asked Tara.

"I don't know."

Tara set down her wine glass and moved closer to Léa, taking her hand.

"I want you to listen to me very carefully," said Tara.

Léa looked down at her toes. But Tara gripped her hand and gave it a tug. Léa met her friend's eyes.

"First, I don't have a problem with this, and you shouldn't either. There are some people out there who do, but we don't. You know why?"

"Why?" said Léa.

144

"Because our parents didn't raise us like that. Okay?"

"Okay."

"Now, second. We've known each other since we were five. We've been through life together. We're closer than family. I think it's safe to say we love each other. That doesn't mean it's sexual. It's just what happens when two special people have shared so much of their lives with each other."

Still gripping Léa's hand, Tara reached for her glass and took a sip of wine. Léa did the same and smiled at Tara.

"You're right about that," she said.

"We've been friends so long that we truly do need each other. Down in that dungeon, you were calm, cool Léa to everyone else. But I know you were still under a lot of stress. You needed me, and I'm sorry I wasn't there for you."

"You're right about that, too," said Léa.

"We're going to be quite a team, and it's okay for us to need each other. Together, we're going to be an unstoppable force, and that's not just my opinion. It's what all the experts in this cave think, too."

Tara took Léa's other hand.

"You know what else is okay?" she asked.

"What?"

"If someday we decide we want something more from each other. Something romantic, something sexual, well that's going to be okay, too, and do you know why?"

"Why?" said Léa.

"Because best friends who love each other are there for each other no matter what."

"Promise?"

"Promise. You too?" said Tara.

"Me too. Promise."

"Good."

Tara smiled, gave Léa's hands a shake, and let go. She reached for her glass and the nearly empty bottle of wine.

"Let's finish this and turn in. Tomorrow could be a busy day," said Tara.

Léa held out her glass as Tara split the last of the bottle.

"Thanks and cheers, my friend," said Léa.

"Thanks and cheers, my friend."

They *clink*ed their glasses together and silently sipped the last few drops of wine.

CHAPTER 27 - SPY SCHOOL, DAY TWO

Léa's Room, 5:30 a.m.

Just like the morning before, Léa woke to music from the iPad on the nightstand. This morning, it played Enya's "Orinoco Flow." Tara always complained when that song came on the radio.

"This is why we have iTunes," she would say.

Léa opened one eye and focused on the iPad's clock.

5:30 a.m.

Under the clock, she noticed a small timer counting down.

0:55 ... 0:54 ... 0:53 ... 0:52 ...

Léa tried sit up, but she didn't make it. She was still sore from the weekend's dungeon test and from running up and down The Castle's turrets.

0:49 ... 0:48 ... 0:47 ... 0:46 ...

"Try again," she said to herself.

Léa rolled onto her back and tried to sit up, but her back muscles screamed in pain. She only made it halfway.

0:43 ... 0:42 ... 0:41 ... 0:40 ...

"Here we go again."

Like her first morning, Léa used her legs as a counterweight. Enya droned from the iPad's small speaker as the clock continued to count down.

0:03 ... 0:02 ... 0:01 ... 0:00 ...

Between a "sail" and an "away," the music changed. Sandro Silva's "Epic" played loudly, not only from the iPad's tiny speakers, but also from the WiFi speakers on either side of the TV.

"Epic" was one of Léa's workout songs. The six minutes of pulsing techno-dance played each morning as Léa hopped out of bed to start her day with pushups, bicycle crunches, full-body planks, dumbbell presses, and kickboxing. Her workout was designed to get her heart beating and her blood pulsing. But most importantly, it cleared her mind to help her focus on the day ahead.

Léa smiled and listened to the beat of the song. Suddenly, it stopped. A red light appeared at the top-center of the TV screen.

Someone had activated the built-in webcam. Suddenly, Tara's face filled the screen, and she wasn't smiling.

"What the fuck are you still doing in bed?" Tara's voice was filled with the attitude that had really annoyed Léa over the past year.

"I just woke up."

"You woke me up more times than I can count with your silly little morning workout. Just 'cause you got to slack off yesterday, doesn't mean you get to skate today."

The screen shut off, and Léa looked around the silent room. Her eyes came to rest on the iPad. The countdown timer had started again.

0:10 ... 0:09 ... 0:08 ... 0:07 ...

Léa smiled and slowly got out of bed. Her blue foam workout mat was unrolled on the floor at the foot of the bed, and her dumbbells were lined up next to the mat. Léa smiled. Only Tara knew her morning workout routine well enough to set up her stuff like this.

The red webcam light still glowed above the TV screen.

"Thanks," Léa said, smiling.

The red light blinked off.

Léa dropped slowly to her hands and knees. She watched the iPad as its second countdown of the morning finished up.

0:03 ... 0:02 ... 0:01 ... 0:00 ...

Sandro Silva's "Epic" began playing again.

Léa stretched onto her elbows and toes, holding a full-body plank as the song's beat wound up. She held the plank for the first minute and half of the song. As the beat changed, she rolled onto her back and rested for thirty seconds.

The beat changed again, and Léa laced her fingers behind her neck and did two minutes of bicycle crunches. Her legs and arms were still sore, but her abs weren't in bad shape. Léa smiled as the song's energy picked up, along with the pace of her bicycle crunches.

Nothing felt better to Léa than the sensation of her heart rate picking up. She closed her eyes. Keeping time with the beat of the song, Léa felt her stomach muscles begin to burn. When she opened her eyes, she saw sweat had appeared on her stomach, arms, and legs as she kept pace with the music.

A minute later, the song ended, and Julien Blend's "Atom" pulsed from the speakers. Léa grabbed two of the dumbbells Tara had left. After twenty-five presses, Léa began one of her own workout creations.

She lay back on the mat and stretched her arms straight out to each side. She pulled her knees up to her chest and then straightened her legs back out. Keeping her feet an inch from the floor, she did a wide leg split, then brought her feet back together. Léa continued her combo knee tuck, leg split until the beat of the music changed.

Léa rolled over for pushups. Her sore arm and back muscles screamed in protest. She fell behind the song's pace, but she kept working until the song ended.

Breathing heavily, Léa rested for a minute, until "Epic" began again, and she repeated the plank and bicycles crunches. When "Atom" began, she did her set of dumbbell presses, knee crunches, and pushups. The music ended, giving Léa another one-minute break. Then "Epic" began again, and she started another round.

Every so often, Léa would change the music on her playlist or would modify some of the moves. But she had started her day with a workout for years. She knew every move by heart.

"Atom" ended, and a new song started. Léa rolled over on her mat, breathing heavily. Her muscles burned, but she felt great. Léa slowly got to her feet. As she stood in the middle of the room, a beat pulsed from the speakers bolted to the wall.

Léa's head nodded along. The song was from one of the *Matrix* movies. Léa listened to the beat of Fluke's "Zion" as it built up energy.

As the beat changed, Léa sprang into action, with a combination of kickboxing and dance. Her fists punched the air in front of her. Her feet struck the air beside her. She spun three hundred and sixty degrees.

Her muscles protested, but Léa didn't stop. Halfway through the song, her nose twitched as she picked up a familiar scent. A smile appeared in the corner of her mouth, but she kept going.

Keeping up with the beat became impossible as her muscles screamed in pain. Léa knew her punches weren't hitting every beat. But that was okay. She was up and moving, and everything worked.

As the song faded, Léa's tempo slowed. The song gave way to silence, and Léa stopped moving. Her breath fell heavily, and she stood still, feeling the blood course through her body.

As her breathing returned to normal, Léa caught another whiff of that familiar scent. After a few minutes of brewing, the coffee machine sputtered and clicked off.

As Léa walked over to the desk for the freshly brewed cup of coffee, she saw a new screen blinking on her iPad. She touched the screen and found her schedule for the day. There was no printed copy today, but it again included several comments that appeared to be just for her.

SCHEDULE FOR: Léa Taylor
5:30 a.m. - Personal workout/coffee
6 a.m. - Gun cleaning (you should have done this last night)
8 a.m. - Breakfast

9 a.m. - Morning class: Good and Evil
10:30 a.m. - Tour of The Castle
Noon - Lunch
1:30 p.m. - Afternoon class: Spy Sex
3 p.m. - Range
4:30 p.m. - Obstacle Course
6 p.m. - Dinner
7:15 p.m. - Deep in the Cliffs Pub
9:30 p.m. - Lights Out

Spy Sex?

Léa cleared the cobwebs and took a big drink of coffee.

The iPad beeped, and a soft voice said, "You have two hours until breakfast."

Léa finished her coffee, grabbed the gun-cleaning kit, and started working on her two guns. As she disassembled and cleaned both of her pistols, she tried to imagine what today's classes would be like.

The first class had to be some kind of ethics for spies. But the second class left plenty of room for speculation.

Léa made quick work of cleaning her guns. Once she put away the cleaning kit, she started the coffee maker again and headed for the shower. As she passed the bed, she slipped her toes under the sweat-drenched workout mat and kicked it into the air. Without missing a step, Léa grabbed it and continued to the shower.

She rinsed the mat under the shower head. As she stood under the hot water, she thought about the day ahead and the scheduled classes. Léa felt the back of her neck tingling.

Sometimes, when something was about to happen, the back of her neck tingled. This morning, the feeling left no doubt.

CHAPTER 28 - GOOD, EVIL, AND RICHARD BURTON

A Classroom in The Castle, 9 a.m.

Just as Léa had suspected, her first class of the day was an ethics class for spies. The teacher called the class Good and Evil. Léa recognized the teacher from the pub. Just before class began, she leaned over and whispered to Cindy.

"That's the woman you were talking to last night."

"Yeah," said Cindy.

Léa could tell from Cindy's bloodshot eyes that she'd had a little too much to drink last night.

"Right then," said Janet Austin before Léa could ask Cindy any more questions. "Everyone ready?"

The small classroom had bare walls and a large LCD screen. Eight leather chairs were arranged in a semi-circle, and a battered leather briefcase sat on the floor beside a small table, which held an old Mac and a Bluetooth remote. Léa hadn't seen Tara all day, even at breakfast.

At breakfast, Léa had noticed a tension in the cafeteria that wasn't there the day before. People had eaten quickly, with no conversation.

As soon as Janet Austin started talking, Léa's neck tingled again. Even though the teacher was clearly interested in the topic, she seemed distracted and a bit on edge.

"So, good and evil in the world of spies. As your friend, Cindy, and I discussed over drinks last night, it's a rather complicated subject." She paused and surveyed the room. "Let me clearly define the scope of our class. Léa, say you were called into Commander Dennis's office, and he gave you an order to liquidate an enemy agent. And just so we understand each other, I mean to kill another human being in cold blood. How would you know whether you're doing the right thing?"

Léa made no attempt to answer quickly. It was one hell of a loaded question. But Janet had framed an exact situation Léa might find herself in. As Léa considered the ways she might answer, Janet spoke up.

"Good for you for not spouting out a quick answer. It's not a question any of us can or should be able to answer easily." She paused and clicked her computer a few times. "Let me try another one. Anyone know what a spy is?"

Charlie raised his hand. "A person who secretly collects and reports information on the activities, movements, and plans of an enemy or competitor."

"Right out of the book you all should have found in your rooms," said Janet. "Did you memorize that last night?"

"Yeah."

"Good for you. It's always best to stay a few steps ahead so that you never fall behind. And for the record, that's a good answer. So let's try another question. Are spies good people?"

"Depends on who they're spying for," said Pat.

"Good start. But it's not as simple as that. Say you're a kid who grew up in the USA and got a job with the CIA spying against the UK. You'd be bad for the Brits but good for the Yanks. Right?"

"Uh, right," said Pat hesitantly.

Janet smiled at her four students.

"You might as well get used to the fact that there will be no easy answers in my class."

"But there are answers?" asked Cindy.

"Sure there are. But they won't be as simple as you'd like them to be."

"How so?" asked Pat.

"In this class, there will be very few questions that can be answered with a simple yes or no. It'll rarely be as simple as right or wrong. In our world, there are many, many shades of gray."

Janet clicked a few more buttons on her computer. She picked up the small Bluetooth remote and smiled. "So we've got some tough questions to answer. But that doesn't mean we can't have a little fun along the way. As Cindy figured out last night, I'm married to the movie guy, Thomas Austin."

She held up the remote and pointed it at the screen behind her.

"My husband spends hours scouring movies, TV shows, and the Internet for ideas and information that we might use or learn from. One day he happened across a movie from the 1960s that might give us a start in figuring out whether or not what we do is right or wrong." She paused. "So what is a spy? Let's put that question to the master spy novelist John le Carré and one of my favorite movie stars, Richard Burton." She turned toward the screen. "Help us out Richard."

Janet clicked a button on her remote. The lights dimmed, and Richard

Burton's face filled the screen in black and white.

"What the hell do you think spies are? Moral philosophers measuring everything they do against the word of God or Karl Marx? They're not! They're just a bunch of seedy, squalid bastards like me. Little men, drunkards, queers, hen-pecked husbands, civil servants playing cowboys and indians to brighten their rotten little lives. Do you think they sit like monks in a cell, balancing right against wrong?"

Janet clicked the remote. The lights came up, and she looked over her class.

"So we're a bunch of seedy, squalid bastards?" asked Pat.

"Not quite." Janet smiled.

"What's that from?" said Cindy.

"The Spy Who Came in from the Cold."

"So, is this the class where we sit like monks in a cell balancing right against wrong?" asked Cindy.

"No. This is the class where we decide whether or not you have the chops to carry out an order to go out and kill someone in cold blood. Balancing right from wrong is about a mile above your pay grade."

"Whose job is it, then?" asked Cindy.

"A special council here at The Castle we called The Five," said Janet.

"What, what? A secret group within a secret group," said Cindy. "You people are fucking amazing."

"Why is that?" asked Janet.

"Don't you think you all have a few too many secrets around here? What's next? Secret handshakes and rituals with animal sacrifices?"

"Nothing quite so dramatic," said Janet. "But I would like to ask you to show a little more respect for the cause to which hundreds of people have dedicated their lives."

"Respect? Secret groups within a secret groups? The Five? Cold-blooded murder? And let's not forget your kinky little welcoming party. I think respect might be a little hard to come by."

"Then perhaps just a bit of restraint until you get all the facts so you might make an informed decision." Janet spoke forcefully.

"I think I've already proved to you lot how good I am in restraints," said Cindy.

Pat looked down and laughed. Charlie looked up at the ceiling. Léa cracked a sly smile.

Janet took a deep breath. She shook her head from side to side and breathed again. Still looking down, she spoke slowly, but with total conviction.

"There's no way you could know this, but I had almost the exact questions you have when I first came here." She looked up. "You may not believe it, but I actually sympathize with how you feel. I really do."

She looked at each of the students.

"I was just as mad as you are. But one thing was different. I wasn't so blatantly disrespectful. Maybe it was because I was brought up in a different time."

She locked her gaze on Cindy.

"You and I are a lot alike. But I'm clearly smarter because I waited until I had all the facts before I made up my mind. You, on the other hand, seem to be going out of your way to piss people off."

"Well maybe if—"

"Maybe if you would just shut the fuck up, you might learn something, as opposed to proving to all of us what a horse's ass you are. You're not talking to a bunch of squalid, seedy bastards playing cowboys and indians to brighten their rotten little lives, here."

Janet took a deep breath.

"Who do you think makes clinically insane dictators stand down when they get their hands on a dirty bomb? Who do you think saved this squalid little world from the brink of nuclear war? Not just during the Cuban Missile Crisis, but repeatedly when fat old men were posturing in the halls of ineffective governments. Men with big egos, small brains, pathetically small dicks and even smaller balls."

Charlie and Pat looked down and smirked. Léa's sly smile grew larger. Cindy looked directly into Janet's eyes.

Janet reached into her briefcase and pulled out a much older model of the same gun the four students had received the day before. She held the gun to one side. With her other hand, she pulled back the slide and snapped a fresh bullet into the chamber.

"And who do you think had the balls to stand up to a cruel, frightening, and dangerous criminal with only her wits and her nine millimeter loaded with just two rounds in the clip?"

Janet paused to look at each of her students. The lecture was going just as she'd planned.

"Governments have rules. Police have rules. And yes, even we have rules. But someone has to stand up to the certifiable maniacs who think nothing of ruining countless lives and bringing our world to the brink of utter destruction."

She looked straight at Cindy.

"You're not in the company of crooks or murderers or seedy bastards playing cowboys and indians. You're in the company of the smartest people in the world. The bravest people in the world. The people who cared enough to make sure the world was still around for you to be born into." Janet watched Cindy shrink back. "And some of us did it with nothing more than a gun loaded with two bullets."

She stuffed the pistol and her laptop into her black briefcase.

"People go their whole lives dreaming, hoping, and praying that they, one day, might find themselves in a position to actually make a difference." Janet walked toward the door. "You have been given the extraordinary opportunity to make a difference in this nasty old world." With her hand on the doorknob, she said, "And I'll thank you, Miss Martin, to not treat us like criminals. At least until you've had the chance to learn who and what we are. Then you might make an actual, informed decision."

Janet nodded her head once.

"Class dismissed." The door closed behind her.

They all stared at the closed door in silence.

Outside, Janet took a deep breath and closed here eyes. A few moments later, she looked back at the classroom, smiled, and walked away.

CHAPTER 29 - SPY SEX INTERRUPTED

The Same Classroom, 1:30 p.m.

Cindy, Charlie, Léa, and Pat arrived in the small classroom at precisely 1:30. After only a day and a half, they were getting good at arriving exactly on time.

Even Cindy was getting with the program. Since the morning class with Janet Austin, she seemed to have had a change of heart. She was clearly hungover, but she'd set her anger aside.

Then again, the four of them had other motivations for arriving at their afternoon class exactly on time.

"Welcome to Spy Sex," said Thomas Austin. "I see you're all in your places with bright, shiny faces."

Something's not right about this, thought Léa.

Thomas Austin was way too cheerful, and the students were way too excited. Léa didn't use much brain power to decide that they were about to get a bucket of cold water splashed in their faces.

"Nothing like a class with sex in the title to get the old blood flowing, is there?" Thomas smiled.

Charlie and Pat looked at each other with big smiles on their faces. Cindy wore a mask of serious determination. As for Léa, she always looked the same. She always appeared to be in control and always looking great doing it.

She'll be our most effective agent of all time, thought Thomas.

"Ready to have some fun?" He reached for a remote and hit the play button. The lights dimmed, and the screen glowed.

Noomi Repace screamed through the gag in her mouth. She had just been handcuffed to the bed in *The Girl with the Dragon Tattoo*. Thomas studied his class as they watched the frighteningly realistic rape scene from the 2009 Swedish movie.

The scene was intentionally uncomfortable, and it clearly had the desired effect on Charlie and Pat. Cindy stared blankly. Léa's eyes never wavered from the screen, but Thomas could tell that she was bothered, too.

As the scene ended, the lights came up.

"Not what you were expecting, was it?" said Thomas.

"No." Charlie looked down at his hands.

"Let's try another one."

The screen played the same scene from the 2011 remake. This time, Rooney Mara screamed through the gag.

Charlie and Pat looked even more uncomfortable. Cindy looked away. Léa set her jaw and dropped her chin, but she never let her eyes leave the screen. When it was over, the lights rose again.

"That's nothing," said Thomas. "You know the actor, Yorick van Wageningen, who played the rapist, was so upset after doing that scene that he spent the next day in his hotel room crying."

The students shifted uncomfortably.

"So what's the point?" asked Pat.

"The point is that you'll be going out into a very dangerous world. You'll be dealing with dangerous, sick people." Thomas pointed to the screen. "People who would think that what you just saw was child's play. This class is about helping you to endure that ... and to not let it kill you."

"How do you teach someone to survive that?" asked Cindy softly.

"By reminding you of what Lisbeth Salander did to the rapist," he said. "If you go out there, there is a chance you'll get caught. And if you get caught, some pretty ugly things will probably happen to you. But if you keep your head and get lucky, you will not only survive, but you will get the chance for payback. That's what'll help keep you alive. The chance for payback."

"My father taught me that only a fool seeks revenge," said Léa.

"It's a fine line. You have to learn the difference between revenge and payback."

As Thomas said the word *payback*, Léa's neck began tingling again. Then the classroom door quietly opened. Alan Dennis and Tara Wells stood in the back of the classroom.

"Ready?" asked Thomas.

"We are." Alan nodded toward Léa.

"Miss Taylor. Class is over for you. Gather your things, and go with them," said Thomas.

Léa picked up her backpack, with a glance at Thomas Austin.

"It's okay, Léa," he said. "You're not in trouble. Off you go."

Léa joined Alan and Tara at the back door. Alan spoke to the other three, still in their seats. "A year ago, we brought your friend Miss Wells into our organization because of a computer crisis. That crisis has just gotten a whole lot worse, and your friends, here, are going to try and stop it." He paused. "Sometimes new people have to grow up faster than we'd prefer. Right, Thomas?"

"Right, sir."

"Come along, you two," said Alan. "I'm afraid we need you to help us save the world."

PART 4: THE UPPSALA MISSION

CHAPTER 30 - THE TRAIN TO PARIS

Seat 211-A, The Next Day

Léa settled into her seat as the train pulled out of London St Pancras station. In a little over two hours, she would arrive at Paris Gare du Nord station. The Eurostar "Chunnel" train picked up speed as the countryside passed by.

Léa blinked a few times and rolled her eyes up and down, trying to adjust her new contact lenses. Her vision was perfect, and she didn't need contacts. But the irritating chunks of plastic were a necessary evil—tools of the trade.

The countryside became a blur as the train's speed maxed out at ninety miles per hour. Léa's hand rested gently on her new backpack, identical to the one her father had given her years ago. But along with the secret compartment for her gun, this new backpack contained other amazing secrets, some buried deep in hidden compartments and some in plain sight.

Amazing, thought Lea as she ran her fingers over the backpack's handle.

Almost as soon as the train reached full speed, it began to slow down. Léa looked up at the electronic sign in the cabin and saw they were approaching the last station before the train began its journey under the English Channel.

The train stopped, and new passengers filled the remaining seats before the doors closed, and the train began rolling.

An older woman eyed the seat next to Léa. "Would you mind, dear? There's only one other free seat and, well ..."

She nodded in the direction of the only other empty seat, a few rows behind Léa and on the other side of the car.

"Please," Léa said, moving her backpack off the seat beside her.

"Thank you, dear."

The woman stuffed her bags on the overhead shelf and turned to sit down, shooting a nasty look at the object of her disapproval.

"Kids these days," she said.

She put on her reading glasses and pulled out a musty old paperback. Léa glanced back toward the empty seat and turned to look out the window, a slight smile on one corner of her mouth.

Tara's having way too much fun.

The heavy metal neck and wrist cuffs had reappeared, along with the tattoos, the black leather pants, the black boots, and the bizarre hair. Her black leather motorcycle jacket was zipped halfway, making it obvious that Tara was wearing nothing underneath. Bad News Girl was back.

Léa tilted her head toward Tara. Sure enough, she could hear Tara's Bose headphones throbbing to the pulse of some obscure metal band.

Léa reached for her iPhone and tapped out a message.

Having fun playing bad girl?

A reply arrived a few moments later.

You know it!

You're going to go deaf.

Not a chance. I'm wearing ear plugs!

Léa shook her head in amazement.

You're having way too much fun.

No rules against having fun.

I'll remember that.

The lights in the cabin blazed on as the train entered the tunnel under the English Channel and plunged into complete darkness. The train headed downhill, picking up speed.. The twenty-mile tunnel would drop over two hundred fifty feet below the Channel before emerging in Calais, France.

Léa's phone buzzed.

Have you checked in lately?

Not since this morning.

Now might be a good time.

Léa reached into her backpack for her Mac. She powered it up and signed on to the train's WiFi. Léa launched the mail program, and, just as expected, over twenty messages appeared in her junk mail folder.

Yesterday, Léa's spam folder had been set to delete automatically. Now she was using the universal annoyance to secretly and securely check in with The Castle.

Léa scanned the spam messages, finding pretty much what she had expected—offers for great new credit cards, spray-on suntans, and even a few ways to buy illegal drugs. Near the bottom of the list, a message offered her fifty percent off her first order of Tea Off, a new diet tea.

Her slight, sly smile appeared as she opened the message. There was very little text so Léa clicked *Load Remote Content*. About ten pictures appeared, with testimonials of happy customers who loved Tea Off. There were several *Buy Now* buttons and an unsubscribe button at the bottom.

As she scanned the testimonials, Léa found the hidden message she was looking for.

Target remains: UPPSALA.
Continue as planned.

Anyone looking over Léa's shoulder would have seen nothing but the happy customer's testimonial for Tea Off. But Léa was able to see the message hidden in the picture.

She scrolled down and clicked the unsubscribe button. To anyone spying on Léa, she was just removing her name from a spam list. In actuality, clicking unsubscribe sent a message back to The Castle, letting them know the mission was proceeding on schedule.

Léa snapped her laptop shut. She watched the passing gray walls of the tunnel and thought about the mission. It was simple. Locate and neutralize a rogue Growler who had been launching a series of cyber-attacks against The Castle.

Recently, the attacks mysteriously stopped, but The Castle's experts didn't take long to figure out why. About the same time, someone began trying to hack their way into transportation systems around the EU.

The hacks began with a series of minor incidents on trains leaving Uppsala in Sweden. Several switches mysteriously flipped, sending trains in wrong directions. Then a train from Belgium to Paris was switched onto a track with a high-speed train traveling in the opposite direction.

Soon after the head-on collision, Léa was pulled out of her second day of Spy School.

CHAPTER 31 - MISSION BRIEFING

Commander Dennis's Office, The Day Before

"If you're still upset that Miss Wells was pulled into our little den of thieves a year before you," said Alan, "now's your chance for some payback."

Léa and Tara sat in the soft chairs across from his oak desk. This was a different office than the one where Léa had first met him.

Old-world, wooden paneling covered the stone walls, and the carpet was deep and plush. Corner lamps lit the room with a soft glow, and a single, green-shaded lamp illuminated the desk.

Alan Dennis scooped up a few file folders and a TV remote and sat on the overstuffed couch against the wall. He gauged Léa's reaction to his offer of payback.

She shrugged. "I'll pass."

"May I ask why?" said Alan.

"My dad taught me that only a fool seeks revenge."

"That's one of our core values. I can see your father trained you well."

"My father 'trained' me well?"

Léa leaned back and glanced between Tara and Alan. "Did you guys set up me, Tara, and our friends with our families here in Stromness?"

"Yes. But you both have suspected that for a long time, and this is not the meeting to discuss that."

Tara's eyes were pointed like lasers at Alan. "I've been waiting for over a year to have that conversation. So I guess we can wait a little longer."

"She's been waiting for you to join us for that conversation," said Alan to Léa.

"Our lack of family resemblances has come up more than a few times over the years," said Léa.

"And we do have some of the answers you're looking for," said Alan. "But time is running out, and we must focus on the mission at hand."

Léa and Tara looked at each other. Alan watched the nonverbal communication that was only possible between best friends. Still looking at Tara, Léa gave Alan the answer he was looking for.

"Sure. Why not? We can hold off a little longer."

"Thank you." Alan opened a file and flipped on one of the big LCD screens that lined the office walls.

"Meet Perry Drilling," said Alan as a face appeared on the screen. "He was recruited in 1990 and, at the time, was considered to be the best at breaking and entering computers hooked to a little novelty called the Internet." He looked up at Léa and Tara and peered at them over his reading glasses. "I believe you kids call them hackers."

"Depends on what they're doing," said Tara.

"Really?" asked Alan.

"Hackers just want to break and enter," said Léa.

"Crackers are the people who not only break and enter," said Tara, "but try to do as much damage as they can."

"Ah, thank you. You learn something new every day," said Alan.

There was a knock at the door, and Thomas Austin stuck his head in the office.

"Ready for us?" he asked.

"Yes, yes. Come on in. We're just getting started."

Dick Boxx followed Thomas, along with Janet Austin and a woman dressed in blue medical scrubs. She carried a stainless steel tray covered with a white towel.

Alan turned his attention back to the file. "Back then, the world of computer security was in its infancy. With very few exceptions, no one here had any idea what Perry did. Computers in those days were vastly different from what you kids have today."

Another knock. The door opened, and David McNally entered carrying a backpack similar to Léa's.

"Sorry I'm late." He held up the pack. "Forgot to bring this."

"Good, good." Alan tossed the remote to McNally. "It's your op so you should probably take over the meeting."

"Right." David pointed to the screen. "This guy is turning out to be bad news."

He clicked a button on the remote, and the face was replaced by news coverage of a fatal train crash. "You may had heard about this head-on train crash over on the Continent. We think he was behind it and a host of other incidents. Up till now, he hasn't killed anyone. I guess he's stepping up his game."

"He seemed content to try to hack The Castle's network and cause as much trouble for us as he could," said Thomas Austin. "But this ..."

"I'm sorry. How are two college girls going to stop somebody who's doing that?" Léa pointed to the screen. "Much less find him?"

"Way back in 1990, we found him at the computer school in Uppsala," said Thomas. "Most of the first incidents were on trains going in and out of Uppsala. So we're guessing he may have gone underground in familiar territory."

"You both speak fluent computer-ese, you both have good survival instincts, and you've got that best friends thing going for you," said Janet.

"Plus, the target—er, Perry has never seen either of you before. He'll be looking for one of us. So you two just might be able to get close," said Thomas.

"And what exactly do we do when we get close?" asked Léa.

Alan looked down at his shoes. He nodded once in determination and looked up. "Give him one chance to accompany you back here to The Castle, or kill him."

A cold silence descended over the room.

Léa looked at Janet Austin. "Just like you said in class today," she said quietly.

"Just like I said in class."

Léa looked down, then at Tara. "Doesn't get much clearer than that."

The video of the latest train crash still played on the screen, and Perry Drilling's face looked up at Léa from photos spilling out of the open file folder.

Léa rested her hand on the zipper of her backpack. She felt the form of the small gun inside. In an instant, her past, present, and future came into focus.

"My mum, my dad, and you. My whole life has been training me up to become an ..." her voice trailed off.

The room remained silent. Léa sniffed once, then she cleared the cobwebs.

"You've all been training me to be an assassin."

"Not just an assassin. But, please. May we go over all that later?" Alan looked at his watch. "Right now we need to finish this briefing and get you two on your way."

Léa watched the screen as rescuers pulled bodies out of the wreckage. Her mind was racing. A week ago, she had been a graduate student. She had ran, played volleyball, and competed in long-distance bicycle races. Her biggest decision had been whether to go for her PhD.

Now, she was sitting with people who expected her to kill another human being. Granted, this human was pretty nasty. Her past, present, and future remained in clear focus. There was no escaping the conclusion. Léa and Tara were the logical choices for the mission.

"Okay," she said.

Alan spoke to the woman in medical scrubs. "Jenny, why don't you help Léa with her new contact lenses."

Tara smiled at her friend. *Time to clear some cobwebs.*

163

The woman uncovered the tray, revealing contact lenses, solutions, and cases. Léa closed her eyes and shook her head sharply.

"So predictable," said Tara under her breath.

Léa shot Tara a sideways glance and looked back to the contacts.

"I have twenty-twenty vision. What are they for?"

"It's a nifty little way for you to communicate with us while you're out in the field," said Alan. "It's one of Miss Wells' first contributions."

Léa turned to Tara. "You?"

"I had a lot of help from Mr. Austin," said Tara. "But like he said, it's a 'nifty' way for us to communicate."

"Okay, I'll bite. How does it work?"

No one spoke. Finally, Alan told Tara, "Go on, it was your idea."

"Okay," she said. "What's in practically everyone's computer that everyone overlooks?"

Léa thought for a moment, then shook her head. "I give up."

Tara pointed at the remote. "May I?"

McNally tossed her the remote. Tara stood up and took the floor.

"Yeah, it's spam. Just like this." She clicked the remote.

Several examples of spam email popped up on the screen, ridiculous messages that overpopulate everyone's inboxes. At the top of each message were buttons reading *Not Junk*, and all the pictures were missing.

"Typical spam, right?" said Tara.

"Right," said Léa.

Tara clicked the remote, and a single message filled the screen. The email advertised something called Tea Off. Once Tara clicked *Load Images*, pictures of young, skinny girls smiling and holding up boxes of tea appeared on the screen.

"You've seen crap like this before," said Tara. "It's basically dieters' tea, and it's all over the place."

"Yeah," said Léa.

"Except this brand and message is from us." Tara scrolled down. "See anything wrong with this?"

Léa looked carefully at the screen. A thin girl in a bikini smiled for the camera and held a box of tea bags. Beside the picture were several lines about why the girl loved Tea Off and never started a day without it.

"Can't see anything aside from her bad spray tan," said Léa.

"Right." Tara smiled and motioned to Jenny.

"Have you ever worn contact lenses before?" asked the woman.

"I may have just said something about twenty-twenty vision."

"Right. Sorry. Well, it's not hard to learn. But it'll speed things up if you let me put them in the first time."

"Okay."

Léa really didn't want anyone shoving bits of plastic into her eyes. But she was curious to learn Tara's new secret communication trick.

Having contacts put in wasn't a fun experience, but once they were in place, Léa looked at the screen, and a big smile appeared on her face. "Awesome."

"It's pretty simple," said Tara. "One image in the spam email has the secret message. The text is written in a color you can only see while wearing these contacts."

The message read, *If this were easy, everyone would do it.*

Tears streamed down Léa's face from the contact lenses. She gently wiped her eyes and looked at Jenny. "It's great. But it's going to take some time before I'm used to these things."

"Start by wearing them a few hours at a time to begin with. Wear them longer and longer. If I can get used to them, anyone can," said Jenny.

"Great, thanks." She blinked her eyes and nodded toward the backpack. "That looks a lot like mine."

"It's an exact match," said David. "But this one has a few new features that you might find useful."

"May I?" she asked, reaching for the bag.

David tossed it to Léa. She unzipped a few pockets, including the secret gun pocket.

"Looks about the same," she said.

"Except that the secret pocket is lined with a special material that'll hide your gun from an airport X-ray machine," said Thomas.

Léa examined the pocket more closely. "I can't see any difference."

"You're not supposed to. Now take a look at the top grip," said Thomas.

The handle stitched into the top of the backpack looked almost exactly like the grip on her bag, except one seam wasn't stitched correctly. Léa tugged on it, and some Velcro unzipped. Two small metal tubes popped out.

"Spare ammo?" she asked.

"Good guess. Those will fit eight nine-millimeter slugs, and since they're in a metal grip, no one will suspect you've got bullets in there," said David.

"Nice." She stuffed the tubes back in the grip and sealed the Velcro around it. "Anything else?"

"Notice anything special about the zippers?" Thomas asked.

Léa inspected all the zippers and noticed two of them were different. She was able to unhook a metal zipper from the track and held it up to her still-watery eyes.

"A handcuff key?"

"Right, again. If you suspect you're about to be taken prisoner, just unhook one of those, and hide it somewhere," said Thomas.

"Not bad." Léa replaced the key. "What else?"

"Have a look at the shoulder straps," Thomas suggested.

An extra layer of cloth covered the strap. Once again, she found a piece of the fabric that didn't seem to be stitched. Giving it a gentle tug, the whole outside of the shoulder strap peeled away to reveal a small throwing knife.

"Careful," said Jenny. "That's about as sharp as a surgical scalpel."

"Good to know." Léa examined the knife and the blade. After gripping it several ways, she placed it back in the small sheath and closed the Velcro cover. "I'm guessing the knives are protected the same way the gun is?"

"Same stuff," said Thomas. "It looks like thicker material to an X-ray machine."

"Wait a minute. What about a metal detector?"

"They only run people through a metal detector. Bags get X-rayed," said Thomas.

"Right. Anything else?"

"There are a few more hidden compartments that I'm sure you'll find. But that's about it."

"Okay." Léa set the backpack by her older pack. "So how do we find your bad guy?"

"Like we said, we think he's gone back to his old school in Uppsala," said David. "From there, he's probably gone underground in the college computer culture."

"Maybe." Léa pointed to the folder on the coffee table. "Do you mind?"

"Sure." Alan slid the folder toward Léa.

She paged through the file, set a few items aside, and looked at Tara. "So this guy was supposed to be the nineties version of us, right?"

"Yeah, I guess," said David.

"Well, if I decided to go rogue, I certainly wouldn't go back to the very place where I was recruited."

"So where would you go?" Alan asked.

"Anywhere but Sweden," said Léa.

"But everything seems to be coming from Uppsala," said Thomas.

"Yeah, but if this guy has any brains at all, he's halfway around the world making it look like he's back at his old stomping ground," said Léa.

"We have on-the-ground intel placing him there less than a week ago," said David.

Léa nodded toward Tara. "You've seen what she can do with an off-the-shelf Mac and a few cheap apps. Give us twenty minutes, and we'll come up with 'intel' making it look like you've been prowling around Uppsala, too."

Tara looked down and smiled.

"So where do we look?" said Alan.

"Since you don't have much to go on, we start looking in Uppsala," said Léa.

Tara nodded. "Right now, it's the only starting place we have."

"Wait a minute. You just said he wasn't in Uppsala," said Thomas.

"But I didn't say we shouldn't start at the spot everything is pointing toward."

Tara mentally flinched. She could tell Léa was losing her patience. Any minute now, Léa would verbally body slam them against the wall.

"You've just shown us evidence that this guy has no problem killing several hundred people in cold blood," said Léa, "and you're sending a couple of grad-school girls after him with some pretty flimsy leads. So please tell me that you have better 'intel' than what you just showed us."

"I don't think I like your tone, Miss Taylor," said David.

"I don't care whether you like my 'tone' or not. Especially because all you've shown me is a little history on a guy who I think is probably smart enough to leave a trail of breadcrumbs for his old bosses to make them believe he's back reliving his college glory days."

Léa paused and took a deep breath. McNally started to speak, but Tara cut him off. "I've only had a year of training with you guys, and my best friend has been around less than a week. She just hit the nail on the head about your on-the-ground intel. So you won't mind if I toss a little of my own attitude your way, too."

Alan laughed. "Bravo, Miss Wells, and bravo, Miss Taylor."

"No intel is ever perfect," said David. "You figured that out in short order, and that's good. One thing, though. You both let yourselves get irritated, and that's not so good."

"But overall, they're assertive when they have to be," said Alan. "Brilliant and highly capable, too. I think we're in good hands."

McNally smiled. "Agreed."

Léa cleared the cobwebs, looked away from the group, and smiled. They had gotten her to make a wrong assumption. Basically, they had tricked her, and she hated it. That was a very important lesson that she planned to learn.

"You know what I like about you?" Alan asked.

"No, what?" Léa asked.

"You were clearly irritated with us, but you quickly decided to learn from it. You're smart enough to keep your temper in check."

"Wish I could do that," said Tara.

"Actually," said Alan, "we kind of like your attitude, temper, and sharp tongue."

"Well, most of us," David groused.

Alan checked his watch and stood. "We need to get you both on your way."

"I have all those files," said Thomas, "and our research on that trail of breadcrumbs you were talking about on this jump drive."

"Now, you two should change clothes and pick up some more equipment," said McNally. "You have a ferry and a train to catch."

"Come on. I can help you pack for your trip," said Janet.

As Tara and Léa got up to leave, Alan put a hand on each of their shoulders.

"You both have tremendous potential, and even though you're relatively new, you already have amazing survival skills." His voice became serious. "Two things. Nothing, and I mean absolutely nothing, is important enough for either of you two to get killed. Rule number one is live to fight another day."

"What's rule number two?" asked Léa.

"Rule number two is more of a suggestion," said Alan. "When you find yourself faced with a complicated problem, try to remember that the best solutions are the simplest solutions." He looked at Tara. "Got it?"

"Got it."

"And you?" he asked Léa.

"Got it."

"Then off you go," said Alan.

CHAPTER 32 - LÉA'S MORNING

A Safe House in Paris, 10:30 a.m.

Bright sunshine streamed through Léa's open window. Sounds of small boat motors drifted up from the Canal de l'Ourcq four stories below her. Léa heard a surprising number of voices for the early hour. She checked the clock on her iPhone.

10:30 a.m.

Not so early after all.

Léa cleared the cobwebs and bounced out of bed. After checking her backpack to make sure no one disturbed it while she slept, she dropped to the floor and started her morning workout.

One-minute plank.

One hundred bicycle crunches.

Her dumbbells were back in her room at The Castle so Léa rolled over and punched out twenty-five pushups.

Then she started the process over again. Another full-body plank, more bicycle crunches, and more pushups. When Léa finished that round, she started a third.

After the last set of pushups, Léa rolled onto her back. Breathing heavily, she felt her heart racing and her blood pounding through her veins. The workout only took ten minutes. But, as far as Léa was concerned, it was the only way to start the day.

After a few deep breaths, Léa jumped up and walked over to the dresser. As her breathing returned to normal, she checked herself in the mirror. Her workout only managed to generate a light coat of sweat on her skin, and her heart rate returned to normal almost immediately.

Léa smiled at the girl in the mirror. The girl smiled back.

A small carafe of water and a glass sat on the corner of the dresser. Léa filled the glass and approached the window. Sun streamed through the glass.

The window was a little high so Léa hooked a chair with her foot. She scooted it a few inches down the wall and used the seat as a step to sit in the open window.

In the Canal de l'Ourcq, a few small pleasure boats approached alongside a tour boat. A few cars lined the narrow lane bordering the canal. Except for the boats, not much moved. Above her, a middle-aged man in the building across the canal was checking her out.

Enjoy the view, Léa thought and looked away.

But her attention quickly returned to the window. The man's wife appeared and slapped him on the back of his head. As he walked away, the woman leaned out the window and shouted across the canal.

"Mettez des vêtements que vous salope!"

Léa's French was a little rusty, but after running through the words a few times, Léa smiled and waved to the woman. She flipped Léa the international sign of disapproval and angrily closed the curtains.

Léa continued enjoying the morning sunshine as she thought back to her and Tara's conversation over that great bottle of wine.

A few days ago, Cindy had all but called her a slut. The woman across the canal *had* just call her a slut.

Léa took a sip of water and looked across the canal. The window was open, and the curtain moved with the morning breeze. Léa heard angry voices from inside. Even with her rusty French, she knew they were discussing Léa, her lack of attire, and the man's enjoyment of the view.

Léa knew she'd caused their fight, but she didn't feel all that bad about it. She just wanted to enjoy the morning sunshine before leaving for the cloudy, cold north. Besides, she was in Paris. More than a few women and men here spent time sitting naked in windows.

Léa leaned out the window to see the side of the building. Below her, a few arms and legs were catching some sun. As Léa looked down, the man in the room below looked up at her. He was dressed the same way she was.

"Bonjour," he said.

"Bonjour," said Léa.

She cleared the cobwebs and looked back at the window across the canal.

"Whatever," she said out loud.

"Whatever?" said a voice behind her.

Léa turned casually and found a man standing by her door.

"I knocked, but no one answered," he said.

"Come on in." Léa smiled.

"I am Henrich Wilden. The morning supervisor."

He was dressed in a business suit and held a large, yellow envelope in one hand. He balanced a tray with coffee and fruit in the other. Léa didn't move from the window.

"As you can see," Henrich said, "you aren't our only guest who enjoys *bain de soleil dans une fenêtre.*"

"What's that, again?"

"Sunbathing in a window. It is common here in Paris."

"I may have caused a fight with our neighbors across the canal," said Léa.

"I wouldn't worry about them."

"Why not?"

"It is a, uh, a *maison de prostitution*," said Henrich.

Léa looked back at the curtained window. She dropped her head and laughed out loud.

"Un-flippin' believable," she mumbled.

"What is ... un-flippin' believable?" asked Henrich.

"Nothing. What have you got there?".

"Along with being told you like to begin your day *au naturel*, I was also told of your preference for Bailey's Irish Cream in your morning coffee."

"Perfect." Léa leapt off the windowsill and headed toward the tray. "Why didn't you tell me sooner?"

"And miss my chance to see you leaping through the air for your coffee?" Henrich smiled.

Léa laughed as she landed in front of Wilden, who offered her the tray. Four mini bottles of Bailey's rested next to the carafe of coffee.

"I brought extra for later today," said Henrich.

"This really is the perfect way to start the day." Léa dumped a mini bottle of Bailey's into the empty mug and then filled it with coffee from the carafe.

She closed her eyes and inhaled the aroma before enjoying her first sip. Léa opened her eyes and looked sideways at man, who still held the yellow envelope.

"What's in there?" she asked.

"A few more things you'll need," said Henrich as he held out the envelope.

Léa took another sip of her coffee before setting down the mug and taking the envelope from Henrich.

"As you were told on arriving last night, this hotel is a safe house for people like you."

"You mean Growlers?" said Léa casually.

"Yes. Although we generally try to avoid using that word outside The Castle."

"Got it."

"Along your love of Bailey's and your most charming personality traits, my briefing included the fact that you are new to the organization. So I am happy to help with any questions you may have."

"You're not French," said Léa.

"German."

171

"You said your name is Henrich. Henrich Wilden?"

"That is correct."

"Wilden. That's *wild*, right?"

The man nodded.

"Great name." smiled Léa.

"Merci," said Henrich. He gestured to the envelope. "You'll find three sets of passports with corresponding credit cards and a Baedeker travel guide of Europe."

Léa opened the envelope and dumped the contents on the bed. She picked up the travel guide and thumbed through it.

"As you know, we have a new technology using specially made contact lenses," he said. "Through the lenses, the maps in the book show places like this hotel in a unique color. Should you need a safe place to go, just look at your travel guide while wearing the contact lenses."

"Wow."

"We've been around for a while. We know how to help people such as yourself do your work in comparative safety."

Léa smiled. "Thanks."

"Not at all." Henrich reached into his pocket and pulled out an airline ticket. "You have four hours to finish your coffee, get dressed, and arrive at de Gaulle for your flight to Oslo. From there, you take the train to Uppsala."

"What about Tara?"

"She will be on the same plane and train, but you must not travel together," said Henrich.

"Oh."

"One more thing. Make sure your weapons are in the special pockets of your backpack before you go through the security checkpoint."

Léa glanced at her backpack and the black overnight bag she'd been given at The Castle.

"Got it," she said.

"Good. Once your train is in Sweden and you're a few stops away from Uppsala, you can remove them from the hidden pockets without risking detection by a security sweep."

"Okay." Léa looked over the passports, credit cards, and tickets. "Anything new on Perry Drilling?" she asked.

"I assume that's your target. But I don't know anything about your mission. Only that you're passing through my station on the way to Uppsala and that I'm supposed to make sure you have everything you need."

"Okay," said Léa.

She threw the papers on the bed and picked up her coffee. She took a sip and looked over the cup at Henrich.

"Where is Tara?"

"In her room. You can join her for breakfast. But remember, you must travel separately."

"Why?"

"In case one of you is spotted by the opposition, the other remains safe."

"Oh."

After a few moments of silence, Henrich walked to the door and left Léa alone.

She sat on the bed and looked through her passports. They all had different names, but the pictures were the same. She reached for the backpack and tugged at the open zipper. Peeking inside the hidden compartment, Léa saw her gun securely snapped in its holster.

The sun was still bright through the open window. The reality of where she was and where she was going struck Léa like a slap across the face. She looked at the mirror. The girl staring back appeared worried, almost frightened.

Léa looked down, then back up. The same worried girl stared back. She cleared the cobwebs and stood. What had she gotten herself into?

"Bloody hell," she whispered.

Léa collected the passports and credit cards and stuffed them in the pockets of her backpack. Léa realized that in less than three hours, things would get real. The girl in the mirror still looked worried.

"Not good."

She looked down at her toes.

"Get it together, now."

Léa took several deep breaths and slowly looked back at the mirror. This time, it wasn't frightened girl staring back at her. This time, a confident and determined woman appeared in the mirror.

"Better," said Léa.

CHAPTER 33 - TARA'S MORNING

Two Floors Down, 10:30 a.m.

Tara's Mac beeped like R2-D2 from *Star Wars*. She pulled the sheets over her head to block out the morning light.

Her computer continued to beep, and Tara slowly pulled down the sheet to reveal the tangled black hair covering her eyes.

The R2 beep was a special alert she had set up, and she had been dreading it. Tara took a deep breath and opened one eye. She glanced at the laptop screen, and her eye narrowed angrily.

"Really?" she said under her breath.

Tara lifted herself onto her elbow and brushed the hair from her face, tugging the laptop onto the bed. She shook her head at the picture on the screen.

"How can you be so fucking smart and so fucking stupid at the same time," she hissed.

The image showed Léa sitting in the window of her room and was spreading across the internet in record time. Tara felt her blood begin to boil as she reached for her phone and texted Léa.

ARE YOU FUCKING CRAZY?

Before hitting *send*, Tara looked back at the picture. Clearly, Léa had no idea someone was snapping her picture. Léa was just being Léa.

Still holding her phone, Tara fell back onto her pillow and stared at the ceiling. She got her temper under control and reread the unsent message.

Didn't Léa realize this wasn't a game? Didn't she remember they were going after someone who just killed over three hundred people?

With her finger hovering over the send button, glanced again at the photo of Léa. She laughed out loud, deleted the message, and tossed her phone on the bed.

Of course Léa knew this wasn't a game. She was just being herself.

Someday Léa being Léa would work to their advantage.

This photo was the kind of thing that could easily cost them the mission and maybe even their lives. Tara wasn't being paranoid either. She was convinced the target already knew that someone from The Castle was coming.

The target, Perry Drilling, was the computer genius at The Castle whom Tara had replaced. If she ever decided to disappear, she would leave back doors into the computer system. Even though she had already found a few, Tara knew that Perry Drilling had left more back doors than she had found.

Worse, Tara suspected that this guy knew about her and possibly about Léa, too.

That picture of Léa would prove to Perry Drilling that Alan Dennis had sent his new computer expert and her friend after him.

An hour before the mission briefing in Alan Dennis's wood-paneled office, Tara had taken part in a heated exchange on that very subject.

"Just how fucking stupid can you guys be?" Tara shouted.

"We generally don't put up with language like that here at The Castle," David McNally said.

"And definitely not in the director's office." Thomas Austin smiled at her.

"I don't give a shit whether it's in The Castle or in the director's office or in the queen's throne room. This isn't just a bad idea. It's stupid and fucking reckless." Tara's eyes were on fire.

"That's enough!" shouted David.

Tara slumped back into the overstuffed couch and closed her eyes. She shook her head and looked at Alan Dennis. As calmly and patiently as she could, Tara tried to explain again.

"This is exactly what I was most afraid of when you brought me in last year. When it comes to computers and networks, Perry Drilling isn't stupid. In fact, he's pretty fucking brilliant. But you guys are anything but brilliant. Simply changing your passwords after he disappeared was in no way enough to keep him out."

"You're not here to explain the facts of life, Miss Wells," David said forcefully. "This is a mission briefing, and you're here to listen to your orders and say, 'Yes, sir.'"

Alan Dennis held up his hand and smiled at McNally. "Yes, of course. But I want to hear what she has to say."

Tara glared at McNally for a second, then looked around the room, outfitted with a desk, tables, lamps, a bookshelf, and several TV monitors.

"Nice office," she said with a rare smile.

"What has that got to do with anything?" David was still clearly irritated.

Alan Dennis smiled and held his hand up again.

"I've been here a year," said Tara. "You brought me in to take over your computer network when Perry Drilling disappeared." She spread her hands, pointing at the walls. "This whole place—this castle—has lots of secrets, and all those secrets are written down somewhere. They're not only on paper in a file. They're also in an electronic file on a computer. And that computer is hooked to your network." Tara paused. "You guys put everything on your computers, and I'm sure you password-protect everything."

"We do," said Alan.

Tara looked at McNally. "Would you be surprised that I know you think I'm too angry, too reckless, and too much of a security risk to have even been recruited? I read your private memos about me to Commander Dennis. And that's not all I've read." Tara looked back at Alan. "That bookshelf. Would you be surprised that I know you press your foot against the baseboard on the left to open the hidden door leading to a submarine pen?" Tara smiled.

McNally stood up and pulled handcuffs from his belt. "I told you she was dangerous! She knows way too much and needs to be locked down immediately."

"Now just take it easy," said Alan.

"Sir. She's way beyond the line and has to be locked down."

"No, she doesn't," Alan said. "Put those silly things away. Sit down, David, please."

McNally glared at Tara. She flashed another rare smile.

"I won't ask you again," said Alan quietly.

McNally sat down, and Tara looked back to Alan. "If I know what's in your memos," she said. "If I know about your submarines, your secret passages, and, yes, even your nukes. So does Perry Drilling." She looked at McNally. "You wrote the mission briefing on your desktop in your office, and that means two things."

"What?" said McNally curtly.

"That means Perry Drilling knows you're planning to send me and Léa after him."

"And the other thing?" said McNally.

"I agree with you that it's a mistake to send Léa."

"Why is that?" asked Alan.

Tara thumbed her iPhone, checking the time.

"Because in less than twenty minutes, you're scheduled to pull her out of her first week of Spy School. She has no idea what's out there or how to deal with it." Tara dropped her gaze. "Léa is closer than family to me. This man is a killer with a serious axe to grind against you and everyone here at The Castle. I'm new, too. I can't kill him while I'm trying to protect someone I'm emotionally attached to. Especially someone with no skills."

McNally nodded triumphantly. "Just like I said."

Tara shot him a fiery look. "If it weren't for you, fuck-head, we wouldn't be in this situation. It was you who drove him away."

"That's out of line," said McNally.

Tara leaned forward and clinched her fists. "Is it? You're nothing more than a fucking bully. You humiliated him repeatedly. You called him foul names at the pub, including 'pussy.' By the way, I happen to have one, and this pussy has already kicked your flabby ass once. I'll happily do so again, if for no other reason than I fucking hate bullies."

Thomas Austin turned his head and laughed.

"And that's not just my opinion either. It's in reports and memos filed by everyone here." She looked at Alan. "It's all over your internal network. If I can read it, make no mistake, Drilling has read it." Tara sat back and stared at the floor. "He already knows I'm coming."

"She's right, you know," said Thomas. "About everything."

Alan sat back in his chair. "You're right, Thomas, and so are you, Miss Wells. Now we need to do what we do best. Let's move beyond this disagreement and get around him."

Alan looked up at the painting of Sir Richard hanging on the wall. He put his fingers together and thought for a few minutes, then made his decision.

"One of the important lessons I learned from Sir Richard before his untimely death was to outthink the enemy. It's what he saw in those crazy, dandruff-plagued, socially inept geniuses who schemed against the Germans and won the war all those years ago. It's why we're here now. In the old days," he said to Tara, "it's what they called 'corkscrew thinking,' and I hope it's something you pick up."

Tara paid close attention. Thomas hung on Alan's every word. Even David, who was still clearly irritated, paid attention.

"So Perry knows we're coming," said Alan, "and he knows we're probably sending Miss Wells and Miss Taylor. But I'm also guessing he knows we know." Alan smiled at McNally. "Your plan is a good one. Despite your misgivings, I'm convinced both Miss Wells and Miss Taylor can handle themselves. So instead of doing what Mr. Drilling expects us to do, let's surprise him and stick with the plan."

Tara interrupted. "But Léa—"

"Léa can handle not only herself," said Alan," but anything else that comes her way. I'm convinced she's just the backup you'll need."

"You mean she has the skills to hit whatever she's shooting at," said Tara.

"That too." Alan checked his watch and spoke to Thomas. "You have a class I'm about to interrupt. Get things going for us."

"Right-O," said Thomas as he got up to leave.

"Thomas," said Alan.

"Sir?"

"Get right to some shocking stuff. Scare them a bit."

"Yes sir." Thomas smiled as he left the room.

"Listen carefully, you two," said Alan. "It's clear that you don't like each other." He turned to David. "I know you have good reason to hate her."

He looked down at the knee David had been rubbing.

"And I know you're still pretty upset about your introduction to this place, Tara. But all that was a year ago, and I must ask you both to set your past aside. You two have things you can learn from each other. You can help each other." Alan looked at McNally. "You've been in the line of fire." He nodded to Tara. "She's heading directly into that line. Please, David, help her and her friend to come back."

McNally hesitated and looked down at his knee. After a few moments, he nodded once.

"My pleasure, sir. I can make this work."

"Good. Let's go get Miss Taylor," said Alan.

The next morning lying in her bed in a safe house in Paris, Tara stared at the ceiling and remembered David McNally putting their angry past behind him. He had given her a second mission briefing with information she found truly priceless. He'd told her how he thought the mission would unfold and had come up with several alternatives. Then he'd told her not only how Léa might help, but also how Tara could protect her.

Tara tossed off the bed sheet and sat up. She bounced herself to the side of the bed and swung her bare feet to the wood floor, immediately dropping down for pushups.

Just like her best friend, Tara had been doing a quick workout every morning for years. Unlike her best friend, Tara was wearing her favorite black tee-shirt and shorts.

As Tara worked up her heart rate, another rare smile appeared on her face.

Tara knew she and Léa would be okay.

CHAPTER 34 - BREAKFAST

The Paris Safe House, 11 a.m.

Léa and Tara were sitting at a small table in Tara's room. Heinrich Wilden had wheeled in a cart loaded with coffee, fruit, and croissants. Before leaving, he'd reached into his pocket for a few more mini bottles of Bailey's.

"Here are a few extras for your trip." He'd smiled and headed for the door. "You have an hour before you need to leave, Miss Wells."

"I thought we had four hours," Léa had said.

"We have four hours before the flight," Tara had explained, "but I leave in an hour to catch the train to the airport. You'll take a taxi in about ninety minutes."

"Oh."

Léa dumped a mini bottle of Bailey's in her coffee and took a sip. They ate in silence for a few minutes when Tara opened her laptop and showed Léa the picture that was spreading across the Internet.

"It's not my good side," said Léa looking cautiously up at her best friend.

When Tara didn't respond to Léa's 'good side' comment, Léa looked down at her coffee. She swirled the liquid around in the mug a few times and set it down.

"This isn't good, is it?"

"On the surface," said Tara.

Léa leaned back. "Okay, I'll bite. How is not so bad?"

Tara smiled and began to explain. "One of the things you're going to learn about the The Castle is that they love it when you turn something bad into something good."

Léa placed her elbows on the table. She leaned forward and rested her chin in one hand. "Okay, professor. Tell me how we're going to turn this into something good."

Tara pointed at the picture of Léa on her laptop screen and began tapping on the keyboard. When she was done, she spun the laptop so Léa could see and leaned back in her chair with a rare, satisfied smile.

The screen showed two identical pictures of Léa side by side. Léa reached over and tapped the laptop keys. She called up the image properties, which showed the only difference between the images was that one file was slightly bigger. Léa looked up and smiled.

"The way I figure it," Tara said, "Perry Drilling knows we're coming. After all, he ran The Castle's computers for over ten years. I'm convinced that he left more than a few back doors into the system so that he could check up on us. I'm also sure that he knows everything about both of us and that, most importantly, he knows we're coming." Tara pointed to the picture. "He's probably drooling over your Internet pinup right now."

"So how does that help us?"

"For the past year, I've been embedding subtle code in every file on The Castle's computers."

"Amaze me." Léa nodded to the laptop.

"Basically, it sends out a ping if you look at a Growler file outside of The Castle. We get a lot of pings from London, which I'm assuming is five and six."

Five and six?" asked Léa.

"M.I 5 and M.I.6," said Tara." We also get pings from Langley, Virginia in the US, along with Tokyo, Moscow, and Beijing."

"That would be the CIA and the intelligence services in China, Russia, and Japan."

"Right," Tara said. "But we also get more than a few pings from Uppsala."

"Uppsala."

"Sweden," said Tara.

"Where we're going." Léa smiled.

"Where we're going."

Léa ran this through her mind. Tara smiled as she watched Léa's wheels spinning.

"You've attached your pinger to my picture," she said.

"Yep."

"But the original picture is already in his computer," said Léa.

"I've uploaded my new picture to the mission files back at The Castle. I'm guessing it'll make its way to his computer soon."

"So any pings from my picture are likely coming from him. We'll know where he is," said Léa.

"That's what I'm hoping."

Léa tapped her knuckles on the table, leaned back in her chair, and smiled. "That'll work."

Tara pulled a small plastic box from her backpack. She tossed it at Léa, who snatched it out of the air. She shook it gently. "New toys?"

Tara nodded. "Open it."

Léa unsnapped the latch and opened the box. A tan ball of plastic was nestled in a foam cutout to keep it from rattling around. Tara had opened her own box and was holding an identical piece of plastic, the size of a small pearl.

"See the small red dot on the clear side?" asked Tara.

"Got it."

"That goes up." Tara shook her tangled black hair away from her head and carefully placed plastic piece in her ear. She nodded to Léa's box. "Your turn. It's molded to fit your ear."

Léa turned the plastic in her fingers until the red dot was positioned correctly and carefully pushed it into her ear. "Now what?"

Tara walked to the other end of the room. She turned her back to Léa and spoke quietly. "Can you hear me?"

"Wow. That's pretty clear."

Tara turned to face Léa, but she continued speaking at a whisper. "The battery should last seventy-two hours, and the range is about a mile."

"Not bad."

"They're noise-canceling, so we should be able to hear each other, even in a loud room."

"Seventy-two hours of battery," said Léa.

"Yep. Be sure to put it in a protected pocket of your backpack to get through airport security."

Léa tugged on her ear, and the earpiece fell out. She carefully put it back in the small case and stuffed it into the pocket with her gun.

Tara snapped her laptop closed and put it in her own backpack. Reaching for her black jeans, she stepped out of her running shorts and pulled off the tee-shirt. She paused with her jeans halfway on and sat on the edge of the bed.

"You know it gets real from here, right?" Her voice was grave.

"That's what I've been thinking," said Léa.

Tara stood up, pulled on her jeans, and reached for her black leather jacket. After zipping the jacket less than halfway up, she walked over to the dresser for her metal collar and wrist cuffs. As she snapped the locks closed, Tara turned to Léa.

"This guy isn't just a wormy little computer nerd. He's mad at the world, mad at The Castle, and he's taking it out on innocent people."

"And he knows we're coming," said Léa.

"And he knows we're coming."

Tara sat down on the bed and reached for her black boots. She drew on socks and buckled the boots. "He scares the shit out of me, and I hope he scares the shit out of you, too."

Léa sat next to her. "We really are leaping into the proverbial fire

181

together, aren't we?"

Just like she had done before breakfast, Léa looked at herself in the dresser mirror. But this time, Tara was beside her. "What I don't understand is why us? Why not someone with experience hunting down awful people like this?"

Tara shook her head. "That was my big question, too."

"And what did they say to that?"

"They're always trying to do the unexpected."

"Not so unexpected when the target knows who's coming," said Léa.

"Another good point I brought up."

Léa shook her head. "I just think this is ... is ... bloody hell, reckless."

They sat in silence for a few minutes, each lost in thought. Tara reached over and covered Léa's hand.

"We're going to be okay," she said. "I have some training in this shit, and we both can take care of ourselves."

"We're the smartest kids in town," said Lea.

"That's what they say."

The two friends looked into each other's eyes. Léa ran her fingers over the thick metal cuffs locked to Tara's wrists. Then ran a hand up the black jacket and down to the zipper.

"You do have the bad girl look down." Léa smiled.

"I guess."

"It suits you, sort of."

"Sort of?"

"The world may see you as some badass, tough-bitch hacker," said Léa. "But I know who's really under the black leather and cuffs." She tugged on the zipper a few times, then replaced her hand on Tara's. "What I don't know is what I'm supposed to be or do."

"Just be you," said Tara.

"And who is that?"

"The smartest girl in town."

"Please. It's gonna take more than brains to pull this off."

"We've got what it takes."

"Wish I could be as sure," said Lea.

"Remember what we talked about in Alan Dennis's office before the mission briefing?"

"You mean when I was asking about my family?" said Léa.

"Yeah. We've known we were adopted for years. Now that you know the secrets of The Castle, I'm guessing you've already put two and two together."

"Our adopted parents have been training us our whole lives." Léa looked straight ahead. The two women reflected in the dresser's mirror couldn't look more different. Tara's black leather, cuffs, and scruffy hair clashed violently with Léa's running shorts, tee-shirt, and bright yellow running jacket. She nodded toward the mirror. "They even planned for us to be friends. Encouraged us to do everything together. Made us closer than sisters."

"I would have wanted to be your friend whether they put us together or not," said Tara.

"Me too." She took both of Tara's hands in hers. "I guess they're not so barking mad to send us after all."

"How so?" asked Tara.

"There really is something special here. We're not just school buddies. I do love you like a sister, and I'd die if something happened to you." Tara started to speak, but Léa cut her off. "This—" She gripped Tara's hands harder. "This is more than just friends. It's an emotional bond. They know that if someone pointed a gun at you, I'd take them out in a heartbeat."

Tara gave Léa a genuine smile. When she spoke, her voice was soft and reassuring. "That is exactly what they and I are banking on."

Léa smiled. "Count on it."

There was a soft knock, and the door slowly opened. Heinrich Wilden stuck his head inside. "Ten minutes, Miss Wells."

He quickly backed out of the room and closed the door.

Still holding Léa's hands, Tara stood up and smiled down at her friend. "You know that little hotel on Mykonos you're always checking out?"

Léa looked up at Tara. "How do you know I've been checking it out?"

"You never clear your browsing history."

"Oh."

"Anyway. Let's get this done and stop there for a week or two on our way back to The Castle."

"Will they let us do that?" asked Léa.

Tara released Léa's hands, picked up her backpack, and walked to the door. She gave Léa her best badass, tough-girl look. "I don't really give a shit what they'll 'let' us do. Do you?"

"Hell no." Léa laughed.

"Put your new earpiece in when we get on the train to Uppsala."

Léa patted her backpack and smiled.

CHAPTER 35 - THE HUNT BEGINS

University of Uppsala, 2 p.m.

"That's the library off to the right," said Léa quietly.

"I'm guessing computer science is one of those buildings to the left," said Tara, just as quietly.

Both Tara and Léa were walking toward the library, but they were almost a block apart.

"The student center is a couple buildings behind us," said Léa quietly.

They walked a few steps in silence.

"Student housing is about a mile behind us," said Léa.

"You'd make a good tour guide," said Tara.

"The school was founded in 1477 and ranks as one of the best universities in Northern Europe."

"Thank you, Miss Wikipedia."

"It was a boring flight," said Léa.

"Great. But we're talking a little too much."

If Perry Drilling or one of his henchmen was watching them, talking to themselves would be a dead giveaway that they had hidden communications.

After a few more steps, Léa couldn't help but speak. "Actually, your attire seems to be attracting more attention than us talking to ourselves."

"I thought this look would blend in with the computer science crowd," said Tara.

"More like the *I'm gonna kick your ass* crowd."

"Everyone's a fashion critic."

As they neared the computer science building, Tara became increasingly aware that her choice of attire was completely wrong. Everyone she passed looked at her, and that wasn't good.

"Okay. You're right. This is bad."

"So how do we fix it?"

"Not a problem," said Tara. "I'll just stop in here and tone things down a bit."

Tara climbed the steps to the building beside computer science—the foreign language building.

"*Attendez ici, je serai de retour dans une minute,*" said Tara.

"Whatever. I'll be over at that coffee cart."

"No Bailey's for you. I need you shooting straight. And none of that foofy French vanilla cream in mine."

"Said the girl who just threw some foofy French in my face."

"Just trying to work on that sense of humor you all say I'm lacking."

"You lost me on that one," said Léa.

"I'm heading into the foreign language building. I switched languages. It's like an international play on words."

Léa closed her eyes and cleared the cobwebs. "It doesn't matter which language you're using. A play on words is also called a pun and is sometimes referred to as the lowest form of humor."

"Don't I at least get an A for effort?"

"We really will be lucky to get home alive." Léa sighed.

Three people stood in line at the outdoor coffee cart. Léa looked over her shoulder. The sun shone brightly on the student mall. In the other direction, students studied and socialized. A few were stripped down to next to nothing, working on their future cases of melanoma.

Everyone in the coffee line moved up one spot. Looking back over her shoulder, Léa saw a group of students skateboarding toward her.

"Click," said Léa.

"What's that?" asked Tara.

"Nothing. Interesting picture coming my way."

She slung her backpack around and reached for her camera. Without looking away from the skateboarders, she found the lens she wanted and attached it to her camera.

"I finally found the bathroom. Be out in a minute," said Tara.

"Take your time."

Léa dropped to one knee and lowered the camera to the ground. The guy in front of her in line turned to watch Léa inch her eye down to the viewfinder and wait for the skateboarders.

"Almost there," she whispered.

She set a focus point halfway between her camera and the skateboarders. The coffee line moved up one more person. The people behind Léa clearly weren't interested in waiting for some amateur photographer to snap a picture. Léa heard them mumbled snide comments under their breath.

"Almost there."

She rested her finger on the shutter. Just as the skateboarders came into focus, she lightly pressed the shutter. As her camera made the familiar *click*, Léa heard another *click* in her earpiece.

It was the sound a gun being cocked.

"Fuck me," said Tara.

"Maybe later if you're lucky," said another voice.

Léa heard the sound of handcuffs being ratcheted closed. Then she heard Tara cry out in pain.

"Shut up."

Léa stood up, casually capped the lens, and stuffed the camera in her backpack. She looked up to find herself at the head of the line. The coffee guy waited for her order.

"Coffee. Black," she said.

She heard a loud thud in her earpiece, then the sound of air blowing out of Tara's lungs.

"Don't fucking try that again," said the voice menacingly.

Léa watched coldly as the guy handed her a cup of coffee and told her the price. She reached into one of the backpack's pockets and handed him some money. She slung her backpack over her shoulder and casually walked away from the coffee cart.

"At least you saved me the trouble of having to search you for hidden weapons," sneered the voice, close to Tara's earpiece.

"Happy to help out." Tara sounded like her teeth were clenched.

Léa's brain shifted into high speed.

What happened? What do I know?

The sound of a gun being cocked and handcuffs closing. Clearly, Tara had been taken hostage. But by whom? As Léa slowly walked down the mall, she sipped her coffee and listened for clues.

What else do I know?

One male voice telling Tara not to try something again and saying something about searching her for hidden weapons. Léa walked casually toward the main doors of the foreign language building.

Too easy.

Tara had obviously made it to the bathroom and had been in the process of changing clothes when some guy had pulled a gun, which had sounded like some kind of revolver.

He has six shots.

Léa had been able to tell from Tara's sounds that her hands were tightly cuffed, probably behind her back. And the crack about not having to search her was easy, too. Tara had been caught in the middle of changing and probably wasn't wearing much.

Good.

Léa looked up and down the mall full of students and realized this guy wouldn't be able to move a naked, handcuffed girl far.

Léa looked up at the doors. It wasn't time to go into the building yet. So she sat down on the steps and pulled out her camera. She flipped a few knobs and looked through the pictures she'd taken.

Then she noticed her heart was racing. She looked away from the small LCD screen.

What is wrong with me?

Looking back at the camera, she saw her reflection in the screen. The expression on her face surprised her. Instead of calm, cool Léa, the face staring back at her was stressed and worried.

She reached into her backpack and for her sunglasses. At least she could hide the fear in her eyes behind her Oakleys. Léa felt her heart pounding in her chest.

It's adrenaline.

The life of being an agent, a spy for The Castle had just gotten real. Her best friend was in trouble. A gun was probably pointed at her head right now. No wonder Léa's heart was pounding. She wanted to leap into action and save her friend.

Not now, she told herself.

She took a deep breath and a sip of coffee. Her heart began to settle down. Léa looked left and right. Everything seemed normal. She took another deep breath. Her heart slowed. She felt herself calming.

She flipped the camera off and detached the lens before carefully packing it away in her backpack. As she slipped the camera body into its padded case, she casually looked left and right again. There was still nothing happening.

"Where are you, love?" Léa said quietly.

She hoped Tara would give her a clue to where she was.

Léa looked left and right again.

Nothing.

Her backpack rested on her feet, between her knees. The main compartment was still unzipped. She casually reached in and pulled out her bright yellow windbreaker. She slipped it on and zipped the backpack closed. Resting her hand on the backpack, she sipped her coffee and glanced around.

Nothing.

She felt her heart rate pick up again.

No. Settle down.

Léa took another deep breath and willed herself to remain calm. Waiting was clearly not one of her strengths.

She felt for the hidden zipper and tugged it open, running a finger over the new gun held securely in place by the Velcro strap.

Just before Léa and Tara had left The Castle, Dick Boxx had handed her a few extra clips loaded with fresh ammunition. Léa told him she didn't like the new, bigger gun, but Little Dick had insisted on it being secured in the secret compartment of her backpack.

Léa had protested, saying it was too big for her smaller hands, but Dick had told her she'd get used to it. She had suggested she'd be more accurate with the smaller nine-millimeter she'd been shooting for years. But no, she'd had to take the larger gun.

Thinking back, one corner of Léa's mouth turned up in a half-smile, half-smirk. Her hand moved causally to a second hidden zipper.

As she tugged on the zipper, she planned her next move. She was alone on the steps. No one was behind her. Using the backpack to cover her movements, Léa reached into the second compartment and pulled out the smaller gun.

With the backpack balanced on her knees, she pulled back the slide and let it snap into place. In one movement, Léa brushed aside her windbreaker and slid the gun into the waist of her running shorts.

Léa reached down and tightened the drawstring of her shorts. The gun almost flopped out on the ground, but she tugged the drawstring tight enough to keep the gun in place, then tied a double knot.

Léa looked around to make sure no one was watching her and slung the backpack over her left shoulder, taking one more sip of coffee.

"I'm ready," she said quietly to herself.

She hoped Tara could hear her and give her a clue about where she was. Her earpiece remained silent.

Léa walked directly across from the foreign language building to a stone planter near an outdoor trashcan. Slowly sipping her coffee, Léa looked from side to side and then directly at the building's entrance.

A few seconds later, Léa heard her best friend's quiet voice in her earpiece.

"*Porte Arrière. Allumer la mèche.*"

Léa smiled. Tara was in trouble, but she was still in good enough shape to throw around some more French.

Léa stood up and dropped her half-full cup of coffee in the trashcan before heading toward the alley leading to the back of the building. Her mind raced.

She remembered the first movie night of her career at The Castle, and a slight smile appeared on her lips as she disappeared into the alley. She needed to let Tara know she was in good shape, too.

"Lighting the fuse," she whispered.

CHAPTER 36 - HOSTAGE

University of Uppsala, 2:30 p.m.

Léa turned the corner of the building and found Tara standing in the middle of the alleyway. A small man stood behind her, with a gun to her head.

Léa walked slowly down the alley.

"That's far enough," said the man.

"Hi, Perry." Léa smiled.

"I said that's far enough."

"Nice to meet you, Perry. Now how about letting my friend go."

The man sneered. "Not a chance."

Léa's head tilted ever so slightly. Something wasn't right. The guy holding the gun and the guy whose file Léa had read didn't seem to be the same person. This guy seemed too nervous.

"Drop the backpack," the man ordered.

Léa let the backpack slip off her shoulder, and she gently placed it on the ground.

"Good girl. Now put your hands up."

Léa slowly raised her hands as she surveyed the scene.

There was no way Tara could escape. Her hands were securely cuffed behind her back, and Perry's gun was firmly planted against her head.

Just as Léa had imagined, Tara wasn't wearing a thing. The man had a tight grip on her handcuffs. He was shorter than Tara and held her handcuffs low, causing her to lean back, slightly off balance. The scene was bizarrely erotic, and Léa actually laughed out loud.

Tara was clearly in pain, probably from the tight handcuffs, but she managed a smile. The man seemed confused and afraid.

"What's so funny?"

"It's a girl thing," said Tara through clenched teeth.

The man gave her handcuffs a sharp jerk, and she cried out in pain.

"Shut up," he commanded nervously.

Something's not right, thought Léa.

The short man held the gun in his left hand and gripped Tara's handcuffs with his right. Tactically, he was in the superior position and shouldn't be nervous at all. But he was sweating. His eyes darted from side to side. And Perry Drilling was right-handed.

Léa looked again to make sure. The gun was in the man's left hand.

He tightened his grip on the gun and tried to sound like he meant business.

"You know how this'll end if you're not extremely careful. So you need to start backing away, *now!*"

Léa took a small step backward.

Tara flexed her fingers and tried to move her wrists. But the handcuffs were too tight, and Tara's hands were going numb. The man's grip on the handcuff chain left her no hope of wiggling free. Even if she were able to pull away, the gun to her head kept Tara from struggling.

From the corner of her eye, Tara could see the gun barrel. It looked like a cheap .38. Tara snorted in disgust. If this was it, she wished it would be from a better quality gun.

"What's so funny?" sneered the man.

"You and your shitty little gun."

"Shut up, or you'll be dead sooner than you have to be," he growled.

He gave Tara's handcuffs another painful jerk.

Even though her back to was to man, Tara could tell he was scared, and she could tell that Léa was thinking the same thing.

Tara and Léa each realized the other was thinking the same thing.

Something's not right here.

Tara's eyes shifted toward the gun pointed at her head. Léa caught Tara's gaze. The gun was in the man's left hand. He was holding it way too tightly, and he was clearly scared.

Tara could tell Léa's brain was in overdrive. Something would happen any second now.

As Léa surveyed the situation, she decided on a plan.

I need a distraction, she thought.

She took another small step backward and surveyed the alley. Nothing but building walls, a few cardboard boxes, and trashcans. But something else was in the alley with them. Léa's eyes shifted from Tara to the trashcans.

A cat, she almost said out loud.

Léa looked back at Tara and slightly smiled as she planned her next move.

It'll take two shots.

The first shot goes to the right side of that trash can. The cat takes off, probably with a loud yowl. *Perry looks over his shoulder. As he looks, the gun moves a few inches behind Tara's head.*

It sounded simple, but if the man didn't turn far enough, he could end up blowing Tara's head off.

Léa's thoughts were interrupted as the scared man barked another order. "I said get the fuck out of here, *now!*"

Léa looked directly into Tara's eyes as she inched backward. "Okay. You're the boss," she said calmly.

"Fucking right." The man adjusted the gun, gripping it even more tightly. Too tightly.

Good, thought Léa.

As she backed away slowly, Léa inched a bit to her left. Never taking her eyes off Tara, she finalized her plans. She could tell Tara knew what she was thinking.

Step one: Stumble to create the first diversion.

Step two: Wave my hands for balance to create the second diversion.

Léa had taken three slow steps and was edging to her left.

Step three: As you bring your hands down, drag your right thumb over your stomach and around your back to clear your jacket away from your gun.

She took two more steps.

The gun is loaded.

No safety.

First round is already chambered.

Two shots.

One to the trash can.

One to his head.

Léa's eyes never left Tara's.

Now, she thought.

It only took a second.

191

CHAPTER 37 - NATURAL COVER

The Same Alley, 2:32 p.m.

The cat *yowl*ed loudly and took off down the alley. The man turned to look at the noise.

The sound of the bullet hitting the man's head made Tara's ears ring. One moment he was standing behind her, gripping her handcuff chain. The next moment, Tara felt the grip on her handcuffs loosen.

The bullet caught the man where Léa had expected it to, and he spun halfway around before falling to the ground. His head exploded, showering Tara in blood.

Tara saw Léa scoop up her backpack as she ran toward her.

"Where's your stuff?" asked Léa.

Tara saw Léa's lips moving, but all she heard was a ringing in her ears.

Tara shook her head. She didn't understand.

Léa held up her backpack and mouthed the word *where*.

Tara nodded toward the back door of the building.

"Come on. We've got to get out of this alley."

Léa grabbed Tara's arm and half-carried her to the door. Léa reached for the handle and gave it a tug. As they stepped inside, Tara looked over her shoulder at the lifeless body laying the alley.

A long hallway stretched in both directions from the back door.

"Which way to your stuff?" asked Léa.

Tara smiled. "I heard you that time."

"Good. But we've gotta get out of this hallway and find your stuff before the campus police arrive."

"Bathroom. Down that way." Tara nodded to her right.

"Come on." Léa gripped Tara's arm and forced her to run down the hall.

"Can't you at least take these fucking things off?" said Tara.

"Later. We've gotta get out of sight."

She tugged on Tara's arm, urging her to run faster. Léa looked over her shoulder to see if anyone was following them. The hall was still empty.

Tara slowed down. "Whoa. Stop. We're here."

As they entered the bathroom, the building alarm sounded, and a voice announced a campus emergency.

Léa checked that the hallway was still empty and closed the door, snapping the deadbolt.

Tara stared at herself in the mirror above the sink. Bright red blood covered one side of her body, contrasting sharply against her pale skin. She shook her head. "If that little shit had any kinky diseases, I'll fucking kill him."

Léa walked behind her friend and looked in the mirror. "Sorry about all the blood."

"Our first time out, and I totally fucked it up," said Tara.

"Bullshit."

"If you hadn't come around that corner, and if you weren't the best shot ever ..."

"No one gets to hold a gun to my best friend's head," said Léa.

She looked Tara up and down and gave her a sly smile.

Tara turned her head slightly and eyed her friend. "What?"

"Ironic." Léa smiled.

"What?"

"I'm the one who likes getting naked and playing with handcuffs."

Tara's eyes flashed open. "Yeah, well, I don't. Get these fucking things off now."

Léa smiled and reached for her backpack. She pulled out a pen. Holding it up so Tara could see, Léa popped off the cap, revealing a hidden handcuff key.

Tara turned around, and Léa went to work on the cuffs.

"Your hands are blue."

Tara brought her hands in front of her. "Those things fucking hurt, even when they're off."

She tried to wiggle her fingers and winced in pain. She turned her hands over revealing deep cuts around her wrists.

"We're gonna have to clean those out," said Léa.

Tara looked at herself in the mirror. "Not just the wrists."

Tara walked toward the line of sinks and turned on the hot water, and Léa looked around the bathroom. A line of five toilet stalls were separated by old-style wooden privacy partitions.

Tara's clothes and backpack were sprawled on the floor of one of the stalls. Near the door, an old metal trashcan had been kicked over, spilling its contents—used paper towels, empty cigarette packs, and an open white box with the letters *EPT* in solid black text.

"Bring me some paper towels," said Tara as she held her blue hands under the running water.

Léa snapped open the paper-towel dispenser, grabbed a hand full and set them in the dry sink next to Tara.

Three sharp knocks sounded on the door.

"Campus police! Is anyone in there?"

"Just us. We locked the door when the alarm sounded," Léa shouted back.

"We are campus police. Open the door immediately."

Tara looked at herself in the mirror. Half of her body was caked with blood, and her clothes were in a pile on the floor.

"Get in the stall, put your clothes and your backpack on your lap, and don't say anything." Léa moved toward the door, looking over her shoulder as the stall door closed. Léa reached up and snapped open the lock. The door burst open, and two, young, male campus police officers entered the room with their guns drawn.

"Are you alone?" asked the first officer.

Léa put her hands up and tried to look scared.

"Just, just me and my friend."

"Come out of there, now."

Léa smiled nervously and took a hesitant step toward the officer.

"Please. She's in pretty bad shape right now."

"I don't care. Come out, now," shouted the officer.

Léa smiled nervously again and nodded toward the overturned trash can.

"Please, she just got some really bad news."

"What?" The officer looked at the pile of trash.

With one of her raised hands, Léa pointed to the pile of trash.

"See that box?" she said innocently.

"What about it?"

"She just found out."

"Found out what?"

"She's, you know, pregnant." Léa gestured over her shoulder toward the back wall of the bathroom, where a used EPT wand was tossed in the corner. She smiled at the officer and nodded. "Pregnant."

"Just now?"

"Just now."

The officer looked over his shoulder at his partner, who took a quick look at Léa, the closed bathroom stall, and the empty EPT box on the floor. He nodded.

"Okay," said the officer as he lowered his gun. "We've had a shooting on campus, and the shooters are still at large." He pointed to the lock. "Lock this door behind us, and don't let anyone in. Don't leave until you hear the all clear."

"Yes, sir." Léa smiled.

The officer holstered his gun and reached into his shirt pocket. He pulled out a hand full of cards and quickly sorted through them. "Here's the number for the campus pregnancy crisis center."

As he handed the card to Léa, a loud snort came from the closed stall. Léa looked over her shoulder. When she looked back, the officer was still smiling helpfully.

"Lots of hormones now, but she'll be okay," he said as he walked out of the room.

As soon as the door closed, Léa snapped the lock shut and walked back to the sink. The stall door slowly opened. Tara was still covered with dried blood, but color had begun returning to her hands.

"Pregnant. Really? That's what you came up with?"

Léa smiled and pointed to the pile of trash. Tara saw the empty EPT box.

"I was just using the, um, natural cover," said Léa.

Tara shook her head as she walked to the sink and started cleaning the cuts around her wrists. "Pregnant."

Tara held her wrists under the hot water, and Léa grabbed a hand full of paper towels. She soaked them in the next sink and went to work on the blood covering Tara's left shoulder. Tara glanced over her shoulder at her friend. Léa was about to get a mild surprise.

As Léa scrubbed, most of the blood came off easily, revealing a patch of black ink.

Léa had noticed a neck tattoo at the coffee shop a week ago. But it hadn't been there a few nights later when they had shared that bottle of wine back at The Castle. Léa had assumed she'd been wearing a temporary tattoo—part of Tara's costume. But the tattoo on her back wasn't washing off.

"How long have you had this?"

"About nine months," said Tara.

As Léa scrubbed, the tattoo emerged from under the blood. It was about two inches across. The design was simple enough, a circle of flames. Léa had seen flames like these before, but she couldn't remember where.

"Nice," said Léa.

"Thanks."

Léa hoped Tara might tell her more, but her friend focused on washing off her arms. Léa was about to ask Tara about the tattoo when the building alarm sounded. A voice over the P.A. said the emergency was not over and that everyone needed to stay where they were.

CHAPTER 38 - WHAT ARE BEST FRIENDS FOR?

University of Uppsala, 4 p.m.

Fortunately, the long lockdown gave Tara enough time to wash off the blood, and she emerged from the restroom looking normal, more or less. She pulled on her black jeans.

"I don't know who helped you come up with your biker-girl getup," Léa said. "But I think we've already figured out that it's not working on a college campus."

Tara's head snapped up, and she inhaled just ahead of a sharp reply. But as soon as she opened her mouth, she closed it again. Tara looked down at the black jeans and nodded. "You're right."

Léa pointed at Tara's backpack. "What else do you have in there?"

"Just my workout stuff."

"Perfect. We'll look like all the other students walking back to the dorm after a workout."

Tara pulled out her favorite shorts and tee-shirt. "These boots don't exactly fit with the workout look," she said.

"What else do you have in there?" asked Léa.

Tara fished around in her backpack. She pulled out a toothbrush, socks, and her big metal cuffs. "That's about it."

"Wait a minute." Léa reached for her backpack. After a moment of searching, she pulled out a pair of flip-flops. "Perfect. They go with your drowned rat look."

Tara's eyes rolled up toward the ceiling. "I just hope I don't have to do any running in these things."

Léa reached into her backpack again. This time she removed a towel and tossed it to Tara. "Drape this around your shoulders. Use it to dry your hair as we're walking."

"Not bad." Tara pulled on her tee-shirt and ruffled her sopping wet hair with the towel before draping it over her shoulders. She slipped into the flip-flops and looked down at her legs. "They're white as a marble statue. I'll never fit in with those tan kids out there."

"We're in Sweden," said Léa. "The only kids with a tan are the two or three who have been fake baking. You'll fit in fine."

Tara folded her leather jacket and stuffed it in her backpack, realizing the pack was full even as she reached for her black boots. "What do I do with these?"

"Just leave them," said Léa.

Tara's shoulders slumped, and she tilted her head. "I am not going all the way back to The Castle in flip-flops."

"I thought we were going to Mykonos," said Léa.

"Where ever."

Léa thought for a minute, then held out her hand. "Give me the leather jacket and the jeans. You put the boots in your pack."

"They'll never fit in that overstuffed pack of yours."

"I'll make it work." Léa pulled out her camera, lens, and wire pouch, along with a small bathroom pack. Then she folded the leather jacket, trying a few different folds to find the perfect fit, and stuffed it into the pack."

"Careful with that," said Tara.

Léa cleared the cobwebs and turned to Tara. "It's a leather jacket. I think it'll survive getting stuffed into a backpack."

"I know. Just wanted to lighten the mood a bit." Tara smiled.

Léa smiled back. "Things sure didn't go the way I thought they would."

"Yeah," said Tara.

Léa crammed the jacket deep into her backpack. The jeans went in next, followed by her camera stuff. She and Tara zipped their packs and looked up at the same time.

"Ready?" asked Léa.

"Ready," said Tara.

They walked to the row of sinks, three of which were full of bloody paper towels.

"What do we do with these?" asked Tara.

Blood was smeared all over the sink Tara had used.

"We can't just leave it like this," said Léa. "It would take those campus cops two seconds to figure out that nice girl and her pregnant friend had something to do with the body in the alley."

Tara frowned at Léa's use of the P-word but quickly returned her attention to the problem. "We could flush it down the toilet."

"There's too much. We'd clog them all," said Léa.

Tara and Léa each ran through possibilities, quickly discarding them as unworkable.

"Use natural cover, right?" said Tara.

"Natural cover. Right."

Tara examined the overturned trashcan, less than half-full of used paper towels. The plastic liner had come loose from the can.

"I wonder ..." Tara pulled the plastic liner completely out of the trashcan. She peered into the can and smiled. "Perfect."

"What's perfect?" asked Léa.

"Custodians usually leave a few spare liners in the bottom in case they run out." Tara reached into the can and drew out a new, unused trash bag. She grinned at Léa and began filling the bag with bloody paper towels. "Start cleaning the blood off that sink," she said.

After a few minutes, the sink looked good as new. Tara held open the trash bag, and Léa tossed in the last of the bloody paper towels.

"Now what?" asked Léa.

Tara picked up the trashcan and crammed in the full trash bag. Standing on one leg, she used her foot to pack the paper towels tightly into the bottom of the can.

Then Tara grabbed the half-full trash bag that had spilled out of the can and a few clean paper towels. She walked to the corner and used the paper towels to pick up the EPT wand and toss it into the bag.

"Get the rest of the trash laying around," said Tara.

Once the room was clean, Tara replaced the first trash bag in the can and arranged the liner so it looked normal. She dragged it over to the paper-towel dispenser and snapped the top on the can.

Standing back, Léa and Tara admired their cleanup work.

"If this spy thing doesn't work out," said Léa, "we could always get jobs cleaning restrooms."

"A lot less stressful, for sure."

Two normal-looking college women stared back at them from a mirror above the sinks. Almost normal. Léa turned to Tara and touched her badly bruised and cut wrists.

"You can't go out like that," she said.

"If only you let me wear my leather."

Léa looked back to the mirror. She took off her bright yellow windbreaker. "Will this work?"

Tara slipped on the jacket and tugged at the sleeves. They just covered her wrists. "Perfect."

They both turned back to the mirror and checked each other again. Everything looked fine. As they reached for their backpacks, Tara caught the glint of black metal tucked into Léa's running shorts.

"Um, we've got one more wardrobe problem."

"What?" Léa asked.

"Look behind you."

Léa turned and saw the grip of her gun. "I didn't even feel it back there."

"Good thing we checked each other before making our big public appearance," said Tara.

Léa drew the gun out of her waistband, careful to point it away from Tara. She dropped the magazine and swiftly caught it. After stuffing the magazine in her waistband, she racked the slide to pop the bullet out of the chamber.

Tara watched Léa expertly checked the gun for problems, then reload the round she had removed from the chamber. Just as Léa was about to slap the magazine back into the grip, Tara said, "I haven't thanked you for saving my life."

Léa pulled back the slide and quickly released it, chambering a bullet and cocking the gun. As she snapped on the safety, Léa smiled at Tara.

"No one holds a gun to my best friend's head."

Léa knelt to pick up her pack and slid the gun into its hidden holster. She trained her eyes on the hidden compartment, slowly zipping it closed.

"I know I just killed someone back there. I know I'm supposed to feel something about that. But I don't." Léa stood up and faced Tara. "When my dad gave me that gun, he told me I might have to use it one day. He told me I would have to decide whether I could use it, and I would have to be confident in my judgment that I'd done the right thing." She gave Tara's hand a quick squeeze. "I made that decision a long time ago. And like I said. No one gets to hold a gun to my best friend's head. So I'm pretty sure I did the right thing."

"You did, and thank you."

"What are friends for?"

The building's public address system sounded, announcing that the lockdown had been lifted.

"Ready to go?" asked Léa.

"Let's get outta here."

They walked out of the restroom and made their way to the front door of the foreign language building.

CHAPTER 39 - JUICE AND BIKES

University of Uppsala, 4:15 p.m.

A bank of dark gray clouds rolled over the horizon. The sunshine from earlier in the day was long gone, and the temperature was dropping. Léa and Tara weren't the only ones who'd been caught in warm-weather clothes. They looked like everyone else racing home as the storm approached.

Pausing at the bottom of the stairs, they looked both directions. There were more campus police than normal, but no one seemed interested in Tara and Léa.

"Which way to the dorms?" asked Tara.

"See, now you're glad Miss Wikipedia checked out the place before we got here."

Tara gave Léa an irritated, sideways glance. "Less sarcastic comments, more directions, please."

"Just trying to make us look like normal students, instead of two spies on the run."

"We're not on the run. But we do need to start heading to the train station," said Tara.

"Well, the dorms are to the left, and the train station is straight ahead."

"Come on." Tara took off toward the dorms.

"So if we're going to catch a train, why are we heading to the dorms?" asked Léa.

"Just trying to blend in. Keep in mind they're still looking for whoever was in the alley. Suspects probably wouldn't be heading for the dorms."

"Brilliant."

Every person they passed seemed on edge. Word about the shooting had quickly spread, and everyone walked with determination. Only a few people were casually hanging out around the coffee cart.

"Speaking of blending in, why don't you run the towel over your hair a few times," said Léa.

"Good idea." Tara went to work on her wet hair.

"Can't have you running around campus looking like a drowned rat," said Léa playfully.

"Is 'drowned rat' your new favorite phrase, now?"

"Just making conversation. We seemed to be the only people who weren't talking."

Tara dropped the towel around her shoulders and casually glanced around. City police and people wearing business suits had joined the campus police. They were setting up barricades and checking the IDs of people heading for the bus and train stations.

Tara nudged Léa and nodded over her shoulder. Léa looked back at the makeshift checkpoint and exhaled. "Good thing I let you take us to the dorms."

"We may have only caught a temporary break. I'm pretty sure they'll be checking IDs at the dorm entrances, too."

"The sooner we get off campus, the better," said Léa.

Even with all the extra cops patrolling the area, campus life was slowly returning to normal. Short lines appeared at coffee, sandwich, and juice stands. Everyone ignored Tara and Léa.

Not everyone.

A man and a woman stood next to a sandwich stand about a block and a half away. They were dressed in black, and their sunglass-covered eyes were focused on Léa and Tara like lasers.

"Who wears sunglasses on a cloudy day?" asked Léa.

"People I think we'd rather not meet," said Tara.

Léa pointed to a juice stand just ahead. There were three people in line, and the stand was in the open, set up next to two rows of bikes.

"Let's stop for some juice and try to figure something out," said Léa.

In line, they kept an eye on the sunglasses couple. They hadn't moved, but they were still carefully watching Léa and Tara.

"We can't keep looking over our shoulders," said Tara.

"Try the side of the cart," said Léa.

The juice cart was covered with bright, stainless steel and made a nice rearview mirror.

"Perfect," said Tara.

They moved up one spot in line. Tara checked out the sunglasses couple's reflection in the metal. "They're still back there. Haven't moved."

"I'll bet they stay there until we get our juice, then start heading our way," said Léa.

"Good bet."

Léa looked around. Nothing but students, cops, and bikes. Lots of bikes. Léa nudged Tara. "Wanna go for a bike ride?"

Tara looked over at the bikes. "That has possibilities." But her smile quickly faded. Almost all the bikes parked at the rack were securely locked to the pipes. "Those locks could be a problem."

"No problem at all. You get the juice, I'll get some bikes." Léa walked toward the bike rack. She slung her backpack around and unzipped one of the front pockets. She looked over her shoulder and smiled at Tara. "I'll take a raspberry apple, thanks."

"Got it," said Tara.

The line moved up again. Tara looked down at the stainless steel. The sunglasses couple still hadn't moved, but their attention had shifted to Léa making her way through the sea of bikes.

In the reflective metal, Tara saw sunglasses woman raise a hand to her mouth, as though speaking into a radio. Then Tara found herself at the head of the line.

"Two raspberry apple on ice," she said.

As the juice cart guy went to work on the drinks, Tara glanced at Léa. She stuffed something in her backpack and slung it over her shoulder. Léa pointed to two bikes and smiled.

Tara nodded and checked her rearview mirror. This time, sunglasses man had his hand up to his mouth. He and the woman both kept eyes on Tara and Léa.

"Here you go," said the juice guy.

"Thanks," said Tara.

She paid him and carried the drinks toward Léa. Sunglasses man and woman walked slowly toward the bike rack.

The look in Léa's eyes warned Tara of approaching trouble.

Léa cinched the backpack tight against her spine. She hopped onto one of the bikes and reached out for the juice in Tara's hand. Léa offered her other hand to hold Tara's cup of juice. "Get your pack on."

As Tara secured her own pack, she checked out the bikes Léa had selected. Both were modern, carbon fiber racing bikes.

"Leave it to you to pick the most expensive bikes in the shop," said Tara.

"Does that mean you like what I found?"

"Perfect."

"If it starts raining," said Léa, "we'll need to let a little air out of the tires."

"Why?"

"Racing tires are highly pressurized, making them very firm so they go faster. But they'll slip in wet conditions so letting out a little air helps them grip the road." Léa looked over Tara's shoulder and pushed her the second bike. "But that'll have to wait. We've got to go. Right now!"

Tara hopped on her bike, then looked up at Léa. The pedals were two pieces of plastic the size of coins.

"I can't pedal this with flip-flops," said Tara.

Léa gave Tara's back a shove and started pedaling herself.

"No time, we've got to go!"

Tara fumbled with the small bits of plastic before she was able to begin pedaling normally. Looking up, she saw sunglasses man and woman were running directly toward them. Then she saw Léa's arm reach out. Her juice cup was in her hand. As she passed the couple, Léa flipped the top off her juice cup and splashed it in their faces.

"Nice," said Tara as one of her flip-flops slipped off the plastic pedal. "Shit." She tried to keep her feet on the pedals long enough to catch up to Léa.

As she passed sunglasses man and woman, Tara flung her own juice and ice at them. She looked over her shoulder when she caught up to Léa and saw them both talking into their hands again, while wiping juice from their sunglasses.

"So how do you like your bike?" asked Léa.

"These pedals suck."

"I've got the same thing."

"Yeah, but you've got tennis shoes. These flip-flops just aren't going to work."

"Let's get off of campus and try to find a quiet place where you can change to your boots."

As they passed one dorm, Léa pointed to her left and turned between the buildings.

"Where are we going?" asked Tara.

"Where sunglasses man and woman can't see where we're going."

"Good call," said Tara as her flip-flop slipped again.

They rolled between the buildings, and Tara slowed her bike. As one pedal rotated up, she reached down and pulled off the flip-flop. She secured it in the waistband of her shorts, then removed the other one.

With both hands on the handlebars, Tara adjusted her bare feet on the small pedals and flicked the gears up and down. She had much better control of the bike.

"Better?" asked Léa.

"Much better."

"There's a smaller road around this building," said Léa. "If there are no cops there, we might be able to slip off campus."

"Just ride by the road and check it before turning in."

"That way they won't suspect us if we see cops and immediately turn around."

"You got it. Here we go."

There weren't any cops so Tara and Léa looped around and slowly pedaled between the dorm buildings. As soon as they cleared the buildings, they heard the roar of a powerful car engine.

A black Mercedes lurched forward, with two passengers looking directly at Léa and Tara.

They were wearing sunglasses.

CHAPTER 40 - BIKE CHASE

Streets of Uppsala, 4:20 p.m.

"We've gotta go, now!" yelled Tara.

"This way!" Léa made a hard right into a residential area.

Tara followed, and they both ran through their gears, picking up speed. Tara looked over her shoulder and saw the Mercedes closing fast. "They're still back there!"

"Let's jump the curb." Léa pushed her bike even faster.

Léa turned hard left and hopped her bike onto the curb. After a hard right, she was riding on the sidewalk parallel to the street. The sudden move surprised Tara, who had to pass a few parked cars before she was able to jump the curb.

With one click of her gears and a little extra pressure on the pedals, Tara was able to catch up. Less than an inch separated Tara's front tire from Léa's rear tire. As they came to a cross street, Léa turned her head to one side.

"Bump," she said over her shoulder.

A second later, Léa's bike flew over the curb and bounced onto the roadway, rapidly approaching the other side of the street as Tara's bike flew off the curb. Léa gave her handlebars a sharp yank, and the front tire barely cleared the curb. Then she pushed herself off the pedals and leaned forward over her handlebars, helping the rear tire clear the curb. In a split second, Tara landed right behind her.

They rapidly approached the end of the sidewalk they were speeding down. As Léa pedaled on, she heard Tara's voice saying something about turning soon. Léa wasn't sure why she was only hearing Tara in one ear until she remembered the plastic earpiece.

Léa glanced over her shoulder, and Tara tapped her ear. Léa looked forward and said quietly, "I can hear you. Can you hear me?"

"Loud and clear," said Tara.

"Now that we're done with the cell phone commercial, I figure we'd better get off this road soon."

"And we might want to think of a way back to the train station."

"One thing at a time," said Léa.

They had two more cross streets before the narrow, residential street dead ended into the river. Léa looked between the houses for a pathway they could ride through, leaving the black Mercedes behind. But each yard was fenced.

"Let's take the next left," said Léa.

"Right behind you."

"Bump."

Léa's bike flew over the curb, and she made a tight left turn. Tara followed. Looking over her shoulder, Tara saw the sudden move had paid off. The speeding car overshot the turn. The driver had to slam on the brakes and reverse. That bought them a few extra seconds.

As soon at Léa made the turn, her right hand shot out, indicating the next turn. Her hand returned to the handlebar, and she cut right onto a four-lane road jammed with cars.

The road was the main route through the old college town. No one was getting anywhere fast, except Léa and Tara. They were able to weave through the cars, putting quite a bit of distance between themselves and the black Mercedes. There was no way the car would catch up.

"I think we can slow it down a bit," said Tara into the earpiece.

Léa looked over her shoulder and saw the black car hopelessly locked in traffic. "Want to stop and get your shoes on?" she asked.

"I'm fine," said Tara.

They pedaled east along the four-lane road. A sign showed the train station was just ahead.

"Looks like we're moving in the right direction," said Léa.

Tara looked back. The black Mercedes hadn't moved. Ahead, another sign said they were about to cross the Fyris River.

"Once we cross the river, we bear right, and it should take us right to the train station," said Léa.

"Looks like we've got a roundabout at our turn," said Tara.

Clouds rolled in, and light rain began to fall as they reached the bridge. The temperature dropped. Léa wiped rain from her eyes and worked her cold fingers to warm them up.

"Roads are getting wet," said Léa. "Remember what I told you about these racing tires?"

"Got it," said Tara.

As they cleared the bridge, the roundabout came into view. Tara looked behind her, and the black Mercedes was nowhere to be seen.

"Next right," said Léa.

As she began turning south, Léa caught sight of an identical black Mercedes heading their way, with two occupants wearing business suits and sunglasses. One of the car's rear windows opened, and a hand holding a gun emerged.

"Bad turn!" yelled Léa.

She skidded into a three-sixty turn and headed back to the roundabout. Tara was right on her back wheel. Over Tara's shoulder, Léa saw the second black Mercedes jump the curb and zip through traffic.

"These guys seem to be a little more serious about catching us," said Tara.

"They're not afraid to show their hardware either," said Léa.

"Hardware?"

"Gun. Looked like a .45."

Tara and Léa exited the roundabout and headed back the way they had come—toward the first black Mercedes.

"Let's see where that road to the right takes us," said Léa.

Léa dodged a few cars and made a fast right turn. Tara quickly followed.

"We're heading away from our train," said Tara.

"We should be able to double back after our next turn. Assuming there isn't another black Mercedes heading our way."

"Speaking of a black Mercedes, we need to step on it," said Tara.

The second Mercedes had cut around several cars and was closing in rapidly. Léa stood up on her pedals and ran through the gears, maxing out her speed. She looked back over her shoulder and saw Tara on her back wheel.

"You're handling those pedals pretty well," said Léa.

"I slipped off a few times when we started, but think I've got the hang of it, now."

Oncoming traffic kept the Mercedes trapped behind slower cars.

Léa felt her legs burning. "We can ease off a bit."

"Aren't they still back there?" asked Tara.

"They're trapped behind a few slow cars, and I'm starting to tear up my leg muscles."

"Me too."

Both bikes slowed down a bit. The black Mercedes honked its horn, and Léa and Tara looked back to see the two slower cars respond by slowing down further.

"We were due for a break," said Léa.

"Where to, now?"

"Next right."

The Mercedes' honking increased as the slow cars continued their passive resistance. The black car fell farther behind the bikes as they neared their turn.

They cut right and headed northeast again. Traffic seemed to be thinning out as they rode away from the campus. The roads in this part of town were wider, and both Léa and Tara were able to keep a steady pace, putting more distance and cars between them and the black Mercedes.

They crossed a small bridge and saw the rail line beneath them.

"We're going to need to head south soon," said Tara.

"Working on it."

Tara noticed how quiet it had become. Something had changed, but she couldn't put her finger on it. She glanced back and realized that the honking had stopped. The black Mercedes made the turn and gained a passing lane. Tara stood on her pedals and poured on the speed.

"Here we go again," said Tara as she passed Léa.

A few seconds later Léa caught up to Tara. A sign signaled a roundabout ahead. Suddenly, the sign shattered.

"Those fuckers are shooting at us!" yelled Tara.

"Not good."

As they approached the roundabout, cars scattered behind them, clearing a path for the Mercedes. No one wanted to tangle with some idiot shooting out the window of a car.

Léa pedaled furiously, easing up next to Tara as they both tried to keep up their speed. The black Mercedes closed the gap.

"Listen," said Léa through ragged breaths. "I think I can take out one of their wheels in the roundabout. But I can't get to my gun."

"I can get it," said Tara.

Tara slowed her pace to slide behind Léa. Pressing harder on the pedals, Tara rode up on Léa's other side and reached for the hidden zipper. She tugged, and the zipper slipped out of her fingers.

"This fucking rain isn't helping."

"It's getting colder, too," said Léa.

Tara made another try for the zipper and was able to open the secret compartment halfway. As her hand slipped again, she heard a second shot from the black Mercedes and saw another road sign disintegrate.

"They're not very good shots, are they?" said Léa.

"Fucking good enough for me."

Tara made another attempt to unzip the backpack. They'd been riding hard for nearly fifteen minutes, and both were getting tired.

Even though Léa hadn't finished a full week of spy school, she was pretty sure that fatigue, rain, cold, and a high-speed chase were not a good combination. Tired people make mistakes, and both she and Tara were getting tired fast. Léa could tell Tara was getting stressed by her increased use of the F-word. But until Léa had her gun, all she could do was try to lighten the mood.

"I think we can get along just fine without every other word being the F-word," she said.

Tara finally succeeded in opening the secret compartment. She was about to fire back a sharp reply when Léa looked over and smiled.

"Fuckin' A," said Tara through heavy breaths.

"Your sense of humor is getting better." Léa gave a breathless laugh.

"I try to please."

"We're going to make it," Léa said.

Tara reached into the backpack, thumbed open the hidden holster's snap, and pulled out Léa's gun. Gripping the gun was difficult in the rain, but Tara was able to spin it around and hold it out to Léa.

Léa gripped her left handlebar tightly and reached out her right hand for the gun. A driver beside them saw the gun and hit his brakes, leaving one car between the bikes and the black Mercedes.

"What now?" asked Tara.

"As soon as we hit the roundabout, you take off ahead of me. I'll have to twist around to get a clear shot."

Another shot rang out from the black Mercedes. The bullet hit the ground between Tara's bike wheels. The ricochet barely missed Léa's foot.

"They're getting better," said Léa.

"Let's not give them too much more practice."

"Almost to the roundabout. Get ready to take off."

Another shot landed in front of Tara's bike, spraying pavement and loose rocks.

Léa and Tara entered the roundabout, and Tara took off, followed closely by Léa, her front tire inches from Tara's back wheel. The black Mercedes entered the roundabout moments later. Another shot rang out, striking the back reflector under Léa's bicycle seat.

I'm running out of time, thought Léa.

She stole a quick glance at the Mercedes as it pulled alongside the bicycles. Léa saw the face of man in the back seat who was pulling the trigger. He was clearly aiming for Tara.

Two shots. Now!

Sitting higher on her bike, Léa pointed the gun under her left arm and squeezed off two shots. The shooter in the Mercedes fell back into the car, and Léa aimed at the front wheel. Two more shots, and the tire exploded. The car veered toward the bikes.

"Faster! Faster!" Léa stood on the bike's pedals.

Léa and Tara pedaled furiously, and the driver of the black Mercedes struggled to keep control of the big car. The vehicle was too heavy to handle the speed. The bumper veered right, missing Léa's rear wheel by less than an inch.

Léa looked back just as the car jumped the curb and crashed into a concrete planter. Tara looked back just as the car exploded. They both pedaled furiously, keeping up their speed.

"Where to, now?" Tara was out of breath and paused between each word.

"We passed a bike path, by those apartments." Léa was still holding her gun. She couldn't reach her pack so she tucked it into the waistband of her running shorts. "There's the path. Next right."

The two bikes hopped the curb and rode along the sidewalk until it veered away from the road. The wet gravel of the bike path made controlling the bikes difficult. As the path twisted under the road, Léa called out to Tara.

"Let's stop under the bridge for a few."

They coasted to a stop. Both Léa and Tara were breathing hard, but not too hard. They were able to clearly hear police sirens approaching.

"We can't stay here long," said Tara.

Léa pulled her iPhone from the pocket of her running shorts and checked the time.

"Not good," she said.

"What's not good?" asked Tara.

"The train leaves in less than fifteen minutes." Léa thumbed on the gun's safety and handed it to Tara. "Holster it, and make sure it's securely snapped."

Two seconds later, Tara had secured the gun in its secret holster and zipped the hidden compartment.

"Come on," said Léa as she shoved her bicycle forward.

Tara followed as Léa took off. They turned left, then right, then right again as they rode through the big apartment complex. Every now and then, a pedestrian would yell at them to slow down.

Gravel wedged itself between the small plastic pedal and Tara's bare feet. Each push of the pedal embedded rocks deeper in the soles of her feet. Tara became increasingly aware of the pain as her adrenaline leveled. She reached for one foot at the top of its path and brushed away the rocks. After pedaling a few times, she was able to clear the gravel from both feet.

Looking up, Tara noticed all the apartment buildings looked the same. They seemed to stretch on forever.

"I hate to ask, but do you know where we're going?" said Tara.

"No sweat."

After a few more turns, Léa pointed straight ahead. They emerged near a road similar to the one they'd just escaped, but traffic moved smoothly, and no one seemed to notice the two bikes bounce off the curb and into the bike lane.

They rode west until they came to another roundabout. It was strangely familiar.

"We've been here before," said Tara.

"Before the second car started chasing us," said Léa.

"So maybe the first car is still around here somewhere."

"Maybe, but I'd guess they're heading to help their buddies."

As they entered the roundabout, signs clearly marked the way to the train station. Pedaling steadily, Léa checked the time.

"We've got about ten minutes so keep up the speed."

More signs marked their progress toward the station. A train whistle blew.

"Don't forget the bags," said Tara.

Léa nodded. "The lockers are to the right."

Both bikes veered right and carefully weaved through waiting passengers. At the luggage lockers, Léa pulled the key from the pocket of her running shorts. Another train whistle sounded as they slung overnight bags over their shoulders.

"We'd better get moving," said Léa.

They raced onto the platform as the silver electric train slowly pulled out of the station. They spotted two open doors as they coasted alongside the moving train.

"You take the first door, I'll get the one up ahead," called Léa.

Tara cruised a little longer before stepping off the bike. She gripped the handlebars and tilted the bike onto its rear wheel before stepping onto the moving train. Down the tracks, Léa had done the same thing.

Once aboard the train, Léa and Tara parked their bikes in the commuter bike rack. A conductor asked to see tickets. Tara fished around in a pocket of her backpack and handed over two annual train passes.

As the conductor scanned the train passes, he looked down at Tara's bare feet and pointed to the sign by the door. Near the bottom of the long list of rules was a graphic of a bare foot overlaid by a red circle and diagonal line. Tara reached behind her back and pulled the flip-flops out of her waistband. Looking up at the conductor, she dropped them to the floor, slipped them on, and held out her hand for the rail passes.

With flip-flops on and rail passes checked, they set out to find the nearest restroom. Léa and Tara were both covered with road dirt and sweat from their mad bicycle dash. The train's bathroom was small. Léa walked in, and Tara peered through the door.

"Both of us will never fit in there. I'll just wait."

"It'll be okay," said Léa. "Besides, we probably should stick together in case there are any sunglasses people on the train."

"Sunglasses people. That's a good one." Tara squeezed into the small bathroom.

Fifteen minutes later, they were clean and dry and settled in their seats. As the train left Uppsala behind, it picked up speed and rocked Léa and Tara to sleep.

CHAPTER 41 - WE'RE NOT SO HOT

The Train to Stockholm, 5:30 p.m.

Half an hour later, the train coasted to a smooth stop. Léa opened one eye and looked out the window. The rain was falling harder, and drops of water streaked down the glass.

Tara scrunched down in her seat, trying to get comfortable. Without opening her eyes, she whispered to Léa, "Where are we?"

"First stop. Six more to go."

Léa noticed that one of Tara's jacket sleeves had risen above her bandaged wrist. She reached over and tugged down the black leather.

"What?" said Tara sleepily.

"Nothing, love. Go back to sleep."

Tara fidgeted in her seat. When she stilled, her head was resting on Léa's shoulder.

"We should call home soon," Tara mumbled.

"Later." Léa shifted in her seat and closed her eyes.

Both Tara and Léa were asleep before the train pulled out of the station. The tempo of the rain increased along with the train's speed. The skies became grayer as the train rolled down the tracks toward Stockholm.

Half hour later, the electric train slid effortlessly into the next station. A slight jolt through the cars woke both Tara and Léa as the brakes brought the train to a stop.

Léa shook the sleep from her brain and sat up higher in her seat. Outside, the rain hadn't let up.

Tara straightened up, too, and stretched her arms toward the ceiling. Léa's eyes went to the white bandages wrapped around Tara's wrists.

"Hey. Bandages." Léa nudged her.

Tara shrugged and yawned. "So what?"

"I don't know. Low profile. That sort of thing."

Tara dropped her hands to her lap. "You think that bandages might tip off our secret identities?"

"Maybe," said Léa.

"I'd probably assume something like a suicide survivor and try to get far away."

New passengers filtered into the cabin, and two young guys stopped next to their seat.

"Afternoon, ladies. Looking for some travel friends?"

Tara reached over and rested her hand on Léa's. She glared at the guys with as much contempt as she could.

"Sorry. Not into guys," she said.

"Your loss," he said, and they worked their way down the train to some empty seats.

Léa smiled at Tara. "What was that we were saying last Christmas about never being asked out on dates?"

"This really isn't the time for romance," said Tara.

"I don't know. The quiet guy seemed your type."

"Not even close." Tara looked out the window.

The rain was pouring, and some of the cabin's windows were fogging up.

"It's getting colder out there," said Léa.

They watched rain droplets roll down the glass. After a few minutes, a voice announced over the PA that there would be a brief delay. The two friends sat in silence for a few minutes.

"We're not so hot at this spy thing are we?" said Léa quietly.

"Royally fucked things up is more like it," said Tara.

A few more silent minutes passed as the rain fell outside.

"Thing is ..." Léa's voice trailed off. "Thing is, I don't really think we fucked anything up."

"How so?"

"He knew we were coming. Knew exactly when we'd get there. Where we'd be."

"Well, just this morning we were saying he probably knew we were coming," said Tara.

Léa looked back out the window at the falling rain. She used her sleeve to wipe the foggy glass. From the top of the pane, a small raindrop slowly rolled down the window.

"Could he have hacked his way deeper into The Castle's computers than we suspected?" asked Léa.

"Possible."

"Could it even be possible that he put a pinger on us, the same way you put a pinger on my Paris picture?"

"It would help explain how fast everything crashed and burned."

Léa's eyes followed a few more raindrops from the top of the window as they rolled down the glass. She thought back over the day and tried to remember everything that had gone wrong. She also tried to remember the little things that hadn't seemed right. She thought of her first instincts about Drilling in the alley.

"I thought something was off with Perry Drilling," she said.

Tara thought so, too, but she wanted to hear Léa's thoughts before tossing out her observations. She doubted she'd been as observant with a gun to her head.

"Like what?" asked Tara.

"I never met him before today, but we both read his file, and he seemed more nervous than he should have been."

"True. But he was all alone in a back alley holding a gun to a naked, handcuffed girl's head." Tara rubbed her wrists. "Remember, he wasn't a trained field agent and probably didn't have too many girlfriends. Makes sense he'd be a little nervous."

"He was more than nervous," said Léa. "I'd say he was terrified. Plus, if he had hacked The Castle's computers like we thought, he should have been very well informed. He had the edge in so many ways, but he didn't act like it."

"And another thing," said Tara. "His file said he was a bit on the hefty side. The guy standing behind me was kinda shrimpy."

Léa watched raindrops, and Tara looked down the rows of seats, roaming around the train before stopping on the window across the aisle. Raindrops rolled down the glass, with no sign of letting up.

Léa nudged Tara. "Okay, if I'm reading all the tea leaves correctly, Perry Drilling knew we were coming. So we need to assume that he's completely hacked The Castle's computers. As for the man in the alley, I don't think that was Perry Drilling."

Tara stared at the raindrops rolling down the window across the aisle. Of course Léa was right, which meant they had a serious problem. She turned toward Léa. "Which means he's still out there and may even know where we are right now."

"Yeah," said Léa. "Plus, he's probably pissed at us. We've killed at least three of his friends."

"And wrecked one of his expensive cars."

"So what do we do now?" Léa asked.

"We need help." Tara reached for her backpack.

CHAPTER 42 - TARA'S SECRET CODE

The Train to Stockholm, 6 p.m.

Tara dug her laptop out of the backpack and gently pressed the power button.

Léa watched Tara sign on to the train's WiFi system. She launched a weather app and waited for the radar frames to load.

"First step in setting up secure communications. Start something like a weather app that will generate innocent web traffic," said Tara.

Then she launched Tweet Deck, and about ten Twitter streams crawled across the screen.

"More innocent web traffic?" asked Léa.

"You got it."

Tara switched to the Mac's second desktop and opened an app that put a small globe on the upper right corner of the screen.

"That's a scrambler," said Tara.

"Scrambler?"

"You start messenger from the scrambler submenu, and all of your messages are encrypted."

"Nice," said Léa.

Tara right clicked on the globe and a short menu popped up. She moved the pointer over the messenger app, then stopped. Her fingers hovered over the keyboard for a few moments. Tara looked at Léa and moved her fingers away from the computer.

"What's wrong?" asked Léa.

"This won't work."

Léa's eyes flicked between Tara and the computer. "Because Perry Drilling has hacked The Castle and is probably reading everything on everyone's desktop."

"Including anything we might send through messenger."

"Even though it's scrambled, he'll see the plain text on The Castle's end."

"That's about it," said Tara quietly.

Léa looked out the window. The train was still at the station. She nudged Tara. "So how do we tip them off that they've been hacked without getting hacked ourselves? And how do we get the help we need?"

Tara's eyes widened. She looked up from her laptop and slowly turned to Léa.

"Fuck me! I may have just given us away when I signed my Mac onto the train's WiFi."

"He knows where we are," said Léa.

"He knows where we are."

Léa reached for her backpack. She glanced around the cabin to see if anyone was watching her and made sure no one standing outside on the platform could see her. Léa tugged at the hidden zipper and pulled out her gun. Leaning forward, she slipped it into the waistband of her jeans.

"Time to go," said Tara.

Just as they started to get up, the train shifted forward. Léa's hand moved toward the gun hidden under her yellow jacket. Tara surveyed the cabin. Nothing suspicious, just other passengers settled in their seats.

They sat back down.

"We get off at the next station," said Léa.

"Right," said Tara.

As the train picked up speed, they kept watch for anything dodgy. After a few minutes, Tara started to shut down her laptop.

Léa shook her head and put her hand on Tara's.

"Hang on, we've still got to warn The Castle, and we still need help."

"You're right," said Tara.

"What is it they're always saying back at The Castle? Always look for ways to turn a bad situation into something good."

"That's what they say."

"So, we don't want to tip off Drilling that we know he's hacked us," said Léa. "But we still need to get a message back to Stromness."

Tara thought for a moment. "We still can."

"How?"

"We do it the old-fashioned way." Tara smirked and pulled a pen, a legal pad, and a small notebook from her backpack.

"I didn't know you still used paper. And do my eyes deceive me? Is that your little black book?"

"Funny." Tara handed her laptop to Léa, uncapped her pen, and scratched out a message.

Drilling still alive. Highly probable he has hacked Castle's entire computer system. Strongly suggest system lockdown Plan Blue be immediately executed. Stripper and Goth

Tara handed the legal pad to Léa. "How does that look, and how many words can we cut?"

"Cut?"

"We've gotta make this as short as possible," said Tara.

"Well, to start, we can replace the *be* with *executed*. That cuts a word. Then we can toss that *still* and drop another word."

"Good. How many words have we got?" asked Tara.

Léa counted. "Twenty-six."

"Outstanding." Tara ripped the old message off the legal pad and handed it to Léa. Then she fished an empty water bottle from her backpack. "Shred that into the smallest pieces you can, and stuff them into this bottle."

Léa went to work shredding the paper, and Tara rewrote the message on a blank sheet. As she wrote, Tara glanced sideways at Léa with a slight smirk.

"How do you like your codename?"

"Doesn't exactly fit most people's image of me," said Léa. "I'm no expert at this spying thing, but I'm guessing that makes it a good one."

"I don't know. After that parade you staged on your first night at The Castle ..."

"I meant the outside world."

"If only the outside world knew you like I know you," said Tara.

"Couldn't we be Double-Oh-Eight and Double-Oh-Nine?"

"Wrong spy story."

Léa made fast work of shredding the message. "Done," she said.

Tara slipped the elastic band from her black notebook. She smiled at Léa, but it wasn't the usual smirky or sarcastic smile. It was genuine. Her eyes came alive.

"What?" said Léa.

"You're gonna love this."

Léa turned her head slightly. "Okay."

"In the world of secret codes, a lot of them are breakable if you're willing to invest the time and the money."

"Sounds reasonable," said Léa.

"History quiz. What was the ace up our sleeve in World War Two?"

"That's easy. The code breakers at Bletchley Park."

"Right. They invested the time and the money to break Enigma so they could read German messages, sometimes even before the Germans had them decoded."

"So what does Enigma have to do with us?" asked Léa.

"We're gonna use something older than Enigma and impossible to crack."

217

"What would that be?"

Tara held up her little black book. Her eyes twinkled. "A one-time pad."

"It's unbreakable?" asked Léa.

"If you follow three simple rules." Tara just smiled.

"Really?"

"Really," Tara smiled.

"Okay, you're having too much fun."

"Yeah. I am."

"Why this sudden appearance of the old Tara?" Léa didn't give her time to answer. "Not that I'm complaining. I really miss this part of you."

"We're in a tough business. For me, it's best that people don't know the real Tara."

"Okay. But you need to let the real you out of her cage a little more often, at least when I'm around. But for now, let's get back to this one-time pad thing you're so impressed with. What are the three simple rules that make it unbreakable?"

"First, make sure the message key is truly random," said Tara. "Second, the key has to be as long as the plain text. And third, you can never, ever reuse it."

"So why do you want it as short as possible?"

"Several reasons. It makes our job easier, and the less you send, the harder it is to crack."

"So how does this work?" Léa pointed to the little black book.

Tara handed her the legal pad and a pen. Opening her notebook, she glanced at the date on her laptop and thumbed through the pages. Tara set the open book on the legal pad.

"Step one. Turn the letters in our message into numbers."

Léa saw the page Tara had turned to was covered with a grid of letters and numbers, all carefully handwritten.

"Every letter?" asked Léa.

"Every letter."

"This is gonna take a while."

"Welcome to the not-so-sexy part of spying," said Tara. "Get to it."

Léa reached for the pen and started scribbling numbers on the legal pad. After she wrote the first few digits, Tara touched the top of Léa's pen.

"As you're writing the numbers, space them out in groups of five."

"Got it." Léa kept writing numbers. Lots of numbers. The first sentence alone contained twenty-nine numbers.

"Why are the letters at the top out of sequence?" asked Léa.

"They're the most frequently used letters in the English language."

Each line of plain text had five blank lines below it. Tara had also spaced out the letters of each word.

"This would go a lot faster on a computer," said Léa.

"If I were to put this code on my computer and someone hacked it, they'd know the code."

"You made this?" asked Léa.

"Yep."

Léa took about five minutes to finish the entire message. Below each line, numbers were written neatly in groups of fives.

"So now we have our secret code?" asked Léa.

"Not yet." Tara opened the black book to a page filled with more numbers. "This is the message key. They're just random numbers, and there's a different one for each day of the month."

"What do I do with these?" asked Léa.

"Write them directly below the numbers you just entered."

Léa took a breath and started writing more numbers. "Like this?"

"Perfect," said Tara.

Copying the new numbers didn't take nearly as long as encoding the first set.

"Done," said Léa. "What's next?"

"Now subtract each key number from the encoded numbers. If you have to borrow, just drop the first digit."

"You didn't say there'd be math on this test," Léa grumbled.

"Like I said, welcome to the not-so-sexy part of the spy biz."

Léa took a deep breath and started printing another group of numbers. The third line of numbers took about as long to complete as the first had. When Léa finally set the pen down, she had three lines of numbers under each line of text.

"Finished."

"Very good," said Tara.

"Now what?"

"Now we send that last line of numbers to The Castle."

"How? Both of our computers have probably been hacked."

Tara produced a small, sealed envelope from her backpack. She ripped it open and shook out a new iPhone. She gave it a few minutes to power up and pressed her thumb to the Touch ID.

"I bought this a few months ago. Never used it, and I won't let it sign on to the train's WiFi."

"Won't that text appear on someone's hacked desktop back at The Castle?"

"No. It'll go to a second iPhone I bought that's connected to an old-style printer in Thomas Austin's office."

"So Thomas Austin receives the message on paper, decodes it, and it's not on anyone's desktop."

"That's the idea," said Tara.

Léa smiled as she watched Tara start the phone's messenger. "This is really quite brilliant. How did you figure all this out and get it set up in time for our trip to Uppsala?"

"I knew Drilling had hacked The Castle. I just didn't know how deep. So I started cooking up this idea with Movie Boy a few months ago."

"The guy who put on the welcome show?"

"That's him." Tara tapped the top line of numbers into the message. "Now, slowly read me that bottom line of numbers."

Tara and Léa both checked to see if anyone was listening. The nearest passenger was three rows away and was wearing noise-canceling headphones.

They looked at each other and smiled.

"We've been reading each other's minds and finishing each other's sentences quite a bit lately," said Léa.

"It's why everyone thinks we'll be so good at this," said Tara. "Let's get that message out."

As Léa started reading numbers, she noticed that Tara had entered another group of five numbers at the top of her message.

"What are those other numbers?"

"That's the key number."

"So Thomas Austin knows which code to use."

"Right. Read."

Léa slowly read numbers while Tara painstakingly tapped them into the iPhone. The process was slow, and the phone's small screen didn't help. Finally, Tara hit the send button.

"Done," she said. "One last thing."

Tara ripped the sheet of paper off the pad and handed it to Léa.

"Rip this up, too?"

Tara nodded. "Right."

She grabbed a plastic zip bag with what looked like aspirin. Tara flicked the bag with her finger until a blue pill emerged from the white ones.

"Hand me the bottle," she said.

Tara dropped the blue pill into the empty bottle and filled it with water from her full bottle. She shook it a few times and stuffed it into the seat pocket.

"It'll completely dissolve the paper."

"So now we're done," said Léa.

"Now we're done."

As Léa leaned back in her seat, she felt the gun dig into her side. She shifted and reached down to adjust it.

"I'm going to keep it handy for a while," said Léa.

"Good idea."

They both looked out the window. The train was picking up speed, and rain continued to streak its windows.

The train hit a curve and rocked hard enough to make Léa and Tara bump into each other.

"Must be trying to make up for the time we lost at the last station," said

Tara.

The train took another curve, jostling the passengers. Then the door that led to the car behind them inched open. The conductor muscled it open wide enough to squeeze through. The passengers watched him make his way to the front of the car and begin pushing the other door open.

As the conductor disappeared into the next car, the train hit another turn. This time, the force of the rocking train car knocked Tara into Léa's shoulder—hard.

"Those doors shouldn't be that hard to open," said Léa.

"I don't think we're trying to make up for lost time." Tara looked out the window.

Léa's hand went to the gun tucked in her jeans. The platform of the next station was blurred by the rain.

"We're not," said Léa.

Tara whispered, "He's got the fucking train."

CHAPTER 4 - PULLING THE PLUG

The Train to Stockholm, 6:30 p.m.

Léa and Tara watched through the window as the rain streaked by. They felt the train moving faster, and another curve threw Léa into Tara. The open computer slid off Léa's lap and was about to hit the floor when Tara snagged it.

Reaching for the power button, Tara's hand stopped in mid-air.

"Look at this," she whispered in Léa's ear.

On the laptop screen, a small window displayed a single sentence:

IT WAS A MISTAKE TO KILL MIGUEL.

Another window opened, and a movie began to load. The black-and-white video was from a security camera perched over the alley from a few hours earlier. The camera was positioned behind the man they had thought to be Perry Drilling. The gun he held to Tara's head was clearly visible.

The video showed Léa start to move slowly backward, away from the camera. In a blur, Léa stumbled, a trashcan flew across the alley, and the man's head exploded. The next frame showed the dead man lying alone in the alley. Then another message appeared under the first:

NICE SHOOTING ... STRIPPER.

Tara began shutting off the laptop's wireless and Bluetooth functions. "Kill your phone and anything else electronic you have," she said.

Léa reached for her iPhone, and Tara punched the laptop's power button and snapped the lid shut.

"Time to go," said Tara.

Walking down the aisle wasn't easy. The train rocked from side to side with increasing force. Just before they reached the door that led to the next car, they looked out the exit window.

"We're going way too fast to jump," said Tara.

Léa edged closer to the exit window.

"No way," she said.

Tara tapped Léa's shoulder and pointed toward the wall by the exit, where a map illustrated the train's route.

"How many stations have we passed?" asked Tara.

"Three. No, four."

"So it's pretty much a straight shot from here to the airport."

"Unless something's in the way, I'm guessing he's hoping to crash us into the station at the end of the line."

"He's not going to kill just us. Everyone on this train will die." Tara tightened the straps of her backpack and opened the secret compartment of Léa's pack. "I don't think we'll need any firepower here. Let's get that out of sight."

Léa touched her gun and looked around before quickly hiding it in its hidden holster. She zipped the secret compartment and slung the backpack over her shoulders. "What next?"

Tara started tugging on the closed door between the train cars.

"Let's get up front," she said.

Léa joined in and muscled the door aside. They made their way through the next two cars before reaching the locked door to the control cabin.

"Now what?" asked Léa.

Tara looked over her shoulder. The train was filled with frightened passengers, all watching the two women standing by the door behind which the conductor had already disappeared. Tara knocked on the door.

Nothing happened.

She knocked again, harder.

Still nothing.

Léa reached across Tara and pounded hard. The door sprang open, and the conductor appeared.

"Go back to your seats and sit down, now," he sneered.

As he turned to close the door, Tara reached out and gently grabbed his arm. He looked down at her hand as Tara squeezed his arm. When he looked back to her face, she was smiling.

"We're guessing you could probably use some help from a couple of kids who know a lot more about computers than you do."

The conductor looked from Tara to Léa, who was also smiling. She nodded toward Tara.

"It's true. We're both certifiable computer geeks."

"But, how did you know?" he asked Tara.

"Two train crashes in less than two weeks. Both on advanced, high-speed, electric trains. Doesn't take much imagination to figure out."

The conductor looked over his shoulder, then stood aside. "Please ..."

Tara and Léa inched into the cramped control cabin. One engineer kept an eye on the tracks ahead, and another had his head buried in an equipment rack.

When the first engineer saw two passengers in the control cabin, he strongly objected to the conductor. The other engineer pulled his head out of the equipment rack and joined in haranguing the conductor.

The conductor patiently waited for the engineers to quiet down and explained why he had let Léa and Tara up front. One engineer pointed to the old-style green screen and keyboard.

"What do a couple of Facebook kids know about this," he said.

"More than you'll ever imagine." Tara moved closer to the equipment rack.

"I haven't been on Facebook for over a week." Léa smiled.

"Let me have a look," said Tara.

"Be my guest," said the engineer.

As Tara turned to the computer screen, the train screamed past another station and careened around another turn, knocking Tara into the engineer and Léa into the wall.

"How many more stations to go?" asked Tara.

"Three more, but they're fairly close together," said the engineer up front.

"We only have about ten minutes to the end of the line," said the conductor.

"Got it." Tara steadied herself.

The conductor leaned down and whispered in Léa's ear. "Promise me she knows what she's doing."

Léa nodded and smiled.

Tara studied the computer screen for a few seconds. She tapped on the keyboard and bent down to see the box at the bottom of the rack.

"Can you open this?" she said.

"Yes." The second engineer reached for his keys, turned them in a few locks, and slid the cover aside.

Tara looked inside and touched a few of the chips. "This thing's toast."

"There's nothing you can do?" asked the second engineer.

Tara pointed to two of the chips. "Those control input from the train and from this keyboard. They're both fried."

"So the train won't know how fast it's going and can't accept new commands," said Léa.

Tara nodded. "No way to stop it in the conventional way."

"How about an unconventional way?" asked Léa.

"That's the only way now."

The train took another curve, jostling everyone in the cabin. Bulbs flickered. Outside, the lights from another station rushed by in a blur.

"We're running out of time," said the conductor.

Tara looked back at the computer cabinet. Léa's attention was on the lights that had just flickered.

Tara smiled. "Of course."

"Let's just pull the plug," said Léa.

Tara eyed the conductor over Léa's shoulder. "This train, it's completely electric?"

"Yes," said the conductor.

"From the tracks?" asked Léa.

"No. From the wires above the train," said the conductor.

Just behind the flickering light was a hatch to the roof. "Can we get on the roof from there?" asked Léa.

"Yes." One of the engineers opened another closet and removed a ladder. Securing the ladder to the wall under the hatch, he reached back into the closet for a fire axe.

Léa nodded hopefully to Tara.

"It is an electric train. So if you pull the plug, it should stop," said Tara.

The engineer climbed the small ladder and popped the hatch. Rain and wind whipped into the cabin as he stuck his head outside. After a few moments, he climbed down a couple rungs and spoke to the conductor.

"Grab my legs so I don't fall," he said.

The conductor edged around Léa and climbed the ladder behind the engineer. He held the ladder firmly with one hand and grabbed the engineer's legs with the other.

A metallic *thud* sounded from the roof. Then a second. Then a third. A bright light flashed, and sparks blazed through the open hatch. The lights flickered and dimmed, but they remained on. The train kept going.

"Shit," said the engineer as he climbed down the ladder.

"What?" asked the other engineer.

"The second power rack on the control cab at the back of the train."

"How long till the end of the line?" asked the conductor.

"About three minutes," said the engineer up front. "Not enough time to make it back there."

Tara and Léa smiled at each other.

Léa shook her backpack off and said to the men in the control cabin, "You guys are going to have to be cool about this."

She unzipped the hidden compartment and pulled her gun from its holster. She dropped the magazine into her free hand, checked it, and slid it back into place. She pulled back the slide and let it snap into position. Tucking the gun into the waistband of her jeans, she began climbing the ladder.

"Don't let me fall," she called down.

Tara followed Léa, holding on to her legs. The train swayed from side to side. Tara knew that would make the shot more difficult. Léa ducked back into the cabin, soaking wet.

"I need the other one," she said.

"What other one?" asked Tara.

"The other gun."

"Hand me the backpack," Tara told the conductor.

The conductor only stared.

"Come on. Now," shouted Tara. The conductor gently picked up the backpack and handed it to her. "What's wrong?" she asked Léa.

"It's too dark out there. The bigger gun has glow-in-the-dark sights."

Tara pulled the larger gun from the other hidden compartment and handed it up. Léa took it and disappeared into the rain and wind. She quickly re-emerged and held the gun under the cabin lights. The conductor and engineers watched in disbelief. She smiled.

"Just gotta charge up the glow-in-the-dark sights."

The conductor nodded. Léa smiled and disappeared again.

The train rocked sharply, and the wind blew cold rain into the control cabin. Even above the loud weather, everyone in the cabin heard a shot ring out.

Nothing happened.

When they heard the second shot, the lights in the cabin died, and the train began to slow. Léa and Tara crawled down the ladder, both drenched. Tara held the backpack for Léa as she hid both guns inside. Tara nodded toward the small crew door behind the conductor.

"Listen guys, we've gotta go," said Tara.

"We can't be here when it's time to answer questions," said Léa.

The conductor moved to block the exit.

"We're not criminals," Tara said reassuringly.

"If we were, we'd just shoot our way out." Léa smiled.

"We just saved your butts," said Tara, "and everyone else's on this train, so you all owe us."

"All we ask is that you let us slip out that door. When it's time to answer questions, you take credit for pulling the plug," said Léa.

The conductor looked at the engineers and nodded. They both nodded back, and the conductor swung open the crew door.

"And what do we say when they ask who shot away the back power rack cable?" asked one of the engineers.

Tara was already out the door. Just before Léa disappeared, she grinned back.

"Just say you noticed something wrong with that power rack at the third station, but the computer fried before you had a chance to check it."

The engineer nodded.

"Hey," said the conductor. "Walk down the tracks ahead of the train for a while. That way the passengers won't see you."

"Will do," said Léa as she disappeared into the night.

CHAPTER 44 - WHAT'S REALLY IMPORTANT

Mykonos Island, A Few Days Later

A gentle breeze blew through the open window. Light, jazzy instrumental music played from the clock radio by the bed. Léa opened her eyes as rays of bright Aegean sunshine streamed through the window of the small suite.

Léa sat up and noticed a pile of brightly colored towels at the foot of her bed, along with a note ...

Come on down to the pool.
(sorry, clothes are not optional here)
t

Léa picked up the small pile of towels, only to discover it was actually a small bikini. She smiled and jumped off the bed.

A few minutes later, she found the door to the hotel's amazing pool and deck. At the early hour, only a few couples were outside enjoying a late breakfast.

"Good morning, Miss Taylor," said a voice behind her.

Léa turned to find the pool's bartender with a mug of coffee.

"Your friend, Miss Wells, said you liked a few shots of Bailey's in your morning coffee. So I took the liberty."

Léa took the mug, tasted the coffee, and smiled. "Perfect. Best way to start the day."

"Your friend is behind the trees to your left," he said before returning to his outdoor bar.

Léa walked slowly around the pool, sipping her coffee and looking for Tara. The past few days—no, the past few weeks had been quite the whirlwind. She had still been amazed to wake up here.

The Mykonos Theoxenia was an Aegean hotel she had always wanted to visit. It was on the west side of the island, near the airport. She had spent more time than she'd ever admit staring at pictures on the hotel's website

227

and Instagram. And now she was here.

Léa turned the corner and spotted Tara, who gave her a slight wave.

"Wow! Look at you," said Léa, taking another sip of coffee.

"What about me?" said Tara sleepily.

"You never struck me as a pool and bikini girl."

"There aren't many places for bikinis and pools back in Stromness."

"True." Léa settled down in the pool chair next to Tara, cradling her coffee and enjoying the view. "These last few weeks ..."

"Not how we thought life would turn out, is it?" said Tara.

"And then to end up here."

"It's an okay place to lay low for a few weeks."

"Perfect for me," said Léa.

"I know."

"How?"

"It's at the top of your browser history. Kinda like a stalker."

"Funny."

Léa lay back in her pool chair and closed her eyes. *These last few weeks ...*

Her whole world had changed in so many ways. The mystery of the haunted castle on the cliff had not only been solved, but had changed the course of her life.

Growing up, she had known many of her friends were adopted. All of their parents had always told them they would understand one day. Now, Léa was one step closer to knowing where she and her best friend had come from.

The best part was that she'd gotten her best friend back.

Léa had been convinced that Tara's life had taken some bizarre route that would drive her away. As it turned out, both of their lives had taken a bizarre route, only to lead them closer together than ever before.

As Léa thought about the changes in her life, conflicting emotions welled up. She was overjoyed to have her best friend back in her life. She felt growing excitement at the new direction her life had taken. And she felt growing dread knowing that she and Tara had made an enemy.

A deadly enemy.

She heard Tara moving shifting in her pool chair. Léa took a sip of coffee.

"We can't stay here forever, and he's still out there," she said.

"He's still out there."

"What do we do now?"

"We stay sharp," said Tara, "we stay brilliant, and you keep shooting straight."

"And you keep coming up with amazing things like your one-time pad."

"And we both remember what's really important," said Tara.

"What's that?"

"We're best friends first, spies second."

"Always," said Léa.

EXTRAS

TARA'S CODEBOOK

TEXT CONVERSION CHART

A	E	I	N	O	T
1	2	3	4	5	6

B	C	D	F	G	H	J	K
70	71	72	73	74	75	76	77

L	M	P	Q	R	S	U	V
78	79	80	81	82	83	84	85

W	X	Y	Z	FIG	.	:	'
86	87	88	89	90	91	92	93

	+	-	=	REQ	SPC
94	95	96	97	98	99